FLASH CRASH

A JAKE RIVETT *HEIST THRILLER*

by

Denison Hatch

THE JAKE RIVETT SERIES

FLASH CRASH

NEVER GO ALONE

For more information about Denison Hatch and the Jake Rivett series, please visit:

DenisonHatch.com

Published by Lookout Press

ISBN: 0-9972812-1-9
ISBN-13: 978-0-9972812-1-7

To my Number One, **MJH** . . .

ONE

Monday

DAVID BELOV WAS LATE for work. He'd never been tardy before, but that wasn't why he was so damn scared. He stood quietly inside the subway car, attempting to display zen while every synapse in his brain burned red hot. Doing his best to stop the fear inside from gurgling up and entering the world, David reminded himself that he just needed to keep it together for a few more hours—one more trading session.

He emerged from the Broad Street station into lower Manhattan on a perfect Monday morning. Only a handful of cloud wisps and contrails arced through the bright blue sky. Crisp enough for David to respect his suit jacket but nothing more. As he paced down the sidewalk, he appeared to be just one more highly-paid, well-educated lemming amongst many.

A few minutes later, David walked through the doors of Montgomery Noyes' headquarters in Wall Street. A storied investment bank, Montgomery was an utter cathedral of finance. If one couldn't identify Montgomery by name alone, then the enormous modernist vaulted glass ceilings that no Roman architect would have conjured in his wildest dreams, and the white Thassos marble walls, made it abundantly clear that what Montgomery Noyes did was close to godliness. Their core competency was refined but simple. They turned money into more money. Montgomery had experienced a hundred years of institutional existence and planned on one thousand more. The firm was led by extremely driven men whose risk palettes had been pushed to aggressive overdrive at a very young age and never slowed down. In some manner of definition, David was also one of those men. It certainly hadn't been destined. He'd bucked the trendline of his upbringing, but he knew that mean reversion always had a knack for bringing shooting stars back to Earth.

David headed through Montgomery Noyes' foyer, past the coffee shop built into the front of the lobby and towards the staffed reception desk at the back. With a nod to a security guard standing sentinel, David brushed his RFID passcard against a sensor. A green light confirmed David's credentials, allowing access. He passed through turnstiles towards Montgomery's private elevator.

▪

David walked across the trading floor on the twentieth story. At nine thirty-two in the morning, two minutes after the open, the place was going nuts. The trading day had begun and the big swinging you-know-what's— in their light blue stripes and Ferragamos and trendy socks patterned after Santa Fe cave dweller scratchings—were in the groove. David couldn't help but overhear a conversation between two gregarious traders.

"I got into the E-mini right as it broke the channel, man," bellowed Rick Stanfield, a robust man who only wore Brooks Brothers but could never quite figure out how to choose an aesthetically pleasing combination of pattern and color. At first glance, in his red lobster corduroys and rainbow-striped shirt, Rick appeared to be an outright caricature of preppy culture. He reveled in that persona, of course. The truth was that his sartorial choices were utterly irrelevant. Rick could read a stock ticker like an elite wide receiver can trace a quarterback's pigskin from sixty yards out. The ability to make money was paramount within the hierarchy of Montgomery Noyes' business—a skill only seconded by the ability to not lose money.

"How hard did you ride it?" Peter Langer asked. Peter was Rick's bullpen best friend. They shot the shit all day long, pounded down drinks after work, and never, ever asked about each other's personal life. Both had wives, children, and homes in the posh suburbs outside of the city, but neither was interested in discussing those taboo topics. Masculinity was always at stake in the game. Especially if your numbers weren't up to snuff. In that case manliness became critical and could in fact be ridden like a wave, at least until the next recession ate everyone's lunch.

"Hard enough not to be the naked guy later," Rick replied.

"I'm babysitting my shit again," Peter said.

"Never babysit. Fuck babies. Drown 'em if they don't make money." Rick noticed David passing by as Peter laughed. "Right, Dave?" Rick held his hand out towards David in a teed-up fist pump gesture.

David grinned awkwardly and slapped Rick's fist with his palm as he passed. David padded alongside the plate glass window towards a back hallway, unable to socialize at Rick and Peter's level.

"Who's that guy?" Peter asked after David had proceeded through the bullpen.

"The quant. David."

"Whatever," said Peter.

David Belov was well aware of where he fit within the pecking order of Montgomery Noyes. He wasn't anything like the blue-blood traders in the bullpen. He was a quant, a quantitative programmer, which meant that he was relegated to the windowless back offices of Montgomery's trading floor. His primary job responsibility was to develop, program, and maintain the algorithms that controlled the timing and manner in which the bank's computer systems traded thousands of securities across the globe.

Fluent in C++, JavaScript, Python, and a handful of other esoteric languages all the way down to binary machine code, David was a commodity within the highly specific world of algorithmic trading. His LinkedIn received plenty of looks. But he was also just that—a commodity, paid ninety thousand dollars a year because he was three years out of grad school and that's what the salary step called for. As far as traders like Rick and Peter were concerned, David was the equivalent of a tool to be utilized, not a person to be respected. He would never have a real, client-facing, trade-generating, revenue-sharing position like the bullpen guys stood on. And it didn't help that David was a first-generation American from a Russian immigrant family who had to scrape for every success in life. If there's anything David had learned about America so far, it was that people who were born with silver spoons in their mouths didn't trust those born drinking powdered milk.

David continued along the back of the trading floor. After the rowdy trading desks in the bullpen came the fast-paced charmers in the sales department. They had names like "J.R." and "Laird" and "Terrence." David listened to the sweet words rattling off the sales guys' tongues like music: "What's really interesting to me, is I'm watching the commodity go up much faster than the miners are. I see a pairs trade there. Short the metal, long miners, and hope they converge." Farther down the row, it was the same thing. Another sales guy raged into his telephone while simultaneously glancing at a tablet cell in the other hand, eyes tracking ticker tape and volume across the large plasma screens set against a back wall. "Anything you want. I'll get you into the GLD index and if it's big enough size, we can buy and store physical gold for you—no problem. We have the second-largest vault in the city."

David padded down a quiet hallway towards the quant desks. Unlike the main floor, the quant section was carpeted. Colleagues spoke in quiet murmurs to one another. Floor-to-ceiling bulletproof glass protected the organized racks of blinking blade computers, and their power supplies and cooling units, which comprised the nerve center of the bank's trading operations. David walked past the twenty-four-hour guarded security desk in front of the server room. He arrived at his own cube and sat down.

David didn't immediately start up his computer as most of the office rats would. He didn't begin checking voicemails, even though the notification light on his phone was blinking. Instead, after a long moment of consternation, he pulled a white envelope out of his pocket. He held it at arm's length and simply stared at it.

"You know I love you, right, dude?" David's reverie was broken by Tyler Stanton, the managing director of the department and David's direct boss. Tyler stood inside David's workspace, leaning against the side of the cubicle with his hand, absentmindedly nudging it back and forth a few inches.

"Watch out"—David pointed—"the desk."

"Oh, crap." Tyler backed up without apologizing. Another fundamental tenet of Montgomery was that one obeyed the hierarchy of command with military reverence. That meant that whatever Tyler felt, desired, or said took precedence over anything that David could possibly emote. Tyler continued to harangue David about his late arrival. "The rest of the guys are here for the FX huddle at six"—Tyler glanced at his watch —"and you're three and a half hours late. Come on, dude. What is that? What's going on? Something you need to tell me about?"

There was no safe way to begin the necessary conversation. The only thing that would save him was action. "I had problems at home," David finally responded, which was literally true but metaphorically a massive understatement.

"Listen, I'm sorry to hear it. I really am," Tyler said.

"Thanks."

"But don't let people see you bleed. It's a bad look," Tyler dispensed his wisdom as he walked away from David's cubicle.

After Tyler was out of sight, David realized that he'd been clenching the envelope nervously throughout his entire interaction with Stanton. His fingers shook while he opened the enclosure. Inside was an anticlimactic, tiny microSD card. David placed the card in his pocket. He tossed the envelope in the trash. The vessel didn't matter—the content did. The result of many hours of panicked programming lay inside the bits and bytes of the microSD card. In many ways, David's entire life had lead up to this moment. No one would ever know it, but the powerful code that rested within that microscopic piece of plastic and copper was the best work he'd ever done.

The air conditioning inside the building was set to maximum spend, but David couldn't feel it. His brow was drenched in sweat. Water dripped off his body like a pot of boiling water with the lid left on too long. He did the best that he could to wipe the physiological condensation off with his hands and then dried them by patting his slacks. David took a final deep breath. He stood up and paced down the hallway towards the glass-encased door to the server room. One of Montgomery's information security officers—a nice enough gent named Roberto, whom David would often chat with about terrible reality television—was sitting in front of the door.

"Had a bunch of flags pop on the code check for three-one," David said.

"Okay. Did Tyler approve it?" Roberto inquired.

"It . . ." David stumbled for a moment. "It should be in the system. That's what I was told."

Roberto checked his computer monitor again, clicking through a bunch of menus. "Oh, there it is. That's weird. Wasn't there a second ago. I got it. All good. Don't trip, buddy," Roberto said as he tapped a button and the door to the server room slid open.

David grimaced. If only that dude knew the beginning of it.

David stepped down the long, silent server room. The custom-built computer systems that lived inside this chamber were absolutely state-of-the-art. The room was always guarded and staffed twenty-four seven. It contained synchronizing software that mirrored all of its data onto colocated servers as far as Sweden and Hawaii, should the East Coast cease to exist at some point in the future. The room was kept at a constantly chilled temperature to prevent the processors from overheating. The system was also protected by massive battery systems from APC, the size of about fifty refrigerators, in case of an extended power outage. The entire network was set up for redundancy in the event of any individual component's failure. If a hard drive, processor, or power supply stopped working, it could be hot swapped out and replaced with no effect on the functionality of the system. Montgomery's information technology team was proud of the fact that they had only lost internet connectivity for a total of three and a half minutes in the last year, which was a better result than 99.89 percent of the entire commercial hosting market. David knew the "Box" very well. He'd coordinated the build out between the programming and operations teams. And in all situations, he'd been a real team player—a true mensch. He'd been the fucking go-to guy and this was what happened to him?

David finally reached his goal, locating a slim black server box nestled deep within the racks. The technorati referred to servers as "blades" because they were only a half inch tall and slid in and out of their cages similar to a sword emerging from a sheath. David placed his hands on his target—one blade amongst many. He yanked the server out and flipped it around, viewing the various inputs on the back. He pulled the microSD card from his pocket and inserted it into a small slot on the back of the blade. Then he replaced the blade into the slot where it came from. A new diode glowed blue on the front of the box, the only indication that the microSD card was present. David gave the server a final lookover, then turned on his heels and headed out of the room.

David returned to his cubicle within the quant section. He sat down.

He loaded up the two stock tickers that most accurately tracked the global commodity trade of pure gold: CME Group Gold Futures and the GLD ETF Index. He watched GLD's stock chart. Not much was going on. Low volume compared to average. The commodity was up a little bit on the day, by half a percent. But nothing was out of the ordinary. It was a boring day for gold. It would not stay that way.

David gazed over the rest of his colleagues in the room. The knowledge of what was about to happen was slowly driving him insane, but the truth was he couldn't expose his predicament to any of them. That was the first rule and the critical one. The second rule was to finish the job —no matter what.

His pupils had reduced to tight little particles. He was perspiring greatly. With his hair slicked back and sweat emerging from his temples, David appeared slightly, but visibly, ill. There was a small part of him that secretly hoped that another programmer, or Tyler, or someone from human resources would pull him aside and ask him what was wrong. Then maybe he could leave for the rest of the day and not be there for the carnage. He shook his head. Not even that would solve his problems. It was a pipe dream. The unvarnished truth was that no one could really tell that something was up with David—because no one was paying him any attention.

David's eyes dipped down to the monitor in front of him. He loaded a programming terminal on his computer and typed quickly, routing the command prompt to a subfolder on the server blade he'd just pulled. He copied his algorithm from the microSD card onto the executable folders of every single server in the stacks. David opened his program's command module. The name of the algorithm played across his computer screen:

\</FLASH CRASH>.

David took a deep breath. His finger hung precariously in the air.

Then he pressed enter.

The program began to run.

TWO

RICK AND PETER BURNED each other back and forth as usual as the afternoon struck the trading floor.

"You see gold today?" Peter prompted.

"Just like my dick on boner pills. You can bet on it being up," Rick replied.

"The mommas and the poppas . . . They still love metals, don't they?"

"Wasn't that a band?" Rick asked, apparently curious.

"Never heard of them," said Peter.

"Just remember this. Without the idiots trading from home we got no muppets to lead to the slaughter. And with no muppets—no cash," Rick said. The two men chuckled. It was funny to them because they weren't joking. They turned back to the monitors as all the green numbers on the ticker turned red.

"Ah, shit. It broke," Peter said.

On the monitors, gold had dipped into the negative for the first time on the day.

"I'm gonna get an espresso," Rick replied.

■

Still as a grave, David continued sitting at his desk. He was having trouble focusing on anything. He finally found himself locked with undivided attention into the framed family photo sitting on his desk. He picked the frame up with his hands and studied it while his crash algorithm ran in the background on his computer monitor. His wife and son—Marina and Mikey Belov—the most important people in the entire world. They were his everything. They were also why this was happening.

David couldn't hold onto the façade any longer. He placed his head down on top of his desk and he cried. Only a few tears came out—a small portion of the frustration he was feeling inside. But it did help. He held the frame tightly in his hands as he crumpled up in his cubicle. Almost as soon as he began, David stopped. Tears weren't appropriate. They were also risky. He dried his eyes a little with his fists and stared across the office with the vacant expression of a dead man.

■

Meanwhile, Peter continued to carefully monitor gold's movement on his screens. He suddenly noticed that the commodity was down 1.5 percent for the day, having ticked down over a percent in less than twenty milliseconds. Peter picked up his phone.

"Gold crashed a hundred basis points in a minute. Something's up," Peter announced.

A few nearby traders perked up. The outer offices of the floor began to rotate open as the news spread. One managing director conspired with another, their attention focused entirely on the gold ticker. They were all watching the beginning of the cascade with bated breath, like a ball rolling towards steps, seconds away from gravity's full force. Within moments the entire floor was rapt as the global value of the commodity continued to fall precariously down by the second . . .

-1.5 percent . . . -1.75 percent . . . -2.4 percent . . . -3.1 percent . . .

As the price began to accelerate further, a panic set in. This sensation was something akin to pure fear, always universal and yet always personal because every person experienced it differently. Panic tends to mirror that which caused it. In this case it was a cascade of numbers. A perpetual motion machine, triggered to descend to infinity. A spaceship sucked into a churning black hole. A running of the bulls through the filter of an impossibly tight street. Time slowed down for the Montgomery traders as they contemplated the nature of what was happening. Surely it wouldn't continue, they thought, and they held onto that notion as though it were a life preserver.

"Who's gonna catch the falling knife?" one of them yelled out, implying the impossibility of predicting whether the price would bounce back or whether this was a one-way trip to intense losses.

"We're too exposed today. This is some spoofing, cancel-order algo, dude," another said.

When panics such as this occur, what happens to most human beings is that they stop thinking about the actual problem at hand and begin to fixate on the personal ramifications of the event. Each and every one of these young men and women had pressure points in their lives, whether it was saving up for that engagement ring of adequate size, or hitting their "number" and getting out of the business altogether, or simply funding monthly heli-ski trips on elite mountains in the West that didn't even have lifts. Because who needs them? Experts hike to their own runs. While gold dropped like a rock through water, finding no bids at all, none of the traders were actually thinking about the commodity. Their minds were fixated on what they were losing. That's why it is so difficult to make good decisions during a panic. The underlying cause that one ought to be focusing upon is far from the mind, while the effect of the potential loss is in the forefront and dominating the cerebral cortex completely.

Finally, the large central office overlooking the entire floor opened and Howard Bergensen came bounding through the bullpen towards Rick's desk. Howard ran like an elderly lion of equal heft and muscle. His personality followed suit. As their royal leader, Howard made it look as though he was for everyone when in fact he was for Howard. That was

Howard's secret. He created a consensus whereby he floated on top. But he also knew that crowd surfing only lasted until the music stopped, and all of them holding him up knew it too.

The phenomenon wasn't unique to Howard. This was how Wall Street worked. The financial industry functioned because it involved vast pools of other people's money, generally public pension funds, and a consistent set of legal procedures that boiled down to limiting liability by always operating behind LLCs and never, ever signing personal guarantees. Howard was the king of it all. He was nowhere near the most intelligent person in the building, but he was certainly the most epic. Every little last piece of financial minutiae, history, and institutional knowledge at Montgomery Noyes sat between his ears. He was indeed one of the only remaining honest-to-goodness Masters of the Universe. A subject truly worthy of Tom Wolfe's attention, Howard ran across the floor towards the gold desk, looking for Rick and reaching Peter instead.

"Where the hell is Rick?" Howard asked immediately.

"He's getting an espresso," Peter replied. Peter immediately pulled out his cell phone and hastily composed a text message to Rick while Howard loomed above him, pissed as shit.

▪

In the bathroom, Rick vacuumed up a line of cocaine off the granite ledge behind the toilet. His head reared up, triumphant. He noticed a text on his cell phone. He picked it up and read Peter's missive. He raced out of the stall.

▪

Back on the trading floor, Peter questioned Howard anxiously. "You want us to get out of the position, boss?"

CNBC was going nuts. The squawk boxes that connected to the futures floors in Chicago and to the NYSE were jammed. The bullpen was utterly wired with the energy of the cascade. The ticker continued to dive negative, the numbers getting deeper and darker, the knife twisting further . . . -3.6 percent . . . -5.2 percent . . .

In the middle of this critically serious moment, Howard seemed to be talking to himself. He was muttering, "It'll hold . . . It'll hold . . . I don't want to get out right at the bottom."

All of a sudden, Rick returned. "This is bullshit. It's gonna trip the circuit breakers. The exchanges will shut it down. We gotta move before that, or we'll get gapped out, Howard!" Rick started screaming while he watched his future and every single vacation to Nantucket for the rest of the decade disintegrate into dead dirt in front of him.

"No. No. Give it time . . ." Howard vacillated.

And then gold kept falling. It was in a full-on death riot like a barrel over Niagara Falls, one of those turn-of-the-century iterations when they weren't outfitted with all manner of airbags and springs. Howard watched with stunned horror: -5.7 percent . . . -6.2 percent . . . It hit -8.1 percent and Howard gave up.

"Sell," he said quietly. The lion didn't roar, he whimpered.

The entire room erupted. Peter and Rick each pulled a phone to an ear, fingers smashing keyboards.

"Sell . . . Sell . . . Sell . . ."

▪

David spent the rest of the afternoon working quietly, in stark contrast to the internal arrest affecting his entire psyche. He had done this. He caused the market to collapse upon itself. That was a fact. He also knew the reason why he had done it, the justification of which he had been forced by necessity to keep only to himself. What David did not know, but surely was destined to find out, was exactly why this was all happening.

As the ominous chime of the market closing resonated throughout the building, David walked through the trading floor on his way to the elevator. After the day's Armageddon, even the sound of the end of open-market transactions wasn't a relief. It was more similar to funeral bells tolling. As David passed by Rick and Peter at their desks, he listened in.

"We got hurt bad. No one knows what happened. My contact at NASDAQ says they're investigating," said Peter into his desk phone. "Yeah. Yeah . . . Overall? Howard lost a billion nominal today—maybe more."

Rick noticed David walking past. "You eat like a bird, Davey-boy. Until you shit like an elephant," Rick said to him. *Succinct, but true.*

David turned to spy Howard Bergensen through the open door in his office, which resembled a war room. Howard sat on a couch surrounded by a handful of senior Montgomery executives. His white shirt was soaked to the bone with sweat. He was bawling his eyes out, a powerful man reduced to tears by the devastation of the market. David couldn't believe it. He wanted to race over to Howard and tell him everything he knew—spill all his guts out across the crystal table. But he knew very well that he couldn't. That wasn't part of the plan. Then he reminded himself that none of this was part of the plan. More importantly, it wasn't his plan at all. David hadn't chosen this. He hoped that meant it wasn't his fault, but he wasn't quite sure. He only knew that he had been given no choice.

▪

David stepped out onto the street. Mother Nature had obviously sensed the market cataclysm and had begun to provide punctuation. Lightning splintered across the thick black-and-blue clouds that patterned the sky, like wounds from the gut punches of the day. The rain pelted down on David and all the other inhabitants of the city. He actually loved the rain. It reminded him of being home, ensconced in love and family. He stared into the sky at the raindrops. Time slowed down, and he felt as though he was watching each droplet in slow motion. He took a step off the street into the moving traffic. He decided that he'd see his wife. He'd see his son. Nothing would stop him. Nothing would separate him from them. It was settled.

A taxi beeped at David as it passed, but he didn't seem to notice. Brakes squealed as a large delivery truck slid across two lanes to avoid him. Angry honking erupted. A large grey sedan came screeching towards him like destiny. But then the vehicle magically slowed to a stop with only inches to spare as it pulled up in front of David. The sedan's back door opened.

"Get in," a voice ordered from inside.

David didn't hesitate. The car was there for him. He obliged. He shut the door behind him and the vehicle swiftly faded into the watery ether of Manhattan.

▪

Inside the grey sedan—his every move watched by an impassive masked man gripping an immense shotgun—David prayed.

THREE

A SHROUD OF STEAM rushed vertically through the pavement vents in front of Montgomery Noyes' stately headquarters. Nothing out of the ordinary for a city that often smelled as though it still had an open sewer system—for an urban landscape that reflected a Batman set on any given street. But if one were to dive down through the vapor and literally descend into the sidewalk vent itself, cascading through the sub-surface infrastructure of the building, he or she would rip along a nerve mass of neon pink, green, and yellow cabling—the true guts of the operation. A serpentine path of ethernet, phone and electrical wires wound its way throughout multiple levels of the bank's sub-basement. The cables plummeted through a series of server rooms, generators, and router stacks. They tracked around HVAC and other industrial systems. And finally the serpent burst through the ceiling of Montgomery Noyes' gargantuan commodity vault.

The Montgomery Noyes bullion and currency depository was built like a fortress. No humans were permitted into the vault itself. The contents were accessed by a robotic forklift stacking system nicknamed the "Stacker," inside an air-sealed corridor of shelves the length of a football field. The Stacker was solely responsible for lifting large pallets of gold and silver bars, and domestic and foreign currency, and moving them from one part of the vault to another for storage. At one end of the vault, a conveyer-belt system led to a secure airlock portal for shipping and receiving.

The security procedures for an actual live person to enter the vault rivaled those of a nuclear-launch control site. After passing through multiple biometric identifiers including eye and hand-vein scans, personal recognition by the guards, and a card swipe, a physical key was required. Two individuals, read in at the highest levels of the bank, had to insert their keys simultaneously within the vault's command center in order to open the airlock. This was rarely necessary, except in the case of servicing or construction, because the Stacker was so powerful. But in case any humans were inside, each bay within the vault contained a built-in scale, accurate down to one-thousandth of an ounce. The scales and sensors monitored any physical movement and cross-checked the bullion weight with a computer database. If any vault was unimpeachable, it was this one. One of the few men who held a key to the vault was Howard. Another was Roger O'Neill.

As the vault's head of security, Roger observed the entire operation through a large window in the command-and-control office situated above the vault. Roger was a second-generation American whose father had emigrated from Northern Ireland in the late seventies, due to rumored affiliations with the Protestant side of the "the Troubles" that were affecting the country at the time. The O'Neill name, of course, had been synonymous with Northern Ireland and Belfast in particular for hundreds of years.

It was in Belfast that Roger's great-great-grandfather had operated a successful ship-building enterprise during the golden age of that region's maritime industry. They had been a family of water people, masters of the seas and adventurers both on and off it. But with the crumbling of the old industry in favor of taxless locales farther east, Roger's family took a few hits. Maybe it came from their experience on the high seas, but there was no male on Roger's side of the family tree who wasn't willing to go down with his ship. Especially if it meant the preservation of the family name. That's how Roger's great-grandfather perished—leaving the family empire in tatters. At that point the O'Neills found it easy to blame others for their misfortune. Especially the Catholics. It was ultimately unclear whether Roger's father was a victim or an aggressor of the religious lines that eventually descended upon Ireland, but it was clear that he was willing to take risks. That's why Roger's father left the homeland. The family bundled up and left for the United States by boat.

The American dream immediately provided Roger's father a job on the local Hingham, Massachusetts police force, a small house on the outskirts of Boston, and a life without the risk of daily car bombings. That peace would last for decades and now was entrenched completely, to the point that the "Boston O'Neills" became a known quantity unto themselves. They were the side of the family who had brought honor back to their lineage. Roger's uncle and cousins owned a few bars and a popular gastropub. His sister operated a general store. His brother was still in the Hingham police force. Roger himself went through the academy in Boston proper and spent twenty years displaying exemplary service for the Boston Police Department. Although Roger enjoyed being a big-city cop, ultimately the lucrative revolving door appealed to him more. And he had no fear of a career change, especially when it might contribute to the continued reascension of the O'Neill family name. When presented with the opportunity to act as head of security for Montgomery Noyes—a bank at the bedrock of the financial system—Roger didn't think about it. He grabbed it with both hands and hung on tight.

With a bit of a paunch from ten years in the office, but a nice strong beard and an accent that still reflected the lingering aspects of his Irish heritage, Roger couldn't help but shake his head as he stared incredulously at the printout in his hands.

"Shite," Roger said simply. He grabbed the paper, reviewed the accounting again, and immediately picked up the telephone on his desk. Sometimes the guys upstairs made clerical mistakes.

"Howard? We're moving a hundred thousand troy ounces?" Roger asked. He nodded as he listened to the affirmative response. He hung up. Two armored truck drivers stood next to him in the office, and others milled outside. They were all intent upon Roger's next command. "Howard confirmed it. The number's right for the overnight transfer. Guess the price of gold ran away from the boys upstairs today. It was carnage. A handful of their counterparties are demanding physical delivery of their allocated metals," Roger said. He turned to the drivers and a handful of his own plain-clothed, former cop, security staff. "Let's use a follow car tonight. You're delivering sixty thousand ounces to J.P. Morgan's vault and then forty to the Fed, okay?" Roger checked his men.

"Over four tons?" the driver asked. His name was Leo.

"Yep."

"Quite a load," Leo said. "That's, like, a hundred million dollars."

"More than that—hundred and twenty million, plus. It's the biggest load we've ever run," Roger replied.

"Right," said Leo.

"So be safe. Run well. Run fast. Don't stop the run—for anything."

■

A steel gate rolled up from the otherwise unimpressive garage exit adjacent to Montgomery's headquarters. The armored truck, filled with approximately a hundred and twenty million dollars' worth of gold bullion, emerged from the garage at street level and carefully navigated across traffic towards Pearl. An unmarked security vehicle exited the garage as well, driven by Roger's tight security crew. They followed close behind the armored truck.

The two vehicles traversed Pearl, a small street cutting towards the Brooklyn Bridge Promenade and FDR Drive. As they drove down the sleepy back street, they passed a nondescript white service van parallel parked next to the sidewalk. Once the two-vehicle convoy passed, the van's engine ignited. The van slowly exited its parking spot and began to follow behind the group surreptitiously, as if by coincidence.

Leo, the driver of the armored truck, and Stevie, his guard, listened to the radio. Stevie sat shotgun and carried one as well. Roger's security team was speaking to them from the car behind, updating the crew on road conditions.

"Okay. Good, good. We'll use Cherry to the bridge ramp to . . ." The security staffer's voice became garbled and unintelligible. Leo glanced at Stevie, who hit the radio with his palm. No sound emerged, except for the choking tinnitus of static. Stevie hit the radio again, a bit harder this time.

"Repeat that? Say again?" Stevie asked.

But radio fuzz was the only message that greeted the two of them back.

"Shitty thing. Restart it," Leo ordered his shotgun guard. Then Leo gazed out his side-view mirror. Immediately spotting the security car still following behind them, he wasn't particularly concerned. "But we should be good, Stevie. They're still behind us," he said. After all, it was just a delivery. Happened once a week—week in, week out. Roger ran a tight ship, just as his ancestors had. No one outside the organization could possibly know that there was more gold sitting inside this truck than there ever had been, or likely ever would be again.

■

The convoy slowly and carefully merged onto the FDR Drive and proceeded to rip north through the clear Manhattan night.

Following behind them, but indistinguishable from the normal flow of light traffic, the white van also merged onto the highway and continued to follow the convoy from about five hundred yards back.

In the follow car, Roger's security man, Ted, played with his radio. It seemed to be malfunctioning from his side as well.

"You have Leo's number, right?" Ted asked.

"No, just Stevie . . ."

"Get him on his cell," Ted commanded one of his passengers, who dug into his own pocket for a cell phone.

"Zero bars. Weird," the passenger said.

The group of vehicles whipped along the highway past the hulking, illuminated city on the left. As they moved north, the white van slowly began to gain on the convoy, until it smoothly matched speed with the follow car and hid within Ted's blind spot for a few seconds. Traffic was sparse in the middle of the night. After a moment of calibrated driving, the passenger-side window of the white van opened just an inch and a barely visible, silenced gun barrel emerged from the crack.

Pop! Pop! Both of the follow car's left tires exploded, seemingly simultaneously—two perfect shots. The three men inside the vehicle were thrown to the side as they began to skid across the highway pavement. They slid across two lanes of traffic with a ghastly shower of sparks and smashed into a side barrier, their vehicle rendered completely immobile. Within twenty seconds, Roger's three staffers, led by Ted, had jumped out of the follow car and were attempting to wave down the armored truck.

▪

Leo and Stevie were already a third of a mile down the highway, past the horizon angle of a sloping turn, completely oblivious to their security's predicament. And they lacked a working radio. Leo powered the truck north. They were only a few miles from the uptown exit of their first drop-off.

Suddenly, two motorcycles flew up the FDR towards the truck. Each motorcycle had a well-built man on front and a female passenger holding on behind him. All four were clad in leather from head to toe, with full helmets covering their faces. The motorcycles crisscrossed behind the armored truck.

Stevie noticed the motorcycles first. "Fucking gearheads," he said. He held up the shotgun in his hands and grinned. "I'll just flash this through the window. That'll scare them off."

"Nah. It's fine. Guys on rice rockets think they own the road. What they don't realize is we just don't want to kill them," Leo responded, staying focused, keeping his eyes on the road.

The motorcycles slowed down to exactly the speed of the truck. The woman on the back of one bike reached into her bag, and her hand emerged gripping what appeared to be a drill. Extending from the front of the drill was a titanium bracket with four industrial suction cups at each corner.

Leo noticed the motorcycle moving even closer to his door. Not able to see what was in her hands, he smiled. "I see them now. Think she'll show us her tits?" he asked Stevie humorously.

It was at that exact moment that Leo abruptly noticed the bizarre drill contraption the woman was holding. She rammed it against the side of the truck—on Leo's door. The suction pads, attached to each end of the bracket system, immediately stuck tight to the armored truck's outer layer. She no longer had to hold the drill, because it had become secured to the side of the armored truck itself.

"The hell is that?" Leo asked Stevie as he craned his neck to observe the device through his side-view mirror.

"Huh?" Stevie didn't have eyes on it.

"I'm pulling over," Leo said.

"But we're not supposed to stop the run," replied Stevie seriously, "for anything." He had learned over time that not obeying Roger's instructions was never deft—always daft.

Leo started to slow down anyway as the woman on the motorcycle initiated the drill with a press of a button on a small remote control in her pocket. Apparently controlled via a wireless connection, the drilling system was topped by a diamond bit with a lubricant pump attached to the side to mitigate friction. Within a matter of seconds, the drill slid into the reinforced-steel side of the armored truck like a knife through butter. The bit ground through the door, creating a small, precise hole in the flank of the truck.

Leo stared down in shock. "Oh my god," he exclaimed slowly. Both Leo and Stevie watched as the tip of the bit stopped moving. Then it began to rip counterclockwise, turning in reverse. As quickly as it had entered, it was gone. Only the small hole remained.

"Don't slow down, man. Gun it. Fucking gun it!" Stevie exclaimed, his fingers gripping the shotgun tight, bracing for whatever was to come.

"Hells yeah, I am." Leo nodded his agreement and jammed his foot onto the accelerator.

Behind the armored truck, the first motorcycle faded away and the second one took its place. A brunette was sitting on the back of the second motorcycle, her long hair streaming in the wind. Once she was within a few feet of the remote-controlled titanium rig suctioned to the side of the armored truck, she pressed another small remote button. On command, the entire drill unit dropped out of the brackets and onto the street below, leaving the open titanium bracket system still attached to the truck and nothing else. A path was now cleared to access the small hole the drill had bored. The brunette placed another device into the brackets. The new unit consisted of a grey cylinder about the size of a soda can, connected to a battery-charged, pressurized gas injector. The injector latched into place. The brunette flicked a switch. Then with a tap on her driving partner's shoulder, the second motorcycle flew off into the night, following quickly behind the first.

As the two bikes departed, Leo could hear the rumbling of another piece of machinery behind the armored truck. He glanced into his side-view mirror, but couldn't quite make the shape out. All he could tell was that a hulking vehicle behind him was blotting out all of the streetlights and casting a shadow over his armored truck. But Leo and Stevie were afflicted by an even more pertinent and mission-critical issue. A light gassy substance had entered the truck, pumped in by the injector on the outside. Visible only around the drill hole, the gas quickly dissipated as it expanded into the space. Leo's eyes started to dilate wildly. His hand slipped off the wheel, and Stevie noticed.

"You okay, man?" Stevie asked. But he received no response. Stevie realized that Leo had stopped moving. He flung his body over to the driver's side, grabbed the wheel and attempted to guide the truck himself. But then he felt it too. The gas began to take him. Stevie barely heard the massive clunking noise on the roof of the truck. He tried in vain to handle the wheel, but while doing so, the truck started to swerve across lanes without his control. It was aimed directly at a concrete barrier adjacent to an exit on the highway ahead. Stevie could barely see. His eyelids felt as though they each had a thousand pounds of weight pulling them down. He was moments from succumbing to the gas's power.

Stevie used the last fleeting moments of his consciousness to brace himself for the certain collision ahead, when he started to feel a new sensation—weightlessness. The armored truck rose a few inches off the ground, then a few feet. Stevie realized that somehow the truck was floating into the sky. The last thought he processed before passing into another plane of existence was that of confusion. Was it just the gas, or was he really flying?

Behind the armored truck, a massive industrial flatbed drove along the highway. An electromagnetic crane rig had been affixed to the flatbed, and had attached itself to the armored truck. The unyielding magnet held the armored truck suspended in the air as the flatbed and crane rig flew down the highway. Once the armored truck was high enough in the air to avoid any collisions, the crane slowly rotated and lowered it onto the flatbed.

Then the flatbed, with its crane and illegally acquired armored truck worth over a hundred million dollars, flew north into the night and away from the bright spires of Manhattan and their phosphorous glow.

FOUR

EXACTLY TWENTY-FOUR HOURS before the gold crash, David wasn't worried about a single problem in the world except for making pancakes. His eight-year-old son Mikey had demanded them and he was fulfilling said request. That's how life should be on Sundays. He was dedicated to being the father he never had, and that wasn't just a turn of phrase.

■

David's own father had died heroically in a gun battle when David was a small child. At least that's what he distinctly remembered his mother, Veronika Belov, informing him at the time. As more time passed, David had realized that Papa's death had been ignominious at best. Veronika had refused to speak about it for years. She was sixty-five years old, and he knew that she would never talk about it again. It was the past—water under the bridge. He still didn't know exactly who was involved, nor even the circumstances that had led to his father's death. Maybe it had been drugs. Or counterfeit cash. Or something worse. All his mother had told him throughout the years was that his father had been a "Russian bear," a fierce man who had known both the limits of his own brain and the power of aggression. He had used the first to a lesser degree than the second. Veronika had always viewed life from the perspective of the various members of the animal kingdom. She felt that the wild kingdom provided a better understanding of humanity. This was presumably because it's easier to objectively understand our motivation by watching creatures that have no subtlety and cannot control their urges.

In the five brief years that he'd known his father, Papa hadn't wanted much to do with David. That's probably because David had been a very intelligent baby. From an early age, he had noticed when something was out of sync in the world. But he hadn't had the vocabulary to fix it. So David would simply scream and carry on as if the world was ending. That was his preferred method of communication as a child—for hours. At age three, there is a fine line between an irrational temper tantrum and the first spark of bona-fide genius. And in general, bears don't like screaming mice. His mother told him that Papa didn't use his head nearly as much as David, and that was a fact David had always prided himself upon. He wished that his dad was still alive, but he wasn't sure what they'd have in common. David wouldn't have wanted to go down Papa's footsteps as a thuggish foot soldier within Bensonhurst's now-indigenous, primarily Eastern European and former Soviet-bloc mafia population.

It was difficult to avoid one's past, no matter how hard David tried. For example, Veronika still insisted on calling her son "Davyd," and pronouncing it exactly as such. Although that was the name on his birth certificate, David hated it. His first form of identification from the DMV read "David," per his choice. He'd never looked back. David knew that his family's past was never fully escapable, because by definition it was the building blocks from which he existed. But at least he recognized the syndrome. When he was a teenager, he'd actually taken a few steps in his father's direction. But he quickly snapped out of it. He had realized that his was a different destiny. The only two keepsakes that remained of Papa's were a wedding photo that sat on Veronika's television at home and an old suede leather jacket. Veronika had given it to him when his shoulders broadened, around age fourteen. And David still wore that jacket every once in awhile. But he never told anyone where it came from.

▪

All of this was why Sunday mornings were dedicated to his own son, whom he loved more than life itself. And it must be mentioned that David's son's name was spelled "Michael" on his birth certificate, when any number of other derivations would have pleased Veronika moreso. While Papa had not provided intellectual inspiration, or particularly positive genetics, David hoped that Mikey Belov would be set up in life to utilize both. He was confident that if he raised his son right, Mikey would accomplish more than anyone in the lineage prior.

David flipped a pancake with one hand while tapping on a laptop with the other. He was browsing through children's animation shows, looking for a particular cartoon.

"There's nothing else you can watch, in the entire span of the media universe, besides the Samurai Cat?" he asked as Mikey padded into the room with a bathing suit on and a towel wrapped around his body like an Egyptian mummy.

"No way, Daddy. It has to be the Cat!" Mikey replied.

David clicked on a link. The video was there, but it was located behind a login paywall.

"That one's not a free play, Mikey," David said. He sighed, thought for a moment, and then muttered under his breath, "Guess that's why I'm here."

▪

When David was a child, Veronika would constantly remind him that in order to succeed in the world, he needed a skill. That was why Papa had failed. His skills were of a low-grade, bulk-price talent that didn't depend one iota on the brain behind it. The key to the American dream was identifying and exploiting one's own personal edge. No edge? No dream. Develop a skill to differentiate yourself from the masses ahead of you and you'd soon find them mostly behind you. It very quickly became evident to David that his skill was not going to involve physical dominance. There was no way he was going to beat his childhood best friends, Vlad and Baranowski, at tag on the school playground or in pickup basketball games in the park across the street. David would always come in last at anything that required muscle mass.

David found his skill in eighth grade. He could solve math problems faster than anyone he knew. At first he had hidden from the talent because when a boy is fourteen years old, in the less-than-posh areas of Brooklyn, it was decidedly uncool to know how to calculate the area underneath a curve. But luckily David had just enough foresight at that age to not cripple himself. He was never going to be the guy to answer a question incorrectly when he knew the right one. Even in his highly impressionable years, Veronika's voice tugged him back from the brink, saying, "What's your skill going to be, Davyd? What's going to get you out of here?" So even as he tried and largely failed to sharpen his elbows in the outside world, David found himself excelling in everything that involved math. That included physics, algebra, and computer science. When his school opened up its first computer lab in a remote corner off the science department's hallway, David was the first to show up. He realized that math controlled computers and that computers would eventually control almost every element of life. This skill gave David his first sense of power, nascent as it was. More importantly, it gave him his edge.

During the difficult years after high school, David used to jog through Bensonhurst, past Fort Hamilton, and into the Shore Road Park every morning. He'd run up the side of the park, against the water, staring out over the upper bay of the Hudson. After a few miles the city would finally shift into view from the right. The pile of capitalism was nothing less than glorious to David, rising above the water like Oz.

At the time, David was running because he couldn't stop himself from waking up before dawn. Every single morning, by five o'clock sharp, his entire body was strung out with the anxiety. Life was an immensely stressful puzzle. He'd spent a few years slowly pulling his way up by the bootstraps. While living in a tiny walkup apartment with his girlfriend Marina, he studied for his undergraduate math degree, followed by his masters in computer science at Stony Brook in Long Island. During that period, David found it hard to stop thinking about what would happen if he failed. The weight of said pressure would seize him each and every morning. It would fling him from his bed, into his shoes, and out the door. The run provided more comfort than sleep ever could have. He craved the consistency as he curved right along the park and was greeted by the looming skyscrapers of Gotham. The buildings were the most beautiful creatures he'd ever seen, and he could even make out the open oval at the top of Montgomery Noyes' headquarters at the bottom of Wall Street. When the sun finally ascended midway through his run, David wouldn't actually watch the sunrise itself. He would watch the sun's reflection off the buildings in the city that he aspired to matter in, and he wouldn't look away until his route forced him back home.

But even though David had eventually fulfilled his mother's dream with his job at Montgomery Noyes, he didn't actually want to live in the city. Or maybe he secretly did. Either way, Marina definitely did not. She cracked the whip and always had, practically since the day they'd met. Marina had saved his life multiple times throughout the years, and he was quite sure that she wasn't done. David was a dreamer. He didn't spend his time thinking about what was. He pondered what could be. He would throw himself into ideas that were doomed from the start and lose weeks chasing them like Don Quixote. Marina was the opposite. She was pragmatic. She was a doer. She often knew, from the very beginning, what the right thing to do was and the wrong. And in life, instinct sometimes worked out better than high-mindedness. The first time they'd met each other was during a school trip. She had drawn a picture of a sheep and a lion and had put her name over the lion and his over the sheep. He had realized later that he'd loved her ever since.

All these years later, it wasn't lost on David that Marina was the reason why he was still in Bensonhurst this morning. She felt strongly that Bensonhurst was where Mikey should grow up. That's where they'd both been raised, and they'd turned out great. They'd found each other. They could afford a large four-bedroom townhouse. And instead of relying on public education, they were able to send Mikey to the Catholic school at the top of the hill that each had idolized from afar when they were kids.

▪

Although David's skills were less relevant in Bensonhurst than in the big city, he could still be put to work on the weekends. For example, he could crack through multiple layers of user authentication in pursuit of a specific cartoon for his son. Piracy is bad, but a son's joy is better.

David worked the computer while he ruffled Mikey's hair. He loaded a custom keygen algorithm he'd written. He ran it. The computer began to parse through hundreds of thousands of username and password options.

"Is there chocolate in them?" Mikey asked about the pancakes.

"Huh? No. Have a seat, little man." Distracted, David turned back to his computer. He'd finally cracked it. He quickly loaded an episode of Samurai Cat. The show began to play on the laptop, which he spun around for Mikey to watch.

"Tada," David said.

"That is so, so awesome," Mikey responded. "Thanks, Daddy."

David threw a plate down on the table. A napkin. Fork. He poured a small glass of orange juice and then finally paused to fully observe his son's chosen outfit for the morning. "Hey. You probably don't need to wear your towel until you're wet," he said.

"I was just pretending to be strong," Mikey pointed to the computer screen. "Like him."

David realized that Mikey was dressed exactly like the cartoon superhero Samurai Cat, using his towel as if it were the Cat's black ninja kimono. David unwrapped the towel from Mikey. He folded it up.

"Nobody's mean to you at the pool, right?" David asked.

"Not really, Daddy."

"Good. Just remember. When you're a guy like us, who can't use his fists"—David tapped his head—"use your noggin instead."

Then the pancakes started burning. David raced back to the frying pan, lifting up the completely charred pancakes.

"I don't want a burnt pancake. And I want chocolate in it too!" Mikey exclaimed in the logically illogical manner that only an eight-year-old can muster.

"That's not good for you," David said.

"Mommy lets me have it," Mikey replied.

"Well, Mommy's not awake. It's her morning off—from you. And if anyone deserves it, she does," David said as he placed the pancakes in front of Mikey, who began to go to town. He snarfed down food amid laughs. David allowed himself just a brief respite to watch his kid enjoy life. The result of two decades of Herculean effort was to watch one's son as he spilled orange juice and pieces of pancake all over his torso and the kitchen table.

"Seems like Daddy is going to be cleaning up the kitchen for the whole rest of the morning," a woman's voice cast over the two of them. David turned around to see that Marina Belov was no longer sleeping. A pragmatic brunette who didn't wear makeup, she was prettier without it. Marina held up a clean shirt for Mikey. "And you better get ready, because Cat is going to be here any moment," she said.

David grabbed the shirt from Marina, who was wiping Mikey's face with a towel. They tag teamed to clean up Mikey, a daily occurrence and one that would pass all too soon.

"Mikey? One more thing—your medicine," David reminded him.

"Fine. Only a little pinch?" Mikey said.

"For only the bravest little man."

David pulled a small insulin syringe from the fridge. He lifted up Mikey's shirt, lightly touching the injector to Mikey's skin, an inch above the beltline. David had become quite experienced with the device by now, and so had Mikey, because it was required for survival. David and Marina should have noticed when he was three years old and started to fall into longer and longer naps. But they didn't. It took until Mikey had his first seizure, and they rushed him to the hospital, for him to be diagnosed as a child diabetic by an increasingly grim series of specialists. The Belov household quickly learned to worship the gun—the insulin gun.

As David injected three units of insulin hormone into Mikey's abdomen, he heard a loud honking noise emanating from outside. David and Marina turned and peered through the window to see a van out front being driven by Cat Zhadanov, with two more kids in the backseat. Cat was a wild woman with a heart of gold and the wife of David's friend Vlad. The kids were close, and so were the women, originally because of the men. Although David and Vlad didn't see each other as much as they used to, they would always be bound by the place where they grew up together. With a kiss on the forehead from Marina, Mikey raced down the steps towards Cat's van.

"Hey, Mikey?" David asked.

Mikey turned back to his dad.

"Got Froggie with you?"

Mikey smiled and held up a small bright-green plastic frog on a keychain strapped to his backpack—the Froggie Finder. He pressed the Froggie's nose and it flashed yellow-green.

"Love you, little man," Marina said.

David and Marina stood together and watched the car drive off.

"I wish I could go with him," David said.

"Let him live a little," Marina replied.

Marina rested her head on David's shoulder for a moment, until their peace was interrupted by the chirping of two cell phones. Marina and David simultaneously pulled phones out of their respective pockets. They'd each received the same notification message from the Froggie Finder iPhone app: "User1: Location is the intersection of 14th. Ave. and . . ." A green dot tracked Mikey's exact location. In addition to being a cute little toy, the Froggie was also a GPS tracking device for a child.

"This is so ridiculous," Marina said.

"Look. I just want to be able to know where he is . . ." David replied before trailing off.

"I know where he is. He's at the pool," she said.

"Humor me."

"That's what I do. Because I know it comes from a good place." Marina continued, "When do you have to go in?"

David glanced at his watch. "About an hour," he said. Marina cocked her head in disappointment.

"It's life," he said.

"It's work."

"Same thing."

"Doesn't have to be."

"I'll clean up," he added.

"Don't. I can think of a way to spend the time. While the house is free . . ." she smiled at him and allowed a brief, lascivious grin to escape her thin lips.

"I don't know. I need to get ready . . . take a shower," David meandered.

Marina pulled David in and kissed him. "That's such an amazing coincidence, because so do I," she said.

David grinned. He kissed her back. They continued to make out as Marina eagerly guided David inside, both of their phones' Froggie apps chirping on the counter with Mikey's new coordinates. Work could wait on Sundays—for an hour.

FIVE

PROGRAMMING LANGUAGE SPIT ACROSS the blank screen. As intended, David was back in the Montgomery offices and tapping away on an endless chain of machine code. Even though it was Sunday afternoon, a quarter of the floor was there. Such was the nature of the old-school hierarchy at the firm. If one wasn't striving to work harder and longer than everyone else, then rest assured human resources would find a replacement who happily would. Even though the bank had survived the financial crisis by going lean, it had not necessarily become smarter in the process. Face time was still a crucial business axiom. Through the windows to the trading floor, David could see Howard yelling into a phone and gesticulating wildly. If Howard was in on a Sunday, there was a simple rule: You better be there on Sunday, too. All of the warm bodies that stood below Howard on the firm's status pyramid would present themselves. It never mattered what the actual work to be done was, nor indeed the reason that Howard was there. He might be checking golf scores or browsing Etsy, looking for a gift for his niece. It was not relevant. If a banker wasn't giving birth, on a planned vacation, so hungover that movement was literally impossible, or already on the way out? Then they were in. And the only legitimate excuse out of the preceding four was obviously the rip-roaringly drunk one. There existed a certain pride about the hours at Montgomery Noyes—an insane pride, perhaps, but a pride nonetheless. Their competitors were trying out casual Friday policies and prohibiting consecutive Sunday workdays, but Montgomery would go nouveau over its dead body.

A bit later in the afternoon, David noticed as Tyler Stanton arrived in the quant section, bedraggled, pulling a suitcase along with him.

"Vegas?" David asked.

"AC."

"You up?"

"Never gamble like me," Tyler replied.

"That's why I like liquidity. Supply and demand in the open market. You can never lose it all. For every trade, there's a counter trade," David said.

"Spoken like a true quant." Tyler grinned. "I'm going to the gym. Need to take a shower before the wifey sees me, and make sure the other wifey," Tyler mumbled and nodded at Howard, "registers the presence of my pretty face." With that, he disappeared down a hallway towards the elevators.

A few moments afterwards, the sandwich guy pushed his cart through the office. Another mark of excellence within the corporate sphere was a lunch man on full benefits. Montgomery's sandwich man was named Hank, and he had mastered the art of unobtrusive small talk mixed with a sticky order memory. Those were his only two jobs. Hank knew very well that hell would be unleashed on the sandwich man who forgot what Howard's "usual" was, but he went above and beyond that by remembering practically every single employee's preferred order.

"'Sup, my man? Roast beef and provo with a dash of honey mustard?" Hank asked David.

"You got it, Hank. Hey. It's game day. Why aren't you at Meadowlands?" David inquired in his perpetually collegial tone.

"Had to sell the tix. Old lady told me to. You know how it is . . . Happy wife, happy life, right?" Hank said.

"Sorry to hear it."

Hank handed David a sandwich from his cart. "Nah, it ain't nothing like that. Respect the proverb, my man."

"I do and will." David smiled back at him. Hank was a stand-up guy. Maybe the only good one. He came in seven days a week, except for the few weekends out of the year when he was at a football game. But unlike the rest of them, Hank didn't show up out of misplaced obligation. He was paid hourly, after all.

David turned back to his computer. He continued to tap along on the program he was working on, when the booming voice of Howard Bergensen careened over the top of his head. David turned and was shocked to find Bergensen, the old lion himself, standing beside his desk.

"May sixth. Two thousand and ten. What happened?" Howard asked David.

David rotated in his chair. While he prepared to answer, all that ran through his head were questions. Why was Howard Bergensen all the way over in the quant section? Talking to him, of all people?

"Uh, Mr. Bergensen . . . Well, that was the Flash Crash. Dow Jones average plummeted a thousand points in five minutes and—"

"It was caused by the computers, right?" Howard asked.

"Frankly, there's a number of highly plausible options. There's the fat-finger concern. A random guy at a hedge fund enters the wrong trade size into his software, types in an extra zero or two, and suddenly the market is swamped with more sell orders than statistically possible. Spoofing is also an option—when false orders are entered in bulk through the system to try to fish out other counterparties' strategies. Or it could all be as simple as a small programming error inside the exchange's matching system," David responded, realizing that he was already losing Howard.

"So what you're saying is . . . Yes?" Howard asked.

"Precisely, sir. Exactly. The computers. An error within a trading algorithm, most likely."

"It's the wild west in there." Howard pointed towards the server room and its server blades. "We used to trade in the pits on luck, spit and a handshake," he said.

"Now it's just luck?"

"No. Now a bunch of black boxes fight each other for supremacy while we sit around with our thumbs up our asses," Howard replied. "Goodbye." Howard sauntered past David and turned a corner.

David was left with a befuddled expression across his face that matched his mind's conclusions. He racked his brain. He didn't think he'd ever seen Howard in the quant section before, much less staring David dead in the eye. The more he thought about it, the more sure he became. Howard Bergensen did not know him from a sheet of paper. Howard Bergensen did not know his name. The entire interaction was bizarre. But perhaps it was positive. Maybe this was what the path out of the back office looked like. It started with Howard opening up the door a crack. Sure, he'd have to bust his ass off. But maybe it all ended with David trading—David with a full account size—David beating Rick and Peter at their own games. David shook his head. *Davyd, stop daydreaming.*

■

David stood in the elevator, finally heading out for the day. The elevator door opened up a floor below and Tyler entered, freshly washed from the gym.

"Howard came through," David told him.

"Where?" Tyler responded absentmindedly.

"My desk."

"Huh? You talked to Howard?"

"I guess so. I mean, really he just sort of . . . wandered past me. While speaking," David said.

"Did you tell him the desk is doing good, dude?"

"Uh . . . No, I didn't," David stuttered.

"I got one word for you: Politics," Tyler replied.

"Right. I know that."

"Howard only cares about leveraging gold this month. He thinks the commodity collapse is way oversold and the time for rebound is now. It's all the guy will talk about in staff, and it'll probably be offshore raw next month, and that's the point. He doesn't give one tit except what makes him money, because it's money that gives him his house on the Egg and his Lürssen yacht and his fucking red-haired Tibetan Mastiff." Tyler gesticulated wildly as he ranted. "It's money that bestows upon Howard the title of the ultimate baller in our universe. So you tell him about our profit, and then you shut the fuck up. Get it?"

"Yea, Tyler. I get it," David said.

Neither man uttered another word as the elevator descended to the lobby. David didn't like the way Tyler spoke to him and never had. Maybe that's just because Tyler was his boss. Perhaps it was the way he dressed, like the T-shirt he had on, which had likely cost more than a week's worth of groceries for David's family. Or maybe it was the fact that Tyler went to Vegas all the time without his wife. It even could have been because he led the quant section, but didn't know how to program a single line of code himself. Tyler was just like the rest of them, which meant he was the opposite of David. Born and bred to a superb family, having attended an acceptable higher-learning institution and pledged the correct fraternity, Tyler just happened to have raised his hand at the right time during a fortunate lecture and had volunteered to take a desk no one wanted. Within three years he was telling all the programmers in the firm what to do. At least that's how David perceived it. Because Tyler had navigated life so well, David had to tell him that he "got it." And he did. Those were the rules. They weren't written down, but they were sacrosanct.

After the elevator arrived on the bottom floor and the doors opened, David and Tyler exited silently and hurtled in opposite directions.

SIX

THE PUNCHING BAG TOOK it hard. David pounded out the sand-filled leather—left, right, jab, hook, short straight. The large bag swung around in an unwieldy oval, almost knocking David down. The power of randomness could sometimes be quite awesome. David tripped backwards.

Not often, but sometimes David liked to show up at the boxing gym in Bensonhurst and take it out on the dumb bag that weighed the same as he did. He was a little irked at Tyler—right hit—and Howard. What the hell was that guy doing? Was he taunting him? Leftie. David ducked around as the bag swung toward him and into the gym's owner, Vlad Zhadanov. A robust man with tattoos spanning fifty percent of his body, all the way up the back of his neck, Vlad was Cat's husband and David's friend since childhood. Vlad grabbed the bag with two hands and pushed it back towards David.

"You're slapping the shit out of it! Come on, I know you got more than that! Give it all you got. Give it all!" Vlad yelled at him.

If there was one truth about their friendship, it was that Vlad had always been able to motivate David. Sometimes Vlad could be a bully. He was impossible to defeat physically. If you punched Vlad, he was largely impervious. He would simply wind up and hit you again when you weren't looking—just like the bag itself. But Vlad's words were often just as powerful.

It was an honor to work out at Vlad's gym—especially for David, who was considered an outlier in his own community. Every single person at Vlad's gym knew him personally. One didn't just sign up at the front desk and accept a keychain and towel. They earned the right to be there. The men in the gym were tighter than tight and thick as thieves. They all grew up in the neighborhood and applied to themselves most of the same assumptions about the general ethical rules of life. Petrov and Roschin, two identical twin brothers, sparred in another ring beside David. Watching from outside the lines was the amiable and bushy-haired Baranowski, standing with Konstantin, who didn't speak a lick of English at all. David continued to pound out the bag ferociously. He wished that one day his own colleagues, like Tyler, could meet these dudes. They were still David's friends when it was convenient for both sides. But they were his people always. They'd attended the same schools since they were babes in diapers, and most of them had graduated from New Utrecht High School as "Utes." Tyler would piss his pants if he could meet David's old pals in their natural state. What did that say about David? God, how David would love to see the tables turned on Tyler for once. But that would never happen. Tyler would never come here in his entire life. Deep down inside, every man knows his true place in the world. That's why David was punching a bag in a dingy boxing gym surrounded by a bunch of thugs who reminded him of his father, while Tyler played squash at the Yale Club.

Left. Right. Jab. From across the gym, Vlad continued to clock David's frenetic activity with cool detachment.

■

After an hour or so, David rested. He padded into the old-school Russian banya in the back of Vlad's facility. The paneled room had a small firewood stove set underneath a vat of water to create a perpetual haze of steam. A series of large wooden tiers were built into the sides of the space. Wearing a towel, David sat on the highest level and soaked up the steam, expelling oxidants. He opened his eyes as Vlad entered the banya.

"Bad day, my peach? Haven't seen you here in awhile," Vlad said.

David looked up and noticed that Vlad was completely naked, except for a diamond-encrusted pendant depicting a scorpion suspended by a gold chain off his neck. Vlad was a big guy, built like a giant oak tree. He sat down as close to the fire as he could muster.

"Saw Cat this morning," David said with a smile.

"Ya. She told me. She said the pool was a nightmare. Every fuckin' ten-year-old Ivan in town was there with three floatin' noodles and a watergun."

"Same pool. Just a whole different experience from ours."

"Yeah. Instead of ice cream bars, we had bloody noses." Vlad chuckled.

"And worse," David said. "Thanks, though. I know Marina needed the day off."

"Anything for you and your family. That's the truth," Vlad replied. He stood again and ambled towards a venik hanging from the wall. The venik was a small broom created from the branches of a birch tree. Vlad soaked the tool in a bucket of ice water. "How's the devil?" Vlad turned back and asked. He handed David the venik. "Do the honors, please."

"You mean the bank?" David asked. David held the venik and Vlad turned away from him. David did exactly what the instrument was designed for and briskly smacked Vlad's back, then targeted the major muscles of Vlad's shoulders. Vlad shook his head as he received the painful whipping voluntarily. His mouth wobbled back and forth humorously, spittle flying from his mouth.

"Buncha' Ivy League pricks. Never know why you're happy working for a bunch of pompous morons," he finally muttered.

"I'm not one of them," David replied.

"I know it. And so do they," Vlad said.

"Hey. I'll do anything for Mikey."

"Ya. I know," Vlad replied. "Remember when we were his age? How good we were at hoppin' those trains on Coney Island down by Gravesend?"

"That was fun. But we were dumb." David grinned at the memory.

"Brave—we were brave."

"Most of the time we were just running away from the five-o. Call it what you want. But I hadn't learned about risk management back then," David said as he finished slapping Vlad with the venik.

"You really do sound like a banker." Vlad laughed a huge guffaw, which bellowed through the chamber. "Been a long time since you stole anything with your hands, hasn't it? Now it's all with your head?"

"I take pennies from other traders all around the world," David said. "Legally," he added after a moment's thought.

Vlad picked up the cold-water pail. He poured the remaining water over the hot coals situated in a cavity above the banya's wood fire. A massive cloud of steam erupted into the room and all visibility was instantly reduced.

"Now the kids hang out more than us," Vlad said ruefully.

"Kids have time. We don't."

"I was thinking . . . What if we did another scuba trip with the girls sometime? Like to Belize," Vlad asked.

"Sure. Sounds good," David replied. He checked his watch. "I gotta run, Vlad." He stood up while Vlad talked to his back.

"Life is going good for you now, ya?" Vlad said. "I get it. But don't forget . . . A rising tide lifts all boats. You don't learn anything about a man when things are good. And you learn everything about him when it all turns to shit."

"You're a poet," David turned and said.

"Nah. I'm just a gangster. But at least I know it," Vlad retorted.

David grinned and exited the banya.

SEVEN

AS THE SUN FINALLY set on Sunday evening, David parked his light-green Honda Civic in front of his house. Hair freshly washed and combed, he walked up the steps with his gym bag in hand. It was at the top of the stairs that David abruptly noticed the front door was wide open. He hightailed it up the remaining front steps towards the glow.

"Hey guys!" David yelled once he was inside. But there was no one in the kitchen. That was unusual around dinnertime, especially for Mikey. As David walked through the kitchen, he noticed a knife lying out on the floor. David instantly became more alert and insistent. "Mair? Mikey!" he called out loudly. No response.

David scrambled around the entire first floor of the house but couldn't find any sign of either of them. He ran up the stairs and into the master bedroom. Nothing. In Mikey's bedroom? No one. The guest room? Nope. Then David heard an unusual ringing noise emanating from downstairs, towards the kitchen. It wasn't a ringtone he was familiar with.

He instantly raced back downstairs towards the kitchen. David noticed an older-model flip phone on the counter. He must have missed the device on his first mad dash through the room. An "unknown" number was calling. The call stopped before David decided whether or not to answer it. He was already beginning to feel a horrible premonition of the future. This was not good. This was an emergency. He stared at the phone and then noticed Mikey's Froggie Finder sitting on the counter as well. All of a sudden the phone began to ring again. It was the same caller. David took a deep breath and finally answered. A man's scrambled and filtered bass voice boomed onto the line.

"David Belov?" the man asked through electronic garbles.

"Who's this?" David said.

"We have Marina—and your son Michael," the man said quickly and confidently. Although David was a cynic, there was something in the man's tone that made it very clear he wasn't lying. David crumbled onto a chair while the man continued to speak. "You have something very valuable to us, and now we have something very valuable to you."

"Who do you think I am? We don't have anything! I barely have savings . . . I'll give you all of it," David exclaimed. This couldn't be happening. He'd done everything he possibly could in life to avoid a circumstance exactly like this. And yet it was occurring, right in front of his eyes.

"On the contrary. It's not your money we want. What you have is in your head, Mr. Belov," the man said slowly.

"What could you possibly mean? What do you want from me?"

"This phone contains a microSD card. There is an assignment on the card. Follow it. Keep the phone on you at all times," the man ordered.

"What's on the card?" David asked.

"All you need to do is read. Do your part—then get out of the way."

"No. Wait. How do I know you have them? I need proof."

"Your wish," the scrambled voice said.

The flip phone suddenly vibrated. David looked down. There was a small pixelated photograph of Marina and Mikey on the cell's tiny screen. They were handcuffed to bedposts on a bed in a blank-looking apartment. Duct tape had been wrapped liberally around their heads. David began to hyperventilate.

"Mikey needs his shots. He's a diabetic," David scrambled.

"Yes. Your wife informed us of that fact."

David raced to a closet in the kitchen. He opened it and found that all of the family's unopened packages of insulin were still in the closet.

"He will not receive any insulin until you save him," the man said.

"No! You can't do that. He won't make it for more than twenty-four hours. I'm telling you—that's the truth."

"You don't even have twenty-four hours. We may call you again. Do not call us back. Do what we ask and save your family. This number is scrambled." With that, the unknown man hung up.

"Wait! Shit!" David screamed. He immediately popped open the battery cover on the flip phone. He pulled out the microSD card as instructed and ran towards his office.

David and Marina's house contained a converted sunporch along its flank that doubled as David's office. It was packed with computers, partially assembled motherboards, and random circuitry lacking a home. The remnants of a technical past. David scrambled for a microSD reader. He found one in a box of other peripherals and hooked it up to his computer. The drive appeared on his desktop. He clicked on the folder, and opened a readme file located within. He stared at the instructions on the screen but he couldn't believe what he was seeing. This definitely wasn't what he expected. There were no programs on the drive. No executables. No algorithms. No raw code. Just a simple text file with instructions:

"Crash the gold index 500 basis points. Tomorrow at 1:15 PM. Don't worry about server room authorization. You'll be approved."

David read the message again and again, trying to parse it for any additional information.

"Oh Jesus. There's no way. Oh god . . ." David whispered to himself. He quickly made a decision. It was a logical conclusion because he was a rule-following man and he'd always figured out how to solve his own problems.

This was a completely insane moment in his life, and he knew exactly what one was supposed to do in a situation like this. He reached for his cell phone and dialed 9-1-1.

After a few rings, the emergency dispatcher picked up, "State your emergency."

"My name is David Belov. I'm at twenty-one hundred Seventy-eighth Street, Bensonhurst. My family's been taken—*my family*. . . . Two—Marina, and Mikey Belov. They're gone—" David stopped as he heard the ringing of the flip phone again. He glanced down to his desk to see the "unknown" number calling him for a third time. He hung up on 9-1-1 and picked up the flip phone cautiously.

"Do not call the police. I am not joking you. This will end very, very badly unless you do exactly what we have instructed you to do." The garbled man's voice was back and much more angry and threatening than before.

David glanced sharply around. *Were they watching?*

"I'm sorry. I'm so sorry," David said. "The gold market? How do you expect me to do that? It's swimming in liquidity. I'd have to send a couple million orders just to move it one percent."

"If the police come to your house, you will keep all the lights off and not answer the door," the man said.

"Okay. I will. I—"

"You're smart, David, but be smarter. Maybe you can find us—eventually. But there won't be enough time for you to save them. When it comes to your task, I know you can do it. You were selected because you are the man for this job. I have full confidence in you."

"That—that's my family you're threatening." David stammered.

"Check your phone."

David looked down. A second photograph had been sent to him. It was Marina. She was still handcuffed, but her clothes had been ripped off and she was exposed down to her underwear. David observed the picture with horror.

"Don't hurt her. Do not hurt her. I'll do it. I'll do . . . anything," David said.

"This is your last chance. Complete your assignment. Only you can do it. If you don't? There won't be a third picture. There won't be any more calls. Your wife and son will simply cease to exist," the man warned ominously and then hung up on David.

David turned off the lights in the kitchen. He walked into the living room and did the same. Standing in the dark, his house phone began to ring, startling him. It was a random New York number that he didn't recognize. Must be the police again. He picked up.

"Hi. . . . Yes. I just called. . . . No. Everything's fine. I found them. Sorry about that. . . . Right. False alarm," David lied to the dispatcher. Then he took a deep breath and sat back down at the computer with the instructions in front of him: Crash the gold index. Tomorrow.

David loaded up his Borland C++ programming application and began to program frantically. His fingers typed incessantly on the keypad, forming a rhythm. The scariest part about the problem ahead was how easy he found it to solve. He had lied to the man on the phone. Considering that he had access to the buying power and trusted exchange connections of Montgomery Noyes' servers, he knew that he would have no problem manipulating the market to do exactly as the kidnappers intended. Then again, they probably knew that already. His obfuscation was useless. David's fingers continued to tap as fast as his brainstem would permit the code to flow out.

But David wasn't really focused on the words onscreen. All he could do was replay the moments of the last ten minutes in his mind: A knife on the floor. Was there blood? He didn't think so. Maybe Marina had picked it up to defend herself? A new cell phone with a microSD card. Obviously whoever did this was well aware of his skills—his edge. The American ideal. He'd have to talk to his mother about that later. He knew one thing for sure: No one would go to this extent based on a fluke. Howard Bergensen kept floating into David's mind as he typed. It had been just a few hours before when Howard was questioning him about the engineering of a flash crash. Did that mean that Howard could be responsible? No way. Why would Howard ever do something like that? Howard had too much to lose. That would be impossible. When you own a house in the Hamptons, you don't kidnap housewives and children. It made no sense. David thought about the kidnappers themselves. They knew that he was calling 9-1-1. Or was it just a coincidence that they called him back? It couldn't have been. So they were watching him in the house. Were they outside? Had they hacked into his computer or his cell phone? Something worse? Cameras? All of these thoughts raced through David's mind like an endless conveyor belt ripping through an Escher drawing. There were too many moving parts to encompass the whole. If he focused too hard on one element, all of the other connective pieces would fall out of line.

What David did know was that those pictures were real and the voice on the line meant what he was saying. He could do the work, right then, that might get his family back to him alive. That's why his fingers rat-atat-tapped. While he wrote the custom code, he thought about whom in the world he could possibly go to.

That's when he realized that he was actually a lucky bastard—because he had a friend named Vlad Zhadanov. And if there was any time that Vlad could be useful, that time was right then. Should he go to Vlad? Vlad solved problems. But unlike David's programming skills, Vlad was never elegant in his approach. And there just wasn't enough time.

David wrestled with the decision in his mind as he typed. But before he could plan a new course of action, he'd already finished the algorithm.

EIGHT

<u>Monday</u>

AT ONE SIXTEEN ON Monday afternoon, David's flash crash algorithm operated like a charm and Montgomery Noyes experienced a brush with Armageddon.

■

On the evening of the crash, Howard Bergensen reclined in a bathtub at Windswept, his mansion in the Hamptons. There were only a few nights a year in which Howard would take a bath after work. His time was precious and he rarely splurged, but his wife and children knew to never disturb him on the rare evenings when he was soaking. They knew that bath days were the very worst ones. He sat in the piping-hot tub with an iced towel over his face and he listened to CNBC playing on the small flat-screen in the bathroom, still unable or unwilling to completely unplug himself from the situation.

"After today's flash crash, you're wondering . . . Is the American dream dead?" one of the anchors pondered and subsequently self-answered,

"Maybe it's just on vacation."

The crash had shaken Howard, even though he was better prepared than the majority to stay on his feet no matter what calamities befell the markets. Howard was a survivor, but that didn't mean he still couldn't be shot out of the sky. He was acutely aware that he wasn't infallible. That's probably what had kept his career going so far. He'd survived much scarier moments in financial history, from the Long-Term Capital Management debacle to Black Monday in 1987, when the Dow dropped twenty-two percent in one day—not to mention the first tech boom and the more recent credit and housing crisis.

But because he was also a human, Howard was worried about the tangential effects of the flash crash. He didn't want this event to negatively affect his wife and kids—the same ones who would furtively glance into the bathroom every hour just to make sure he was alive. Marjorie was actually his third wife. And the kids still living in the house were his fifth and sixth kids. Howard had already planted two earlier generations of family tree, with whom he was certainly still intertwined, plus he had the newest version to worry about. All of his progeny required constant payments—"annuities" as he viewed them—because the bloodletting never stopped. Once child support was over, the kid was going to college. And Howard was not a cruel man. He loved his children. So he was going to pay for all of them to go to school. At that time it was Sebastian, from Howard's second and shortest-lived marriage, who had just started at Columbia. What Howard had learned recently, via family unit number one, was that even after college graduation the expenses didn't end. His second-eldest had moved to Los Angeles to be an assistant in the film business. Howard was convinced that he paid his gardener more to trim rhododendrons than his son was paid to coordinate big-budget movies. And rent wasn't cheap in Santa Monica. More payments. And then his oldest, Caroline . . . Well, she'd gotten married. That costed money. And like clockwork, the baby came along. Hell if Howard was going to allow his first grandchild to grow up in an apartment in downtown Chicago. He knew that he was soon to be on the hook for a substantial deposit on a nice house in Evanston or Lakeview.

Howard made a ton of money, and he spent a ton plus one. If the first part of that equation experienced more than a hiccup, he was in trouble with the second, because the latter would not abate quickly if ever. There were a few other debts as well—negative account values that he may have conveniently forgotten to tell Marjorie about. He and a couple partners from the club had invested in a hotel in Taos that specialized in basalt rubs and steam rooms. The problem was that the establishment was never more than twenty percent full, no matter how much money they poured into it. It was in the midst of a second renovation, and Howard sensed that the money was literally taking a mud bath. Finally, he had doodled around with some futures trading strategies in his personal account. Those moves were in the red by a couple million, and his broker-dealer was giving him as much time as he needed because he ran Montgomery. But the time-out wouldn't last forever.

Howard still had some tricks up his sleeves. He had made plans to deal with his debts and he was carrying them out, but one deadly characteristic of money was the way issues snowballed. Such was the nature of the cascade. Inertia was a hell of a force. Objects in motion stay in motion, and those that are falling? Gravity is relentless.

Beyond everything, Howard was guilty of neglecting the fact that Montgomery's liabilities might become his own. He was reaching the conclusion that he had to stick his finger in the dike immediately. He needed to stay on top of all this, slowly start making the bank's money back, cement the board of directors' full confidence in him, and continue doing exactly what he'd done for over thirty years in the fiduciary business: Win at all costs. He knew he could do it, but he also knew that the next few weeks would constitute a precarious tightrope walk over the raging rapids.

Howard stirred when his cell phone started to vibrate on the marble surface of his tub. His bad night was about to turn into a nightmare. He picked up.

"This is Howard," he said. He listened. At first he was incredulous but calm as Roger O'Neill briefed him about the robbery of their armored truck on the FDR just a few minutes before. Then Howard slowly became enraged. Luckily he had insurance for this circumstance, but the one-two punch of bad trade management and a physical loss was not something he was expecting in the lovely twilight of his career. He contracted all of the muscles in his body as he screamed from the depths of his belly, "No, that will not suffice!"

Howard lifted himself out of the tub and stomped out of the bathroom, dripping wet and screaming for his wife. "Marjorie, call Steve. I need a car back to the city. Immediately!"

▪

Roger O'Neill stood at the scene of the crime listening to Howard berate him. Far from resolved, the situation was turning further grim with each passing minute. The more details Roger had learned from pressing the police, the less secure he had felt. This was momentous. It was one of the largest heists the city—hell, the country—had ever seen. As the bank's visible security chief, Roger knew that he was on the hook. And if there was any value imperative to Roger, it was that his good name not be dragged through the mud on any condition. What he was seeing and hearing made him a very unhappy man. Three security staffers stood behind Roger, mirroring the completely despondent look on their boss's face. They were slowly jacking up their disabled car on the side of the road and inspecting the tires that had been ripped to shreds by two silenced pistol shots. There were two police cruisers present, but Roger watched as a third police squad car sped onto the scene with sirens blaring and burned rubber to decelerate. It parked behind them. Then another squad car arrived. Soon the entire FDR highway was completely blocked off by the NYPD. Red and blue light ricocheted everywhere.

▪

Red and blue lights rocketed across the Bitter End as well, a rock spot in Greenwich Village on the other side of the island. Jake Rivett opened his mouth and delivered a manic yell.

"Yayaayayayaaaaaaa!" Jake's scream completely overtook any of his band members' instruments or any audience member's desire to maintain a coherent conversation with friends. Jake Rivett got in your face with his music. He liked it that way. It kept people off balance, and that was exactly the point. Spit sprayed from Jake's mouth and coated the microphone in front of his lips as he crushed his latest original screamo track. Twig skinny with blonde spiked hair, an all-leather-and-denim-façade worn skintight, Jake rocked the mic hard.

"Is anyone out there breaking free of this plastic shell encasing me?" Jake sang, and he truly wanted to know. His band went absolutely nuts on the last line. Jake climbed up a three-foot speaker to the side of the stage and did a backflip off the tower to end the song. He didn't completely pull it off, under rotating and smashing into the ground with his whole body. But it was the thought that counted. He stood up to greet the crowd.

There wasn't much of one. Just a sprinkling of applause greeted Jake and his band at the end of their set. Throughout the dark music venue, Jake noticed a small collection of punk-rock chicks and their boyfriends, a bartender taking care of a couple of winos, and an older couple in a booth. That was it. But the key to turning a hobby into a career was to start and not quit. Because of that, Jake had thrown himself to the ground many times before and would be doing the same again in the future.

The lackluster crowd didn't stop Jake and his band from jumping off the stage, hooting and hollering and truly pumped up. A performance was a performance—and also a good night. One was compelled by the spirit of rock n' roll to act like a rock star while becoming one, even if that placed oneself at the expense of the dream before even getting there. As many wannabe rockers had realized only in hindsight, the efficacy of that philosophy was never clear until many years later. And then it would be crystal clear—hopefully not "crystal meth" clear, but instead, "crystal chandelier" clear.

Jake immediately headed for his backpack, which was on the ground underneath a side table, when the band's drummer, Schaub, pulled him away.

"See those babes at the bar? They know about a party in Brooklyn," Schaub told him. "We gotta take them up on that, bro."

"That's chill," Jake replied. He found his cell phone and checked it. There was a missed call. "Shit," he said. "I can't."

"Seriously? It's midnight."

"Assholes never sleep."

Jake placed a black motorcycle helmet over his head and walked out of the bar without any further ado. Sometimes it hurt to leave his bandmates high and dry, but they could handle the after hours all by themselves.

The cold, hard truth was that even if Jake had been in the middle of a song, he would have responded immediately and left the stage. His hobby would remain just that for the time being, because he had his orders. No one is truly obligated by a job. One can always quit. Jake could too. But he never would. Because what he did for a living provided him with even more exhilaration than a couple shots of J.D. and blasting extreme decibels ever could. He could always become a rock star after retirement.

▪

Having been beckoned, Jake ripped through the deserted streets of the city on his super-powered Ducati bike. Without activating its blinker, a lumbering delivery truck moved into the lane in front of Jake, almost cutting him off. Jake accelerated past the truck at the last moment. The driver honked and moved up near his tail, just a few feet away. Jake reached behind his back and pulled a crowbar off the back of the bike. He reared back towards the truck and swung the crowbar wildly in the air, gesticulating for the trucker to stay away. Needless to say, the truck backed off.

Power was a tricky thing. For three years of high school, Jake had attended a military boarding school in upstate New York, where the force of intimidation had been cemented into his young mind. Boarding school had been his father's idea, which was ironic because his father was the one who taught Jake the most about fear in the first place. Sometimes one didn't need to actually do anything to get one's way. Simply projecting a mental image of the horror that was to come compelled many into submission. That's not to say that Jake figured out how to use this power for himself. Similar to home, he'd remained the whipping boy in boarding school. After graduation he was just happy to get out of there in one piece and finally make it to the city where he belonged. In the city, he'd succeeded in turning the narrative around. He started going to a Krav Maga gym. As he became more lethal, he felt better. The haze lifted. He started to perform on stage, where he was allowed to be himself. He wasn't meek—he was aggressive. He didn't stumble—he stepped forward. He stopped getting bullied by becoming a bully himself. At least some people might describe him that way. But only the bad ones.

Jake continued to spin through the city. He finally arrived in the front of a tall building in Wall Street. But it wasn't just any building. Jake strode off the bike, past a police SUV parked at the front door, and into Montgomery Noyes' headquarters.

▪

Jake raced up to the turnstile by the elevators. A security guard eyed Jake's black-and-denim ensemble with suspicion.

"Can I help you, sir? This is a private entrance," the guard asked.

"Yeah," Jake held up his NYPD detective badge. "You can bring me up to the twentieth floor."

NINE

HOWARD BERGENSEN SAT IN Montgomery's glass-encased boardroom on the twentieth level, across from Tom Marks. Marks was chief of police, the head honcho of the entire police force for the five boroughs.

"So this guy—he's your best?" Howard asked.

Marks nodded. "Give him a bone and he'll stomp after it like a rabid pit bull. But he's like all our undercovers. My only word to the wise is don't ask him to explain himself."

"What does that mean?" Howard asked quizzically.

At that very moment, Jake Rivett entered the conference room and everyone instantly comprehended Marks' directive.

"Gentlemen, this is Rivett," Chief Marks announced. The rest of the conference table took a beat while they processed Detective Jake Rivett's outfit and persona. Jake nodded at the table and then launched right into it. He had spent his entire motorcycle ride, even while maniacally swinging the crowbar, on the phone with his team of investigators who were spread out at various sites all over the city.

"At this moment, we have two hundred units of traffic and aviation out, two SWAT contingents on standby, and major crimes, robbery apprehension and tech working with me out of SID," Jake said succinctly and confidently. Howard was taken aback for a moment but then leaned in. He was only familiar with detectives who wore suits with horrible thread counts and clashing shirt-tie combinations. But in recent years Howard had seen young men walk through his office in jeans and ratty T-shirts and leave holding fundraising checks worth more than even he could dream of. The world was changing and so were the uniforms. So maybe they could work with this guy. There would be a lot of pain ahead—Howard was sure of it. But what kept him going was the light at the end of the tunnel. Everything in life was a means to an end. This situation was no different.

"Don't you have cameras out on the streets?" Howard asked. "On the FDR? Traffic video or whatever you call it?"

"Indeed. You're right. The crime was pretty well captured. We've got workable angles from seven or eight city cameras and some adjacent shots from others. We'll also be pulling as much private footage as we can get our hands on. Real Time Crime Center sent over a visual patchwork of the heist—at least what they've been able to cobble together so far. It's quite," Jake searched for the best word, "sublime."

"Highly professional," Marks added with a nod. Marks always felt the need to explain Jake to others. It had only taken about three years of Jake's employment before Marks had heard his name for the first time, because one fact kept bubbling up through staff meetings and into the higher echelons of management: They had a newbie detective with zero unsolved cases. But that wasn't even why he respected Jake. He'd seen numerous stars turn into supernovas and then collapse into their own hubris during his career. And he didn't love how the kid looked. But as Marks had begun to listen to Jake's process, hopping from one critical case to the next, and as he learned that Jake's father had been the chief of police in the state's capital of Albany, he began to warm to the guy. It didn't hurt that Jake's record was still largely unblemished. Of course there was still a case or two on the roster that Jake hadn't been able to solve. But that was a function of the fact that the hardest cases in the city were being assigned to Rivett regularly.

"There are five persons of interest," Jake said. He flipped around a laptop handed to him by one of Marks' assistants, displaying the video footage from the FDR. Jake controlled the playback as he showed the footage to the assembled executives. "There were two motorcycles involved —two perps on each motorcycle. It looks like a man and woman each. And then there's the crane. It's basically ingenious. They picked up that armored car with a magnet, like it was some prize in a coin-operated machine at the boardwalk. In terms of the whois, there's very few clues about these individuals' identities. All wore helmets, except for one guy— the driver of the crane rig truck. He's our mystery man," Jake said. He paused the video and zoomed in on the magnetic crane rig and flatbed. The side profile of a young Asian man was clearly visible inside the cab of the truck, eyes wide with adrenaline, straight black hair to his shoulders. "Facial algorithms haven't pulled up a hit yet. Frankly, with the blur and the angle on his face, the databases may never find him. That also assumes that he's been booked before. The entire heist was an exercise in utter precision, including their escape route," Jake finished.

"Why do you say that, exactly?" Howard asked.

"Because they exited in Mott Haven, which has the distinction of being exactly one ramp beyond our networked municipal cameras," Jake replied.

"With four point two tons of our gold," Howard said.

"What's that worth, exactly?" Marks asked.

Howard Bergensen stared out the window. "A hundred and twenty-seven point one million dollars," he finally said.

"The press are going to self-immolate with excitement," Jake chimed in.

Howard glared at Rivett.

"Howard, is your bank prepared to announce the loss?" Marks asked.

"Immediately. We did nothing wrong—except pick the wrong damned armored-car company," Howard said as he rotated his laser eyes towards Roger O'Neill and then continued. "My singular interest is our shareholders. We will communicate the truth. Our insurance will cover the loss by the end of the quarter. The robbery doesn't alter my bottom line by a dollar. But the flash crash . . . affected everyone."

"The what?" Marks asked quizzically.

"Gold market crashed earlier," Jake added.

Howard nodded. "That's the entire reason we were forced to settle up. Normally we don't actually move the physical gold from our depository. There's no need. Instead we just mark who owns what at the end of each night. We'll say, 'This rack used to be owned by A, but now it's owned by B.' But ultimately the clients and other banks we trade with do have the contractual right to take physical delivery if they want to. Gold fell over eight percent yesterday in the flash crash. That's an abnormal event—total black swan. And the biggest players in the market all know what everyone else is doing, even if by hearsay and innuendo. It's no secret out there that we were building our gold position up and using leverage to do it. We thought we'd finally reached a solid bottom. So our counterparties got freaked out. We experienced a margin call. A bunch of the organizations that we do business with demanded their physical gold. And that's why we were moving more gold at one time than we ever had before," Howard said.

Jake thought about this. "So no crash, no robbery?"

"Right," Howard confirmed.

"Okay. Then the next logical question is: What caused the flash crash?" Jake asked.

"We don't know yet." Howard sighed. "We're actively looking into it, but there's no guarantees. Maybe we'll figure it out. But sometimes the market's too big, and too complicated, for simple answers."

"There are a number of plausible options: fat finger, high-frequency malfunction, or something predatory," a Montgomery lawyer in the back of the room said.

Howard jumped back in. "The market has no soul. It's like the sea. You build your ship to be watertight, but a tsunami will still destroy it, drown all the sailors, and not even remember doing it."

A heavy silence pervaded the room. Jake watched a blur of motion through the plate glass separating the conference room from the rest of Montgomery Noyes' bullpen. A man was running their way. After another moment, a breathless Tyler Stanton dashed into the conference room.

"NASDAQ called. They've tracked the routing patterns of hundreds of thousands of cancelled trades made just as the crash started," he said. The entire room turned to hear Tyler speak. "It was definitely an algo. This was intentional. But, uh . . ." Tyler struggled to select the appropriate words to express the next shocking statement. "The algo was running off our servers."

"What the hell are you talking about?" Howard fumed.

"We found the executable in fourteen machines, spread across the entire intranet system. Someone put it there—on purpose. The logs indicate that we ran it all day long," Tyler said.

"How is that possible?" Howard asked.

"It's not."

"That is not an answer. Did a hacker do this?" Howard asked again.

"I really don't think so."

"Why not?" Jake asked.

"Some of these computers aren't even connected to the internet. They only provide processing power to our ecosystem, behind fierce firewalls.

And to get into them you'd need to literally have physical access to our server room," Tyler responded. "So unless someone Mission Impossibled themselves into our office, an insider is responsible—an employee."

Howard leaned over to the company lawyer. "Report this confidentially to the SEC." Then he turned back to Tyler. "Is it still in our system?"

"No. IT just shut the last one down."

"We have logs of who went in and out of the room, right?" Howard asked.

"We do. Not only that—we have cameras, too," Tyler said.

"Then who was it?"

Tyler gazed around the room for a long, pregnant moment. He took a deep breath. "The quant," Tyler said. "David Belov."

TEN

WHEN A COMPANY SUCH as Montgomery Noyes is physically robbed for over a hundred million dollars, they can easily handle the loss. That's why insurance exists. What Howard and the bank were not as well prepared to deal with was the inherent reputational risk. There's a large gap between the theory of something and the execution of it, and nowhere is that more evidenced than in the money business. There were trillions of dollars of gold and cash floating around the world, and Montgomery Noyes had always been known as one of the most secure places to store that loot.

Howard Bergensen was quite aware that Montgomery's reputation must stay intact. That's why he gave Jake Rivett the address of his quant within a moment's notice. If David Belov was responsible for this, he was going to pay, and do so dearly. The first force of reparation that David would encounter was an elite counterterror-trained SWAT team, pumped up on sugar-free Red Bull and adrenaline, and their own personal demons, ripping deep track marks into his front lawn in Bensonhurst at five o'clock in the morning with merciless intent.

The SWAT team spread out around David and Marina's house, covering all the exits. A decidedly "no knock" situation, they announced their arrival by means of a reinforced-steel entry battering ram. SWAT splintered the door into multiple fragments. The ram crashed a few times more before completely destructing the wood and the SWAT team filed into the house quickly, screaming bloody murder. The SWAT philosophy, part and parcel from military doctrine, was one of extreme violence of action. They did not disappoint.

Fortunately or unfortunately, depending on one's perspective, the Belov household turned out to be a bunk target that evening.

"Kitchen clear!" one SWAT member screamed. The rest of the team fanned out in all directions with precision. But as the seconds ticked into the minutes and the chaos cleared inside the home, all Jake could discern was the cacophony of "clears" echoing throughout. He finally entered the house himself and conferred with the SWAT team's captain, Markle.

"Nobody's home," Markle said.

"Personal items in there?" Jake asked him.

"No sir—no cell phones, no wallets," Markle replied.

Jake thought for a moment. "Then start dusting." Jake turned to Tony Villalon, another detective from SID who was trailing him. "What's Verizon saying?" Jake asked Villalon.

"We put the pen-register request in six minutes ago. Let me see if they've gotten anything yet," Tony said as he walked off, cell phone already glued to his ear.

In the meantime, Jake wandered throughout David's house. The place was a picture of domesticity. It reminded him of his own childhood home in Albany. But Jake knew to never trust a first impression. On the surface, everything might look great. Especially when the sun was shining. The flaws lay underneath. Jake proceeded through each room on the first floor. He eventually found himself in David's cluttered sunporch office. Jake's gaze immediately fell to the garbage can. It was filled to the brim with shredded paper. Jake pointed to the paper. He nodded at Villalon, who was still on the phone.

"Scan that shit," Jake said. Then he was reminded of his manners. "Please," he added. Jake always had to remember to be polite, especially to his own colleagues. It wasn't so easy for him. It didn't come naturally. Actually, the whole charade was a bit of a curse. There was nothing worse than the knowledge that his social deficiency was so evident to the world. His indifference to protocol and normal human relationships seeped through his personality in an unavoidable manner. His mother had taught Jake to be polite, and he loved her, but she didn't teach him to stay that way. She hadn't listened when he needed her to hear, nor protected him when his father was raging and screaming and pushing him around after getting home from the bars with the rest of the ol' boys in blue.

Jake snapped on a pair of evidence gloves and began to pull David's desk drawers open. He found financial records, letters regarding health-insurance coverage at Montgomery Noyes, a couple of programming manuals, and old student ID cards from Stony Brook. Jake pulled out his phone and began taking photos as evidence, even though he knew that he wouldn't necessarily find a smoking gun there.

That's not how big cases worked. The highest-priority investigations were generally solved in one of two ways. Primarily, a person who was one or two links of the chain away from the evildoers would hear something implicit, but understand it as explicit, and allow an informant or police connection to become aware. That was the main way in which crimes were solved. The suspect's name came first, and the evidence to put him or her away was subsequently acquired in whatever manner possible.

The other method that Jake found his crimes resolving themselves was the hard way, which thankfully occurred less—the slog. The slog could manifest itself in a million different ways, but it usually began with the evidence itself, and not just one piece of evidence. It would be through the relationship between two or more information points that Jake would build a case. Cross-referencing, collating, mosaic-building—these were the ways that the rubber really hit the road for Jake and his detectives. So while Jake was well aware that the Belov's random files and personal detritus would yield very little by themselves, he also knew they might be his only hope in the long run.

Scanning atop one of David's bookshelves, Jake's eyes eventually fell across an old, worn photograph. The picture captured two couples in the Florida Keys: David and Marina Belov and another couple that Jake didn't recognize. The foursome was sitting on a boat with used scuba tanks and gear lying around their feet. Jake took a picture of the photo for the slog. Then Tony appeared at the door again, cell phone glued to his ear as per usual. But instead of Villalon's usually dour demeanor, there was a wide smile on his face.

"We got it Jake," Tony said. He listened to whatever the Verizon technician was telling him over the line and then continued. "The family has three lines on their plan. Two are off. But the third line is still connected to the network. Position coming in as . . . Union City, New Jersey."

■

Forty-five minutes later, the sun rose on the morning after the crime over the vast warehouse districts of Union City. Markle and his SWAT team snaked their way through the extensive, rough industrial zone. They were tired, but this was their bread and butter. It had only been about ten hours, and every single member of the team could operate at an efficient and professional level for twenty-four consecutive hours. Following protocol, they covered one another through firing zones until they located a side door. They quickly breached entry with an explosive charge, and the door swung open. SWAT moved slowly into the building. They took care to examine the most dangerous angles of exposure. First, a visual check around the door for booby traps, and then a ninety-degree scan with separation to the left and right of the inside of each door. All seemed clear. The entire team moved inside.

SWAT pulled down their night-vision goggles. Infrared lights lit the place up in an otherworldly green. It was completely uninhabited.

"SWAT! Hands up!" Markle screamed.

No one responded in any way.

Markle couldn't hear anything—not a single footstep or shuffle, nor the distinctive clack of a round entering a gun barrel. Nothing but silence. The inside of the building consisted of a graveyard of towering milling machines once used to manufacture enormous engine gears for submarines, each a few stories tall. The SWAT team snaked around every nook and cranny. As they neared the far side of the warehouse, Markle noticed a table sitting out in the open. Three cell phones sat on the table. One of them was still on. *Odd.*

Markle took a step back, and SWAT reformed their assault formation. Under no circumstances would Markle simply pick up one of the phones without Villalon and his technical team present. The gyroscopes inside the devices could be rigged such that a slight movement would blow up an explosive charge. While deciding on the next course of action, Markle heard a slight moan. Definitely human.

Markle ran swiftly towards the noise. Something was undulating behind the table. His flashlight caught sight of three black shapes on the floor—huge black duffel bags. They were human sized, and they were moving. Each bag was padlocked. Markle pulled a knife from his belt and ripped away the zipper around the padlock. He opened the first bag to find Mikey Belov, shaking and losing consciousness. The second and third bags contained Marina and David. All three had duct tape wrapped around their mouths. Their feet and legs were bound, but they were alive. Markle and the SWAT team rapidly unbound the hysterical family.

Just a moment after he'd been freed, Mikey's entire body began to spasm. It was a seizure. David and Marina pulled Mikey towards themselves, trying to comfort him. After a few moments of shaking, his motions turned into a horrific, full-fledged grand mal.

"No! Mikey . . . Hold on, honey. You'll be okay. You're good. We're here," Marina cried out. "We need an ambulance here! Right now!" David and Marina held Mikey's body down as the seizure continued. They rolled him on his side when he went unconscious. None of this was particularly new for Marina and David, except that it had been a long time since Mikey had been completely off his medicine. Having been saved, the last thing they wanted was a cluster bomb of seizures blowing their son to Kingdom Come.

Jake Rivett watched both of the parents working to console their son. Whatever he'd hypothesized about David as it related to the case at hand, he could tell that the man was dedicated to Mikey. He nodded at Markle, who used his radio to call up the ambulance that was waiting a few blocks away. Within a minute or two, paramedics came racing through the warehouse to aid Mikey. Jake kept his eye on David the entire time. Yes, David was a victim. But Jake was already beginning to sense that there were many moving parts to this crime's equation and that he was nowhere close to seeing the whole game board for what it was. Mikey's tragic circumstances aside, Jake was sure that David Belov was the man standing closest to the epicenter.

ELEVEN

AT KINGS COUNTY HOSPITAL in Brooklyn, David and Marina stood vigil while Mikey rested in the hospital bed. The doctors had described his condition as a severe hypoglycemic coma. IV tubes fed potassium, sodium and insulin into his body. The parents didn't hear as Jake entered the room.

"Mr. Belov?" Jake asked.

David turned around.

"I'm Jake Rivett. The sooner we can speak, the better."

"Who are you?" David asked.

"NYPD. Lead detective," Jake replied.

"For us?

"Yes"—Jake nodded—"and a number of unfolding situations."

"Situations?"

"It sounds like you know more than I do, David."

"Excuse me?" David asked.

"Can we speak outside?" Jake said.

■

Out in the hallway, David recounted his version of the last two days exactly as they had occurred. He told Jake his truth. It had been a normal Sunday—just a tad over perfunctory. He went into work and talked to a few co-workers, including Tyler Stanton and Howard Bergensen. He hit the gym.

"Where?" Jake asked.

"Bensonhurst. The boxing ring down on Cropsey," David answered. He then completed the rest of his nightmare.

Jake wasn't able to divine the truth from a lie. He wasn't omniscient. But as his years on the force had progressed, Jake had become increasingly adept at separating an open witness from a closed one. There were familiar threads to narratives that desperate men told. Jake's ear was picking up on something like that, in this situation, but he couldn't be exactly sure what. The rhythm was off—like his drummer's tempo a half step late. He hated when that happened. It put him on edge. This particular set of crimes was starting to make Jake feel as though he'd found a line in the inside stitching of his leather jacket. Once he had started to pull the thread, an infinite web of complications had begun to manifest in the fashion of a fractal series. He didn't like that. That's why Jake usually simply cut threads with his teeth. Unfortunately a case is much different from a garment malfunction or an errant bandmate, and Jake knew he had to dig further on this one, no matter what pure craziness was bound to result.

"Do you recognize this man?" Jake asked. He held up his cell phone to David. On the screen was a surveillance frame of the mysterious Asian man—his face in shadow—who had been driving the magnetic crane rig during the gold heist. David stared at the photograph intently.

"Never seen him before," David said with confidence.

"How do you know?" Jake asked.

"First of all, the only time I saw anyone was when they picked me up from the office on Monday afternoon," David said.

"Go on," Jake prompted him.

"And even then, they were all wearing masks."

"What type of masks?" Jake asked.

"Just like, wool—black. Holes for the eyes and mouth."

"Balaclavas. And what time did they pick you up?"

"After the regular market close. So that's four—probably four-fifteen."

"Where?"

"Right in front of the building," David said.

"How did you know that was going to happen?" Jake asked.

"What do you mean?"

"How did you know to leave the building and be picked up?"

"I told you about the phone on my counter. Right after the crash, they texted me—told me exactly where to go at the end of the day," David said.

"Where's the phone?"

"That was the first thing they took when I got in the car," David said. He could sense that Jake wasn't enjoying his responses, so he continued. "You have to understand, this wasn't some prank. They had my family. They sent me photographs of Marina, tied up on a bed. I knew I could do it, and I also knew that it was the only way to see my wife and son alive. Think about my position. Are you saying you wouldn't have done the exact same thing?"

"I'm not saying a thing, David. I'm asking questions."

"You don't believe me."

"I trust what I see. I trust what I can prove," Jake said. Jake observed David. He was nervous—tapping his fingers on the chair he was sitting on. "The problem I have right now," Jake wound up, "is that you're a liar."

"What?" David replied, astounded.

"What you did . . . wasn't all you could do. You could have called the police. Correct?"

"I . . ."

"I listened to your 9-1-1 call. You hung up. And when we called back, you said you'd found her. You lied to us there. Why'd you do that?" Jake asked.

"Oh, come on, sir. There was only one safe bet: I had to do what they wanted. I do that and I get my family back. That's all I could think about."

"What does one have to do with the other? Why not inform the authorities and keep working on your program?"

"Because they were watching me," David said.

"How do you know?" Jake asked.

"Right as I was talking to your dispatch, they called me again. The voice told me to hang up the phone on the police and never try them again," David answered.

"Pretty convenient," Jake said.

"Not for me."

"Then the next obvious question is . . . Why you?"

"That's been on my mind—obviously."

"So who knew you were capable of writing this type of program?"

David shrugged. "Thousands of people? Everyone I work with? It's not so simplistic, sir. My thesis at Stony Brook was on industrial control system kill switches—"

"Sounds like complicated shit," Jake retorted.

"Microchips control everything. Not just computer programs. Your car. The electric grid. The water system . . . I found flaws in systems. Then I hacked them. A few years ago I wrote a virus that could destroy a refrigerator. At Stony Brook I built a device that forced the power supply into thinking that it could provide a higher voltage than it could. I'd run the current through the circuit board, fry every chip and make the milk go bad. I spoke at Black Hat about it. I was originally headhunted by Montgomery for my systems capabilities—because the quantitative work . . . you know . . . the computers at the bank? The software's important. But it's the hardware design that really can make or break a trading strategy . . ." David trailed off.

"Okay. So you're a very smart, very logical man."

David didn't respond.

"Right?" Jake asked.

"I wasn't sure if that was a question or a statement."

"Don't get sharp with me, Mr. Belov. You wiped away billions of dollars of net worth across the globe. I've listened to your story, and even then I don't have a semblance of an idea if the ends justify the means. You are definitely still sitting on the wrong side of the table. Your fingerprints are all over this, and guess what? There's nobody else—just a whole bunch of ghosts. So why don't you help me figure something out, instead of acting like you're some sort of savant who's above the gutter that you're finding yourself in? A hundred and twenty million dollars. That's like, dynasty money," Jake said. "Right?"

"It's a lot," David confirmed.

"So if I'm the mastermind behind this job? I need at least a handful of guys. I need to steal a big crane, some real estate to prep and store it all, a programmer . . ." Jake pointed at David. "That's you. And then after all that planning and all that time, I finally get my hands on the gold. Enough to move to Europe and eat the Rothschilds for dinner. Oh, and I leave no tracks at all. Except, I leave David. I leave David's wife and kid—alive. I even leave your cell phones on so that the police can find you. Why the hell would I do that?"

"Mikey's in a coma," David answered.

"This wasn't his fault, and I'm not saying that."

"But you're going to stand there and tell me that because I'm alive . . . I'm suspicious?"

"I didn't say that either," Jake replied.

"You implied it—logically."

"Okay. I did."

"Are you here to arrest me or something?" David asked.

"No, sir. But if you're tied to this crime in any way—"

David jumped in to interrupt him. "We were terrorized!"

"If that's true, then you've got nothing to worry about," Jake said.

"If that's true?" David thought about Jake's response and then stood up. "I'm going to go take care of my son," he said.

"David?"

David turned.

"People get blinded by money and forget about the law. I am the law. I am going to break this thing open. I just hope you're not there on the other side when I do," Jake said.

David slammed the door to Mikey's hospital room in response.

"That was not super chill, Jake," Jake muttered under his breath. He was a human too and he knew he shouldn't have been so confrontational, but sometimes—scratch that—most of the time, he just couldn't help it.

▪

Back inside the hospital room, Mikey's heart-rate monitor was steadily rising. He began to motion with his arms and his head slowly turned to the side.

"He's coming out of it!" Marina yelled with joy. Two doctors entered the room and conferred with one another. Mikey coughed. All attention was focused on the child in the bed as he opened his eyes and the world came into focus for the first time that afternoon. He stared at his parents for a minute or two before speaking.

"Daddy?" Mikey asked shakily.

"I'm right here, little man," David said as relief washed over his body.

"I'm so hungry. Can I have chocolate pancakes?" Mikey said.

Tears streamed down David's and Marina's faces as stress released from their bodies. Mikey started to drift off again, holding his parents' hands.

▪

Jake watched the reunion occur through the hospital window until he received a text on his cell phone. He checked it. Tony had sent him a photograph from the police lab. The strips of shredded paper from David's trashcan had been matched and put back together by a scanning algorithm to reveal a Google Maps printout. A red circle was drawn around a random street intersection in Pelham, New York.

"What's this?" Jake muttered. He quickly tapped out a return text to Villalon and then leaned towards a cop guarding the hospital door.

"Don't let the husband leave without my permission, understood?" Jake instructed him. "The man in there with the kid . . . He's my number one."

▪

Jake rocketed towards Pelham on his bike. As he neared the exit, he could see four police helicopters circling above an area just off the highway. The police presence in the air was abundant.

Jake pulled up and was astounded to find the flatbed truck, the magnetic crane rig, and the armored truck from the robbery. All three machines sat placidly along a lonely street. Jake leapt from his motorcycle and approached the scene. Although it was fortuitous that the recovery had occurred so quickly, the pit inside Jake's stomach was not subsiding. It was growing.

The side of the armored truck, where the gold had been located, had been cut through and replaced with a gaping hole. An abandoned gas-powered torch sat on the sidewalk next to it. This indicated a number of facts to Jake, but the first was that the criminals knew exactly what they were doing. An amateur would go for a door or window, not realizing that the portholes of armored vehicles were actually better protected than the side flanks. It was clear that this was not the work of first-timers, but then again, Jake already knew that. This simply cemented it. Jake's mind had already raced a hundred steps ahead, as usual. But as he snapped back to real time, Jake realized that in addition to being the first detective on the scene, he was also the first responder.

Jake sprinted towards the front of the armored truck and became nauseated when he noticed that the bank's driver and guard were still inside the cab. Neither man was moving. Jake tried to open the door. It wouldn't budge. He stepped back and pulled his standard-issue Glock from a shoulder holster. He shot the door lock. Nothing. The steel was impervious. Jake sprinted back to his motorcycle. He spied the power cutter on the ground. The irony was not lost upon Jake that whoever had perpetrated this crime had been better prepared to save a life than he was. But instead of reaching for the cutter, Jake retrieved his trusty crowbar. He had an idea. He'd piggyback off the work already done. Jake jumped through the hole in the armor, into the back of the truck.

He tripped over a few pieces of electronic equipment lying on the floor, seemingly left behind. Glancing down quizzically, Jake noticed a portable device the size of a brick. The handheld unit was made of grey metal, with six identical walkie-talkie-esque antennas emerging from the top. He couldn't identify what it was, but neither was this the time to do so. An access door inside the cargo hold of the truck separated him from the armored truck's cab. Since Jake was already through one line of defense, the door was significantly less fortified. He used the crowbar to painstakingly lever the door open. He opened it a few inches, just enough to push his hand through and manually unlock the door. The small door swung open. Jake shuffled into the truck's cab on his knees, leaning towards the driver immediately. The driver didn't respond to Jake's touch or yelling. He felt for a pulse on the driver but found nothing. Jake scrambled over to the passenger to see if the other man was alive. No. Both guards were dead.

Jake shook his head and extracted himself from the truck. He could do nothing in this moment except sit down on the ground against the truck and try to control his emotions. His chest heaved. Not only was Jake chasing a gang of highly sophisticated and coordinated bank robbers—he was up against murderers as well.

That wasn't a huge surprise, in the sense that eighty or ninety thousand dollars could get a man killed on the streets in the current day. With eighty as the going rate, a hundred million could buy a citywide massacre. But the deaths did change the complexion of the case. They also stood in contrast to a specific set of humans—the Belov family—who ought to have been sacrificial lambs.

Jake stood up and walked to his bike while police sirens rang out and multiple squad cars finally arrived on the scene. He'd made his decision. He reached for his police radio.

"Arrest the quant—immediately," Jake ordered.

■

In Kings County Hospital, a large group of officers rushed down the hallway towards Mikey's hospital room. The police officer at the door jumped to his feet and opened the door. But Marina stood in the way.

"Out of the way, ma'am."

"No!" Marina screamed. "Not in front of my son!"

"Mr. Belov! You are under arrest. Do not resist!" the cop yelled. Marina pushed back against the door as more cops piled on. She couldn't hold them any longer. Inside the hospital room, Marina fell onto the ground, tears running down her face. The cops finally gained entry and discovered that David wasn't there.

■

David walked briskly down the hallway. He was wearing an extra set of scrubs that he'd found hanging in the room next door to Mikey's. Luckily there had been an adjoining door that allowed him access to a hallway just around the corner from Mikey's wing. For a brief moment, visions of Hollywood movies flashed through his head. He was like Harrison Ford in *The Fugitive*—on the run. David didn't want to be a fugitive, but he had no other choice. He could already sense the overbearing crush of evidence pointing his way. The detective's demeanor and hypotheses had said it all. It was also all fabricated, but why would the police believe that? Whoever had done this to him and his family had prepared their gameplan at a granular level. He knew that if he didn't work outside the system, there would be no way of pulling himself back above the surface. The death spiral of coincidence and circumstance was poised to take him under—unless he could do something about it. Unless he could fight back. He couldn't do that from a cell. Jail would cement his fate —not to mention the fact that Rivett obviously hated him. That really pissed David off. It fulfilled much of the stereotypes about the police from the old neighborhood he thought he'd left behind. It was all splashing up back around him in a form of psychological blowback that David wasn't quite prepared to address. There was still a part of him that didn't trust the police. He never just believed what they said. Sometimes they spoke the truth, and sometimes they didn't. They did what they wanted—what was good for them. They weren't on his side. No one was. It was David against the world.

David pulled a clipboard off the wall when he noticed a pack of police officers walking his way. He ducked into a random patient's room, emerging after the phalanx of cops had passed. They hadn't noticed. A character inside his own narrative, David became acutely aware of his senses. His heart pounded on overdrive. His muscles contracted, ready for anything. The surge of adrenaline that accompanies survival kept him fully charged. He reached a set of service stairs. He popped into the stairwell and tore down the stairs.

▪

David emerged from the side exit of the hospital to encounter another squad car. He couldn't help but engage in eye contact with the two officers in the car, then walk past them as calmly as possible. Once he felt that they weren't looking at him any longer, David jackknifed across the street. Cars squealed their brakes to avoid him, honking loudly to display their displeasure. David checked the cops again. It seemed that his jaywalking had not raised the ire of the authorities. Such was the chaotic patchwork of everyday Manhattan. He turned a corner and peered over his shoulder again. Nobody was following him. *Incredible.* David concluded that he'd actually escaped. But he had to stay gone, which would prove much more difficult than slipping through the hospital's security cordon.

After a few blocks of quick pacing, David eventually spied a pay phone inside the vestibule of a McDonald's. He stepped inside.

David took a deep breath while he thought about the next step. The truth was that he ought to have made this move two days earlier. He comforted himself by remembering that it also might have killed his wife and child. But the situation had changed. Since Marina and Mikey were finally safe, he was ready to ask for help from the one person whom he knew without a shadow of a doubt would be there for him. The quarter rested above the coin slot of the pay phone. He decided. He jammed the change into the public phone and dialed a number.

He reached Vlad Zhadanov's voicemail.

"It's me. I need your help. I'm at the McDonald's on Flatbush—south of Church. Can you pick me up? Please. It's an emergency," David begged his old friend.

TWELVE

<u>Twenty Years Prior</u>

THE FIRST TIME DAVID met Vlad Zhadanov was in fourth grade, when they were both ten years old. Their grade school, P.S. 128 on Twenty-first Avenue, was an institution in Bensonhurst. At five stories tall, the building towered over the two-story townhomes that constituted the majority of the neighborhood. It was regally constructed, primarily consisting of stacked brick but also accented and outlined by grand limestone bulwarks. David's memories of the time were fleeting, as the fresh side of youth often is, but he would never forget the day that he met Vlad. It was in the bathroom on the second floor, and Vlad was conducting a peeing contest.

At the time, the boys' bathrooms in P.S. 128 were old enough to be considered antique. With aqua tiling from floor to ceiling and original bronze fixtures, the design would also be completely en vogue at a hipster gastropub in modern day. On one side of the bathroom, a long row of white porcelain troughs extended about four feet up from the floor, one after the next. When David opened the door, Vlad was standing about ten feet from the urinals, arcing his back and attempting to articulate his urine all the way into the latrines, like a human park fountain. A few other boys stood around, watching with admiration as Vlad yelled at them, "Bet ya can't go any farther than I can!"

David was unsure what he was witnessing. Soon the rest of the boys had lined up and were trying too. That's when David realized that it was a competition. Vlad noticed that David was still sitting this little exercise out, so he made sure to turn David's way and belittle him.

"If you don't try it, Belov, I'll piss on you, too!" Nothing like the threat of an embarrassing afternoon soaked in urine to get David motivated. He reached down and unzipped, stepped back to the imaginary line, and joined in. At that very moment, their social studies teacher, Mr. Morgan walked into the men's room with an incredulous look on his face. Morgan went berserk. He started screaming at the top of his lungs, letting them know in no uncertain terms that they were all a bunch of shitheads who would never get ahead in life if they spent their time and effort aiming sterile liquid into a urinal. Mr. Morgan wasn't a puritan. He just couldn't handle the preposterous nature of what he was seeing.

The moment defined Vlad forever in David's mind, and not only because he'd achieved the longest distance. Vlad was as consistently provocative as David was thoughtful. Deep down inside, Vlad did it all for the reaction. The competition wouldn't have been complete, wouldn't have gone down in history, without Mr. Morgan's wide eyes and crazed demeanor. Vlad was always busy daring people, cajoling them, threatening them, and palling around with them. And from that day forward, Vlad's relationship with David would simultaneously incorporate all of these aspects.

■

The next four years of middle school were defined by the accelerating blur of adolescence. David and Vlad were quite different animal spirits, but they became fast friends. After Papa died, it had taken David a few years to come out of his shell and not feel as though he was floating along the treadmill of a muted dream. Middle school corresponded with David's ability to finally socialize and get along with other kids. David wasn't quite sure why a rascal like Vlad had even been interested in fostering a friendship with a boy like him in the first place. But there were a few obvious reasons and one deep, unspoken one.

It wasn't lost on David that Vlad consistently helped himself to a peek, or two or three, of David's homework for about six or seven years running. But it didn't really bother David. He didn't feel used. Even though David was acing all of the aforementioned tests and homework, and Vlad was copying him, Vlad still only managed to scrape through school with a C-plus average. In both David's mind and reality, he was actually just helping the poor guy survive. And what did David get out of the arrangement? Vlad had his personality issues, but he was a loyal friend. It was always a two-way street. He included David in the bustle of their burgeoning social life. David would have otherwise spent his lunches alone in the cafeteria if it weren't for Vlad. And that's exactly what David needed at the time.

Vlad was a boy who seemed to have the world at his fingertips. But he was peaking early, and maybe he even knew it. He recognized skills in David that he desperately needed. David was smart—precociously talented, even. But more importantly, he was polite. Veronika had raised him right. Vlad's main interest at the time had nothing to do with the classroom. It was all about what he could do in the wild world that was becoming both bigger and smaller at the same moment, every passing day of childhood. It was infinitely helpful for Vlad to have a buttoned-up friend like David next to him, with his clean shirt tucked in and his hair parted neatly. It was important to Vlad to have a guy by his side who already talked as though he was a studious twenty-year-old when he was actually thirteen. And the primary reason that a nerdy, serious, straight-talker like David was helpful to Vlad was that the police in Brooklyn didn't take very kindly to juveniles with larceny in their blood.

Vlad and David spent countless hours loitering in Coney Island. When they were bored with the sights and sounds of the boardwalk, they'd wander north and explore "Gravesend," a huge municipal parking lot and subway terminus. David was the one who figured out that if they timed it just right, they could hitch rides on various subway cars and traverse them through the subterranean depths of the city to basically any destination they desired.

When one is fourteen years old and lives in New York, the oyster of the city is just beginning to open and reveal its secrets. One learns how to ride the subway without parents, discovers that turnstiles can be jumped if there isn't enough cash for an MTA card, and begins to grasp what the effect of three or four beers at the Rockaways has on body function. A young man of that age stops using the deodorant that his mother has bought for him for years and begins to intensely study the various brands in the aisles of the convenience and grocery stores. The clear-gel deodorant, with the neon lettering printed on its packaging, becomes far more enticing than Old Spice. Of course, in ten years he'd be wearing Old Spice again. But that was neither here nor there. Ten years is a lifetime for a young teen.

Vlad was just like any normal fourteen-year-old at the time and so were all his friends. Baranowski, another one of the urinal offenders, was a constant presence in Vlad's life by this point as well. But unlike a teenager growing up in an exclusive enclave such as Greenwich, Vlad had the specific disadvantage of not having any money at all. He couldn't afford the choice deodorant he wanted. That's the reason why Vlad, Baranowski, and their pal David started shoplifting.

At the highest level, shoplifting is a gentle art. But Vlad didn't learn that the first time around or even the tenth. At its lowest echelon, the sport involves running away from a proprietor who's swinging a hammer down the sidewalk and will stop at nothing to make you their newest lesson to all would-be thieves. All of the shop owners in Bensonhurst proper knew

Vlad, and if Vlad had tried anything in their zones, they would have just marched over to his house and told Arseni. Vlad's father Arseni was a hell of a man. He was masculine. He was from the old world. He was no nonsense. Had such an event occurred, Arseni would have given Vlad a whipping with his bare hands that inflicted much worse damage than a hammer ever could.

Ultimately that's why the three of them would go into Brooklyn or if they were feeling particularly aggressive, all the way to Manhattan in order to find the stuff they coveted. The necessities—like energy drinks, or headphones, or the newest Eminem CD. At first David hadn't been interested in partaking. But he also didn't want to look bad in front of his friends. So he would grab little things from the aisles as well—a candy bar, a lighter—small and inconsequential items like that. Most of the time they got away with it.

▪

One late spring day in Manhattan, Vlad noticed that David was wearing a bulky suede jacket. He decided that they'd be loading David up with the contraband that day, because his outer garment could practically fit a watermelon without looking unusual. Sherpa duty would be David's. They entered a Walgreens in the East Village, and David followed behind Vlad and Baranowski as they surreptitiously grabbed whatever their little hearts desired. They would hand the items back to David, who would stuff them into the various pockets of his jacket.

As the three boys stepped out of the store, David tracked the eyes of the woman behind the cash register. She was fiddling with her nails and not paying him any attention. He thought that was a little strange, because most cashiers were hypervigilant and on the lookout for kids who came in, browsed, and left without any items. But David didn't have much time to think about it, because there were already four cops standing outside. The officers picked up the three boys by their collars and flung them to the ground. All three were arrested. They later found out that a security guard had watched through a video surveillance system from an office in the back of the store as the "heist" occurred.

▪

The flashbulbs of the mugshot, followed by the dark stain of fingerprints, greeted them at the police station a few blocks away. Vlad and Baranowski were released within hours, but David spent the night there. That wasn't due to the fact that he was the only one with the jacket full of contraband; it was because Veronika refused to pick him up immediately. She wanted him to learn his lesson, and he did. The Walgreens experience was the last time that David ever shoplifted.

▪

It took a year and a half for their case to work its way through the system. Arseni pulled a few strings. What that actually meant was that he either did a favor or bent someone's arm in order to get a halfway decent attorney to represent the three boys. They received a nice talking to from the judge, a slap on the wrist, and a fine that would take another two years to pay off—but no time in juvenile hall.

As they were leaving the courtroom, Arseni tried to pull Veronika aside and speak to her. With a sharp word, Veronika twisted out of Arseni's grasp and pulled David down the street in the opposite direction.

"Why'd you do that, Mum?" David asked. After all, Arseni was the reason that they were free and clear.

"He's a bad man," Veronika replied simply.

"What do you mean?"

"If your father had never met Arseni, he might be alive today," she finally emoted. That was the end of the conversation. It didn't take much detective work for David to figure out that Arseni and his own father used to run together in the same crew. Arseni was the boss—Papa, the muscle lackey. And the muscle always faded before the brain did.

The shoplifting incident didn't become the final straw in David's relationship with Vlad. But it did have a cooling effect. David spent more time in the math-and-science department. He saw Vlad less. After school let out, David started to go home instead of crossing the street to hang out with the boys. Vlad didn't take it personally. He knew that David felt ashamed about what had happened. Even if they weren't always best friends, their futures would always be bound together by their pasts. Anyhow, Vlad was real busy with other hobbies by the time freshman year in high school rolled around—getting drunk, smoking clove cigarettes, and learning to box with no gloves against the older boys in the park.

THIRTEEN

Tuesday

DAVID REMAINED INSIDE THE McDonalds. He was sitting at a corner table with his back against a grimy wall. He picked at a small bag of french fries, keeping his eyes low and regulating his breathing. He'd wiped his body down twice in the bathroom in an attempt to reduce the amount of sweat coming out of his pores. That had worked to some degree, although his heart rate was still high and would likely remain that way permanently —or at least until this was all resolved.

There was a small television in the corner of the restaurant. David froze as the words "Highway Heist" scrolled across the bottom of the screen. The news was out, and the media had started to sink their teeth into the FDR Drive robbery. An animated anchor chatted away with multiple "experts." Always "former this" or "former that" from three-letter agencies, the specialists knew nothing except for the long-altered procedures from a decade before and were just happy to make their appearance fees.

As the minutes ticked by, David relaxed enough to observe the inhabitants of the McDonalds in their natural state. They all looked normal. Except for the ones who were obviously homeless, the rest of the people looked as they were—people. Each and every one of them had his or her own personal trials and tribulations. It was impossible to tell if they were eating lunch there because they didn't have a job, were just taking a lunch break, or were the target of a manhunt. He realized that they were probably looking at him and thinking the same exact thing. Like the surface of a lake at sunset, all one can perceive is the peace of the steady plane. What's under the surface might be very different. It's impossible to know. The story of David's last two days was incredible, but there was no one inside this McDonald's who cared. With this theory as his psychological ammunition, David was finally able to calm down and avoid another lengthy trip to the bathroom.

The universal lesson of the prior forty-eight hours began to sink in properly. The surface was irrelevant. It hid everything and said nothing. Working for Montgomery Noyes had appeared to be the perfect goal—a career bullseye. But it wasn't. Maybe Vlad had been right all along. Maybe perfect was impossible, acceptance was peace, and striving for something else the original sin.

David heard a car horn outside, and his heartbeat skyrocketed. He glanced up to notice a large black Mercedes swooping up to the sidewalk. The door opened. Vlad was driving. Without a moment's pause, David rushed for the car and shut the door behind him.

"Turn your phone off and remove the battery" were the first words out of Vlad's mouth as they accelerated away. "I got your message. Cat told me the police were all over your house. What the shit happened, David?"

"The gold—the FDR—the robbery—I didn't do it . . . I didn't. And it's all on me," David said as he tried to pull the battery out of his phone.

"Give me the battery," Vlad said. David handed it to him. Vlad rolled down his window and dropped it onto the pavement. "So what you're saying to me is that the pigs think my little peach, David Belov, who I know for a fact would never hurt a flea, robbed that gold truck yesterday?" Vlad asked inquisitively.

"Th-they're coming for me," David stuttered. "They had a warrant. What do I do? That's what I need to know. I need help, Vlad. You always told me that I could come to you—that you'd be there for me. This is that time."

Vlad thought long and hard as he drove out of the city. "Konstantin keeps some apartments for me. They're safe," he finally announced in silent acceptance of what was yet to come.

▪

The apartment was a studio—a tiny pixel within a sprawling, labyrinthine apartment complex set back from Cropsey Avenue in Brooklyn. David paced back and forth across the room while Vlad sat on the bed with his hands in his pockets, watching him intently. David was, as always, racing to keep up with his brain's anxieties.

"I can figure this out. It's not unsolvable. No problem ever is. That's the first assumption. Therefore it is possible to get to the bottom of this," David said.

"Instead of skipping to the end, let's start at the beginning. How much gold was stolen?" Vlad asked.

"I dunno. The detective told me a hundred and twenty million. What they said on the news was that the truck was completely loaded. Your average truck can hold about twenty-five hundred ounces. But that doesn't mean anything."

"The detective?"

"Jake's his name—this blond guy—young. He was asking me questions and he said a hundred million plus."

"Let's say it was half the truck's load . . ." Vlad pondered.

"That's about eighty million dollars," David said, calculating in his head.

"Okay. So it was probably more than that."

"Sure. Could be," David said.

"Over a hundred million dollars' worth of gold?" Vlad whistled loudly.

"What's the point? Who cares about the exact number?"

"The number doesn't just matter—it's everything. The ramifications are endless," Vlad said as he slid his hand inside his jacket pocket. "Ambition, skill and experience all play together in this world. This was a high-line job. Only a few crews in the entire country could ever run it successfully, let alone get away with it after," Vlad said.

"We don't know that it was successful."

"On the contrary, my peach. It's been, what, twenty-four hours?"

"Yeah," David said.

"A lifetime. You can't steal that much gold without knowing what to do with it. Your average criminal is going to have trouble getting rid of fifty or a hundred thousand dollars worth of product. Anyone who successfully takes a hundred million dollars and leaves nothing behind? You're talking about an utmost professional. I said only a few crews could do it. That's true—statistically. But I don't know them. I'd have a real major difficulty naming a single team that could pull that off." Vlad thought through the logic further and then continued, "And they made it look like you did it all and know much more than you do. Right? So whoever they are, they're very focused on you. If you go to jail, they'll know. And they'll keep moving the gold again and again—until it's completely untraceable."

Vlad finally removed his hand from his pocket. It emerged holding a handgun. Vlad gripped it by the barrel. He placed the gun into David's tentative hand. "Don't give it back to me. You need to feel how serious this is. Now listen. That's a shit ton of metal that was stolen. You wanna dance down the yellow brick road, ya? But if there's really that much gold at the end of it"—Vlad gestured to the gun—"lives will end."

"I don't care."

Vlad paused upon hearing David's response. "I'm your friend. I know you. A long time ago, you decided what your life was going to look like. Right?"

"This is different," David said.

"Bullshit. What went down at the payday shop, my peach—years ago? It was because you made a choice. I was there. I watched you find yourself back then, and I'm watching you now. It's not too different. Remember this. If you pace back and forth all night like I know you will and then make a decision to jump down the rabbit hole . . . You might never get out of there."

David stared at the unfamiliar object in his hands. He knew that Vlad was right. But there were no alternatives. "I know. But if I can't get the truth, then I'm in jail and my life's over. All that matters is that I get the time to figure this out. I know what happened to me. I'm sure. Now I have to prove it. I do that, and everything goes back to normal. And if not . . . There's nothing left for me anyways," David said. He tossed the gun onto the bed next to Vlad.

"Ya," Vlad said as he pocketed the gun again. "Well in that case, my business is just like your business. At the highest levels, everyone knows their competition intimately."

"What do you mean?"

"I mean that while I may not know who did this, I know a guy who knows all the guys. If there's so much as a whisper on the street, he'll have picked it up. His name's the Pie Man and he sells pizza," Vlad said. "He may be able to help."

■

Jake and Villalon stood aside the street in New Rochelle and observed their investigators going through the flatbed truck and remains of the armored car with a fine-tooth comb. Temporary light poles had been erected around what amounted to a second crime scene, aiding the police in their job. Tony's gloved hands handled the unusual router-like device that Jake had first discovered inside the armored car.

"You want the bad news or the worse? I think I know what it is. Probably won't make you very happy."

"Do tell," Jake commanded.

"It's a signal jammer—six band. I'd have to test it, but I bet it could strike out 4G, GSM, 3G, and LTE—maybe more."

"So it blocks cell phones?" Jake asked.

"And data," Tony confirmed.

"What about radio?"

"These types of devices are completely off market. They're illegal at the federal level. Because of that, some electrical engineer will just make 'em in their basement with standard parts. We don't have full visibility on what they can do. But I'd make a strong bet that if you can block cell phones, it would be even easier to block radio."

"That helps. Explains why none of the bank's guards could talk to each other," Jake said and then paused as he contemplated further. "Why leave it?"

"Only if they didn't need it," Tony said as he shrugged.

"To scare us?"

"You're the wrong guy for that," Tony said.

Jake grinned. "No prints, right?"

"No. Of course not. Not a single print across this whole scene. Maybe we'll get a hair sample or two, but these guys took careful to the extreme," Tony replied.

"All right. The jammer. Where do you buy one of those?"

"Nowhere in the United States. A couple dozen websites will sell them to you, label them as a router and risk it at customs—no questions asked. But those businesses and servers aren't based in places that will respond to a subpoena with any alacrity."

"Give that to me," Jake said. He turned the grey box around in the light, examining it from all sides. One of the plugs in the back had a few characters etched around the edges. "Did you see the etching?"

"Yeah. It's Chinese—or Korean," Villalon replied.

"That's a lead . . ."

Tony shook his head. "I don't think so. Like I told you, the device is made up of components. Those components are mostly made in Asia."

"Yeah, well, our getaway driver was made in Asia, too," Jake replied. "Maybe I need to go back downtown to the electronics marts."

"Chinatown?"

"It's not like anyone's going to tell me anything of substance—not off the bat. But I have a rule for that too."

"What?" Tony asked.

"The less they talk, the more they know."

"Be careful down there, Jake."

"I'm always careful," Jake said.

"Yeah? And I'm always carefully cleaning up after you."

▪

Joe's Pizza Pies was a hole in the wall, tucked into a corner of Little Italy. David eyed the classic, red-and-white checkered tablecloths and framed photographs of Joe with celebrities and other ultra-wealthy patrons on the walls. Joe and his restaurant were famous in their own right. Unlike a traditionally thin Italian pizza, Joe subscribed to the Chicago mold. His pizzas were an inch thick and actually resembled pies, filled with layer after layer of delicious dough, sauce, proteins, and vegetables. As David trailed Vlad through the establishment, he concluded that one of the best features of mobsters was that they really did know how to create incredible dining experiences. The authenticity shone through. It was a damn shame that the back offices were the real reason this business existed, especially when the pizza up front was so tasty. But then again, without what was happening in the back, there would be no food at all. Vlad and David approached the sixteen-year-old kid at the counter.

"Get us a truffle and mushroom—extra large," Vlad commanded.

"And tell Joe that Vlad's up front."

▪

Ten minutes later and into the back it was. Vlad and David sat on boxes of ice-cold food inside the food freezer in the rear of the establishment. Perched across from them was the Pie Man himself, Joe Raffaeli. In his early seventies, Joe operated a multidisciplinary business. Of course, he was a restaurateur and a pizza maker, but he was also an entrepreneur. One could even go so far as to call him a trader. At this age, and like most men in senior positions, his hands didn't touch the heat any longer. Joe simply traded on information. Now, if that information led to a bank robbery, or a bribe intended for the police to look the other direction when it came to a prostitution ring, or to someone's death . . . so be it. That's not to say that Joe was evil. He was not. He was simply immoral, and he had a reputation to uphold and a family to support.

"When you met me, I was young, fly, flashy," Joe started up. He cracked a hand warmer and ran it between his palms. "Now I stalk Kmart for deals on fucking hand warmers." Joe glanced at David. "Sorry about the cold. Keeps all the bugs out—except for mine." Joe pointed to a small surveillance camera positioned in the upper corner of the freezer.

"As long as there ain't any worms eating your brain out, I'm happy," Vlad said.

"No worms—at least not brain ones. Maybe in my intestinal tract," Joe replied with a chuckle.

"Less pepperoni. More salad," Vlad suggested.

"The missus says that to me too. I told her that salad can literally go fuck itself. Ever fuck a salad?" Joe asked.

"Can't say I have," Vlad replied.

"I did when I was fourteen. Lotta water in those icebergs. I bet this guy has," Joe said as he pointed at David. "I know you have fucked some things you wasn't proud about in your life."

Not sure whether that was a dig or compliment in Joe's book, David attempted to keep a straight face. "Why do you say that?" David asked.

"Because you're a human," Joe replied.

"Joe. You heard anything 'bout the gold carriage job?" Vlad asked.

"Didn't even take a little birdie on my shoulder to know that you'd come callin' about the heist. I guess I'm getting more and more prescient in my old age. Whaddya want from it? Gonna try to find the crew that did it and double tap that shit?" Joe asked.

"Actually, no. I'm trying to save my friend's life." Vlad nodded at David.

"Honestly? I ain't got much besides what they said on CNN. It's sad but true. I do know that every family in town been ringin' me the last couple days. I mean, Dom himself called. Fuckin' Poles, LA, Miami, tons of calls from Toronto . . . even Skinny Joey's old boys in Philly. And there's one constant in every single call. None of them know who did it, which is surprising, and they all wanna know—which is not surprising in the slightest."

"So it wasn't the Italians?" Vlad asked. "I figured it coulda' been. They got the transit connections to get the stuff off the continent."

"Nope." Joe shook his head.

"Then who the hell else is there?"

"Fuck if I know. Maybe the Chinamen or the Belarusians. I'll make some more calls," Joe promised.

"What about the cartels?"

"It don't play. You know the esés are savages, and the problem with a bunch of coyotes is they'll eat their young, and they'll eat their old. They don't care one bit about the organization or each other. To pull something like this off, you need elders, you need brains, you need brawn, and you need it all to get along with each other. If anything, it's the Europeans. They've been runnin' big crews and blowin' up ATMs with gas for a couple years now. Only problem I have with that theory is they haven't come stateside yet. And you're telling me the first heist you do, once you're in

America, is on a moving armored car in the middle of Manhattan? Don't think so," Joe said.

"Ya," Vlad agreed.

"Truth is I'm drawing full blanks on this one. That means a dark element's moving around the streets—some whale taking outsized risks. Someone who I don't know," Joe opined. "That's unusual, and a little bit scary." Joe stood up. That's how conversations, and relationships, with Joe operated. When he was done, you were done. He opened the door to the freezer. "Your pie's ready," he said.

"How much do we owe you?" David asked.

"A grand will do."

David whistled lightly through his teeth, but Vlad pulled the cash from his wallet with no complaints.

"Hey, truffles ain't cheap," Joe added. "My cousin in the old country had to buy his own breeder so he could train the finest group of Lagottos in the province. Did you know a premium sniffer goes for fifteen grand and you need a pack of at least ten of 'em to pull truffles out of the forest with any reasonable volume?"

"No. I didn't know that, Joe," Vlad said.

"Stick with me. I'll always keep you up and up 'bout the ways of the world," Joe replied.

▪

Driving down a back alley and away from Joe's Pizza Pies, Vlad and David sat in silence. They were soaking in what Joe had just told them, which had been more than a little disheartening. All of a sudden Vlad perked up out of the malaise. "I've been thinking about something, but I don't really know how to tell you this . . ."

"What?" David asked.

"I have a theory. You won't like it. But damn it if I won't be right when we come down to the end." Vlad took a deep breath. "We're looking for the wrong crew. They're right in front of our eyes. It's your guys."

"My guys?" David said quizzically. "I don't have guys."

"Ya. The bankers," Vlad said resolutely. "The bankers did this to themselves."

"That's . . ." David searched for the right word.

"What?"

"Insane. Completely impossible."

"Ya, ya. You say that. Of course you'd say that. But hear me out. You heard Joe. Nobody did this. Nobody in our world. No one from the outside. There's only one more option, and that is the whole robbery was orchestrated from the inside," Vlad said.

"It's just too risky. My colleagues have too much to lose. They're all about limiting liability, not raising it. What would someone who worked at Montgomery have to gain from robbing their own bank?"

"How about a hundred million dollars?" Vlad snapped.

"Okay. But if you work for thirty years at a million bucks a year, and you compound that money by seven percent, you'll have your hundred million dollars at the end—legally. But if you get caught stealing . . . goodbye to all of it. Hello to divorce and your kid calling another man 'Daddy.' Doesn't make any sense."

"Money doesn't mean anything." Vlad shook his head in ardent disagreement. "Money doesn't make a man respectable. It won't satisfy someone who wants more, believes without a shadow of a doubt that they deserve it, and is watching everyone else around them do even better than they are. Just a little bit ago your whole system crashed tens of millions of careers, destroyed millions of lives, and kicked families out of their houses. What type of person knowingly creates and fosters a world that would do that? One type—a psychopath."

"All the bad weeds were pulled," David replied, but this time less resolutely. While he couldn't bring himself to fully agree with Vlad, he was starting to see the logic.

"Let's just play this out from your side. This thing you said you wrote

—this computer thing. Can you run any program you want at any time from your office?" Vlad asked.

"No. We need permission to get into the server room."

"Who gave you permission?"

David thought for a moment. "Tyler Stanton. My boss. But the thing is that Tyler trusts me. So he'd approve me no matter what—even if I didn't actually have a real reason for going in there."

"Had he done that before?"

"Not usually. I'm just saying . . ." David trailed off. "Besides, that was part of the plan."

"What do you mean?"

"My instructions—on the phone I found in my kitchen. They wrote, 'Access will be provided to the server room.' Then they sent me a text during the day: 'Enter server room at twelve sharp.' I received it just as I was walking into the building."

"So they knew Tyler would give you access?" Vlad asked. "Why the hell did your boss give you permission?"

"I don't know. I'm in and out. I remember the guy at the gate said Tyler approved it. But the thing is . . . who knows? Tyler could be under pressure just like me. Or they could have gotten a RAT into his machine, or the server itself . . ." David trailed off. The list of options was too immense.

"What's a RAT?" Vlad asked.

"Remote access tool. Gives you control of someone's computer. You can see what they see, but you can also do whatever you want—without them noticing," David replied.

"So someone could have tricked Tyler's computer into approving you. You don't have antivirus programs?" Vlad inquired.

"We do. They don't always work."

"No. The whole grab plays on one thing: you getting into that room. You don't crash that market, then Montgomery doesn't move any gold. If

Montgomery doesn't move gold, there's nothing to steal. So it all hinges on your access to the server room. And from what you've told me, everything else was planned down to perfection. So whoever did this . . . they can't just live on hope. They had to be absolutely, positively sure you'd be let into that room." Vlad became worked up as he proceeded. "Tell me more about this Tyler Stanton character. I already hate his Waspy-ass name."

FOURTEEN

Wednesday

DAVID ASCENDED ANCIENT LIMESTONE steps, stopping to admire the ornate ironwork that comprised the railing of a grandiose brownstone in the Upper West Side of Manhattan. The macabre faces of gargoyles were carved into each step of the house. Each expression was different. A man has truly made it in the pyramid of life when his hand-carved gargoyles are each as unique and beautiful as God's own snowflakes. David finally reached the front door and rang the doorbell. He could hear the chime echo throughout the various cherry-accented chambers of the house inside. After a few moments, the door opened. This was Tyler Stanton's house. He stood in front of David.

"Are you serious, dude?" Tyler asked. Tyler hesitated at the door. Then he reached for his pocket to grab his cell phone. David put his hand out as a gesture of peace.

"Please, Ty. Just give me three minutes. That's all I want. Then you can call the police and tell them you were out walking and I accosted you.

Whatever makes you look good," David proposed.

"Right now?" Tyler asked.

"All I want is a walk around the block. Just a few minutes," David pleaded. "What's it to you? I'm the one whose life is ruined."

"It's fucking cold out. And you're a fugitive. Do you realize that?" Tyler glanced outside. He gazed left and right suspiciously. It was a blustery night, with a light rain beginning to sprinkle. Trees swayed around the old converted gas lamps, casting eerie shadows across the city street. But Tyler didn't notice anything otherwise off. It was just the quant standing in front of him, after all. Tyler ducked back into the house and yelled to his wife, "Steph? I'm going out for a second. Getting cigarettes." Tyler emerged with a coat. The two men padded slowly down the sidewalk while the wind howled over their heads. Or maybe it was the gargoyles.

"This isn't my fault—" David started.

"Seriously? Don't tell me that's what you wanted to say. You did this, dude. You ran the algorithm. I mean you're the only guy who could even write it in the first place, so of course you ran the thing. That's not even a question. What I really want to know is why? Why'd you do it? What are you getting out of all this? Did you trade against it? You'll never get away with that. Doesn't matter what account you used—they'll trace you, man. Do you know how sophisticated brokerage record keeping is in this day and age?" Tyler said.

"I never said I didn't write it. I did. I wrote it. I admit that," David said.

"No shit. SEC is going to sue us. We'll probably sue you. Oh, also, you're fired—in case that wasn't a fact of extreme abundance for you."

"The least of my worries," David said. "Listen. There's just one thing I wanted to ask you—the reason I'm here. The server room . . . Why'd you let me into the server room?"

"You requested it"—Tyler shrugged—"and I trusted you."

"I didn't request anything. The approval was already in the system, or it came in within seconds of me being at the door. I'm crystal clear on that."

"I was sitting at my computer, David," Tyler said. "Don't you remember that morning? I was a little pissed at you honestly. 'Cause you were late. Saw it pop up. I figured that meant you were working, trying to get back on my good side, which is all I ever wanted out of you and the rest of the team anyways. So I approved it—right then and there."

"Without asking me why?" David pondered out loud.

"So what?" Tyler stopped walking and peered directly at David. "Are you telling me that you're pissed that I trusted you? How the fuck is that logical?" But before David could respond, Tyler kept prodding. "Dude. Is this what this is about? This is why you knocked on my door? Just to ask me why I believed in you?" he asked David.

"Yeah. I guess it is."

"Clearly I made a huge mistake with you. And because of it, I'm trying not to get fired next. I don't know what the hell is going wrong in your life. I probably don't want to. But take me out of it, 'cause it has nothing to do with me," Tyler said. He pulled his phone from his pocket. "Oh, and your time's up, man. We're not going a block. This is all I got."

"I should have known you wouldn't lift a finger for me," David said.

"Well, yeah. Duh. Be careful, dude," Tyler responded as he turned and walked the other direction. The rain rotated from light precipitation to an utter downpour, slinging curtains of water across the city. Tyler's long trench coat billowed behind him as he paced hurriedly back towards the safety of his house. David stood still in the downpour, observing as Tyler passed a nondescript van parked on the street.

In a flash, the door to the van slid open and three men in balaclavas charged directly at Tyler Stanton. One of them was holding a knife. He jammed it into Tyler's neck, about a half inch in depth. Blood spilled from a scraped vein, but not enough to threaten Tyler's life—yet.

"You will be sliced if you scream," the masked man said in a tone very distinctive and recognizable to everyone except for Tyler. The other two thugs tossed Tyler into the back of the vehicle. The van drove off down the street. It stopped for a brief moment to pick up David, who had known this was coming well before he had ascended the steps to Tyler's brownstone.

▪

A barrage of fists pummeled Tyler's face. Left. Right. Right. Left. Right. Each strike was surgical—the motion and marks of a professional fighter. David sat in the back of the van behind Tyler. He winced and slowly slid a black balaclava over his own head as he observed the onslaught.

Vlad was doing the punching. Tyler's hands had been secured, pulled taut by handcuffs to each side of the van. His wallet and Blackberry were ripped from his pockets. As with most young princes who have always achieved their goals in life through a combination of aggressive bluster and above-average intelligence, Tyler remained utterly defiant.

"Who the hell are you?" Tyler screamed between the onslaught of punches.

Tyler's affront was greeted by an enormous smack to the face from Vlad's open hand.

"I'm a nightmare for you," Vlad said as he played with a small gadget in his lap that was built to mirror the contour of a gun but was decidedly not one. The device actually looked like a neon-yellow Nerf weapon. "Ever stick your finger in an electrical outlet before?" Vlad asked with menace.

Tyler's brain immediately clicked. He knew what he was staring at—a taser. The maximum physical intimidation that Tyler had experienced in the past was limited to drunk fistfights on the sidewalk outside of Dorrian's. Although he was perched halfway to unconsciousness, the worst was yet to come. Vlad unbuttoned Tyler's shirt.

"Did you know that an electrical outlet contains about two hundred volts? But this piece of shitty plastic made in a sweatshop in Indonesia delivers four hundred times that charge—directly to your heart cavity. In milliseconds," Vlad orated as he ran the taser gun in circles over Tyler's bare and hairless chest.

"What do you think I know?" Tyler begged plaintively.

"I'm a man with an interest in gold."

"Are you serious?" Tyler asked. "You cannot be real right now."

Vlad took one final look. That was definitely the wrong response. He was deadly serious. He was Vlad. His emotions were binary. He was either messing around or he was gravely definitive. Nothing existed in between. The trick to remaining on Vlad's good side was the ability to divine which emotion he was feeling in any given moment. Tyler didn't know that, and he never would.

Vlad turned the safety off on the taser gun. He aimed it at Tyler, lined up the front sight, and pulled the trigger. Two gas-powered fléchettes accelerated through the air directly into Tyler's chest. All of Tyler's muscles contracted simultaneously as the charge raced through his body. Tyler screamed bloody murder, his cry like a rippling earthquake from his lungs on out.

"One down. Four to go. These things are goddamn expensive. And you know what happens when I run out of cartridges?" Vlad asked. Vlad pantomimed a gun with his hands. He put his fingers to Tyler's temple. "Boom," Vlad threatened. His lips slowly blew air over his index finger, as though there was smoke sailing from the top of a gun.

"I don't know anything about the goddamn robbery. I'm a trader, not a criminal," Tyler said. Tyler jerked back without warning. Rearing up with his arms still securely attached to the sides of the van, he gazed around as best he could. All Tyler could identify were a bunch of masked men. "Did the quant do this?" Tyler screamed and then asked, "Are you in here, David?" Obviously no one responded to him. "Are you going to kill me? I have alot of money! I'll pay you whatever you want—whatever you need to get me out of here. Everyone has a price."

"Nah, you don't got what we're looking for. You gamble. You may have a rich life, but if I were a betting man, I'd presume that you don't have shit," Vlad guessed.

Without waiting for Tyler to respond, he shot Tyler with the taser again. The electricity racked through Tyler's body relentlessly. Tyler puked. The vomit ran down his body to the floor of the van.

David's hands tightened as he dug his fingernails into an armrest with each electrical shock. It had all felt so logical when Vlad had pitched the idea to him, but observing the intimate details of his boss's torture was starting to make David feel unsure about his choices.

"You scheduled David into the server room on Monday morning," Vlad continued.

Tyler glared at Vlad. "I don't know who the fuck you are, but you're in deep here, doing this."

"Says the drowning man."

"No. What's happening around us . . . It's like the world itself. There's too much going on to get your arms around it. You won't be able to understand it even if you try. The walls are falling down. Dust to dust. You get it, man? Anything can go down—even Montgomery. This is bigger than me and much bigger than the quant," Tyler warned.

"Then what's it about?"

"Same thing it always is—money, power, debt—whatever. Bullshit," Tyler said.

"Give me the details!" Vlad screamed.

Having processed Tyler's outburst, David stuffed all of his tentative, peaceful thoughts of resolution into the deepest part of his mind. Tyler did know something. Vlad had been right. David leaned forward and gripped the handcuffs holding Tyler. He pulled as hard as he could, twisting Tyler's wrist even farther against the side of the seat. Tyler retched with pain. Vlad held the taser up, his finger slowly and precariously applying trigger pressure again.

"I don't have anything. I don't know anything about the crash!" Tyler said.

Vlad shot Tyler again. The pure agony of sickening electrical current coursed through Stanton's body.

"Stop!" Tyler screamed out, his decibels rising to the point where David glanced out of the windows to make sure no one had heard. But the van was in motion, speedily ripping through the rain. Tyler would have no savior. David turned back to him and witnessed a final shift. Just like a clam under heat, Tyler began to open up.

"I . . . It . . . It's . . . I didn't cause this crash. I knew nothing about it," Tyler said.

"That's all you have? If this is the way you've chosen to save your life, you picked a piss-poor way to do it," Vlad said.

"I did a favor. That's all."

"What favor?"

"I want proof that you'll let me go," Tyler demanded.

"I don't negotiate with bankers," Vlad replied. He prepared the taser again, but this time he jammed it into Tyler's mouth.

Terrified, Tyler began to emote a muffled scream. "Waahaitt! Waiihhitt. Okay . . . How—"

Vlad pulled the taser out of Tyler's mouth. "What'd you say?" Vlad asked.

"Howard. Howard. I did it for Howard," Tyler said.

Hearing this, David couldn't help it. He lunged at Tyler in anger and frustration. Vlad pushed him back.

Tyler became emotional as he bared his soul. "I gamble and he knew the size of my side book in Vegas. It was bad. That's the truth. My debt service with the bookies is more than my mortgage. Anyway, Howard knew. Stephanie didn't. I needed to fix the problem. He told me he has a hedge fund client. They're called Tsunami. They wanted to run a trading program off our servers directly. He told me he'd settle me up at bonus time—hit me with two or three mil—if I cleared the algorithm through compliance. I thought it was just slightly illegal, you know? A front-running bot or something like that, where it reads the volume of orders coming through our system and places its own orders ahead of the rest. The type of thing we do and we just look the other way for a few days. Mix it in with all the trades together and regulators can never tell. But, I mean, I couldn't . . . couldn't tell the police about all that. They'd ask questions and I mean, the computers . . . We run all sorts of dark shit—shit that who knows if it's legal. Our own lawyers don't. I wasn't going to go down that road, dude."

"That was the flash program?" Vlad asked.

"I guess so. At the time, I didn't know it would be David. Howard told me that morning—on Monday. I approved David's install on the server. That's all."

"For three million dollars."

"Yeah."

"And you didn't think to ask any questions?" Vlad asked.

"No one asks Howard questions. That's sacrilege. God's never wrong," Tyler said.

"So what's Tsunami?"

"I don't fucking know."

"Who runs it?" Vlad changed his line of questioning.

"I have no idea. They're Howard's client. Not mine. I only did one other thing for them, so I know they're in shipping."

"Shipping?"

Tyler nodded and explained. "Tsunami owns a couple hundred shipping containers. A couple months ago, I was told to turn those containers into off-balance sheet assets. So we sold them through a bunch of shells to a controlling entity."

"Why would you do that?" Vlad asked, becoming more and more confused by the second.

"Sometimes companies do it when they're losing money and want to hide it or slow the burn." Tyler shrugged. "Sell them to someone else, even if it's really yourself. Report the cash on your balance sheet as income. It's shady, not illegal."

"So you hid the containers from the company's balance sheet?" Vlad asked.

"I was just doing Howard a favor."

"Then where the hell are they?" Vlad inquired.

"All over the world—on boats, ports . . . It's a real business—a commodity thing. They just rent them out. Look, I can get you the exact locations. There's a spreadsheet on my Berry," Tyler said.

Vlad thought for a moment. "I only have two more charges."

"I'm telling you the truth. That's all I got, dude. I don't know you. I don't know what you're going to do with this. You could ruin me now, and if you don't, then a hundred other people might. I wish I could take it all back. I can't." Tyler began to weep in front of them.

Vlad gazed at him, disgusted. But it finally did seem as if Tyler had been telling the truth. Vlad grabbed Tyler's Blackberry and handed it to David. "Let's get him the fuck out of here," Vlad said. Then he pulled Tyler close to him. "Hey. Maybe you don't want to call the police. You call, and you'll have to tell them what you told me. And then they'll know what you told me, ya?"

"I know. I'm kicked." Tyler's eyes cast down to the floor.

The van stopped, and the men threw Tyler out forcefully. He landed in a puddle of water, completely soaked and ruined.

FIFTEEN

JAKE'S BIKE WHEEL SPUN a stream of wet grime up the back of his coat as he sailed down Canal, in the heart of Chinatown, on Wednesday afternoon. The dirt didn't faze him. His mind was focused on the case at hand. He'd spent the last three hours scouting every electronics store and open-air mart he could locate in the district. He had sauntered in like a customer, never flashed his badge, and yet still emerged empty-handed. No one sold the jammer he was looking for, and they'd all been vociferous in their denials. That meant something. This part of town wasn't afraid to do illegal business right on the streets. If he couldn't find it, it might not exist.

Jake knew Chinatown well. The first time Jake ran away from home, he'd taken the train from upstate into Penn Station and had walked all the way to Chinatown. The sights, sounds, and smells hadn't changed one iota. At the time, he'd been exceptionally mad at his father and didn't think he would ever go back. The strength of emotion in the searing permanence of memory was amazing. This one remained crystal clear in his mind, all these years later. He had been fifteen years old at the time. Jake had walked right into a store a few blocks away from where he was currently standing and had ordered his first piece of fake identification. The guys behind the counter hadn't been much older than him and hadn't glanced at him twice. They had asked Jake to choose a state and had given him a form to fill out with whatever information suited him, including his birthdate. Jake had taken that ID, still hot from the laminator, and had walked into a local bar. He'd gotten shitcanned by himself. It was the first time he'd drunk in his life—his first time being drunk—and he hated it just as much as he thought he would. He slept in an alleyway and went home the next morning. A week later, his dad sent him to boarding school.

Jake's experience and intuition told him that the shop owners he had just quizzed, at stores with names like "FONG ELECTRONICS, LTD." and "SUN COMPUTER IMPORT-EXPORT," were not lying to him at all. If they had possessed devices he was looking for, they would have let him know and made a buck. Jake concluded that he was either barking up the wrong tree, or he wasn't in the right grove.

But he had another idea. He ran the bike down Canal and turned south on Mott, glancing up at the lit decorations strung across the city street. Jake pulled up to a small restaurant called Palace. A lone middle-aged Chinese man with wraparound sunglasses from the eighties leaned against the door and stared at him. Jake parked the motorcycle and hopped off. Recognizing him, the man nodded imperceptibly and held open the door.

"Won't have a problem with the bike, right Guo?" Jake asked.

"As long as you don't have a problem with us," Guo replied.

"Just here for a meal and a little chitchat with Sunny."

"Both are here, twenty-four seven," Guo said. He began cackling at his own joke as Jake entered the restaurant.

Jake walked through the center of the dimly lit Palace Restaurant, illuminated by the ghostly blue of two large fish tanks that framed each side of the room. A pack of piranhas followed Jake as he paced past. The killer fish resembled a screensaver, or a nightmare, but this was neither. It was real life, and the piranhas were one of Palace's signatures. A thick layer of smoke hung in the air like Beijing smog. Environmental restrictions weren't on the forefront of Palace's proprietor's mind.

Nor was health. Sunny weighed five hundred pounds and held court inside his restaurant all day long. Although he was gargantuan in size, it never brought him down. His disposition was cheery and he always had a huge smile on his face. That's why he was named Sunny. He was also happy because he was rich, and he was rich as shit because he had controlled the majority of Chinatown's Triad sects for the last twenty years. Jake approached, and Sunny looked up from a laptop on his desk.

"Mr. New York," Sunny bellowed through the mostly empty restaurant. "What did I do?" Sunny held up his hands in a mock surrender.

"Got an egg roll for an old friend?" Jake asked.

"My friends give when they take. But I still got an egg roll for you," Sunny said as he raised his finger and gestured for one of the petite waitresses standing invisibly in the dark shadows of the restaurant. Sunny rattled out an order in Chinese. She nodded and disappeared again. "It's been a year, Mr. New York. What do you think I do now?" Sunny asked.

"Nothing. I got a case, though—and questions," Jake said as he took a seat. "Who sells phone jammers in your hood?"

"What's that?"

"Don't play," Jake retorted.

"Is this about the robbery?"

"If you want it to be. What do you know?" Jake said.

"I watch news too—your bossman there talking—Marks."

"I wish he'd shut up," Jake replied.

"Jammers are illegal, Mr. New York."

"Oh, so now you do know what I'm talking about?"

"I remember," Sunny said as he shrugged.

"Well, yeah. They are illegal. And you run a completely legal business, Sunny?"

"I'm telling you. It's truth. You know me. I'm not a sophisticate.

Jammers? That spy shit. I like dupin. Mess with your mind for a couple hours. That's all. There's a million normals in city that wanna buy the white. That's as far as we go. Well, not me. I don't touch it, and I don't sell it."

"You can quit it. I'm not here for you," Jake said.

"Just saying. No one wants to buy a jammer, and if they do, there's a half chance they a nerd and a half chance they a Fed and I don't play fifty-fifty games—never. Need to have way more luck on my side, Mr. New York."

"You sure?"

"I tell you straight. That's not my business. DVD with Ryan Gosling on it? Sure. Beside that? No technology."

"Then whose business is it?"

Sunny laughed. "So those robbers used jammers? To do what?"

"I'm asking the questions—not answering," Jake said.

"Don't forget the generosity of your boy Sunny. Maybe two years till you come back next time?" Sunny grunted.

"Generosity?"

"Yeah, skinny boy. You get fattened up."

Jake heard a rustling behind him and turned to see three waiters arriving at the table, each holding multiple platters overflowing with all manner of delectable Chinese food.

"I said an egg roll, Sunny."

"I'm a giver, not a taker. Want a drink with that?"

"Nah. I'm on the job," Jake replied.

"Eat up, Mr. New York. It's your city. I just pay taxes," said Sunny, having lost none of his ebullience throughout their interaction.

■

Jake stepped out of Palace later in the evening. He noticed that Guo had helpfully moved his motorcycle out of the rain and onto the sidewalk. Guo didn't have the key and the bike weighed close to a ton. He must have had help, but Jake didn't see it. Such were the mysteries of Chinatown. Jake stared at Guo. "Still have the salon?" Jake inquired. He had one more idea.

Guo nodded affirmatively.

▪

Inside Guo's massage parlor, conveniently located just a few storefronts down from Sunny's restaurant, Jake lay on the massage table in the dark. The room was barely illuminated by two small wall torches on each side of the room. It smelled fresh, like wild lavender in a country field. Chinese instrumental music wafted lightly through the central speaker system that connected to each room.

Jake focused on nothing while a young woman worked his body much harder than a man at the uptown salons would dare. Jake kept his eyes closed mostly, until the lights slowly came on and the woman smiled at him from the door.

"You're all done, mister," she said.

"No happy ending?" Jake asked.

"You're a cop."

Jake chuckled. "Just kidding."

"You testing," she replied.

"Testing. Right," he said. As she turned to leave, he stopped her. "Hey. Hold on." Jake pulled himself off the massage bench, just managing to cover himself in the nick of time. He could tell he was scaring the girl, but he didn't care. "Who sells all the electronics you can't buy in the store?"

"What?" she replied blankly.

"If I wanted to buy an iPhone that was jailbroken and bring it back to China?"

"I have no idea."

"You sure?" Jake asked. She didn't reply and his attention was suddenly piqued. "Tell me. Cell phones, laptops, radios—stuff like that. But not from a store. Who sells it?"

"I just massage," she replied.

He stepped closer to her, towering over the little woman. "You massage. Right. And you do whatever—for men who aren't cops, I mean. I don't care. But you do. Because that's how you make your money. Let me tell you how I make my money. I get bones by busting people like you—places like this. I could have fifty cops blow down the front door tomorrow if I'd like. But I don't. 'Cause I respect you. Do you respect me? You tell me right now. Where can I find it? Illegal electronics. Where?" Jake was practically spitting into her face.

"Illegal?" she asked.

"Yes."

The petrified woman wasn't sure what to do. She opened the door behind her and slipped out. She turned and stared at Jake again. "No idea," she said once. Her eyes flicked down the hallway towards Guo's office. "No idea," she said and again flicked her eyes towards Guo. Then she disappeared.

Jake padded slowly down the hallway. He could see Guo in his office, laughing on his cell phone.

"This your only business, Guo?" Jake inquired as he leaned against the office door.

"Massages? Yes."

"I'm looking for cell phone jammers," Jake said.

"I'll sell you this." Guo pointed to a Casio boombox from the nineties on a shelf above his computer. He started cackling again. Everyone in Chinatown seemed to be lost within his or her own personal sphere of ironic mirth—the outside world be damned.

"I've been containing myself here, Guo. I know one of you is lying to me. Sunny's on everything that happens, and if he don't, then the only reason for that is 'cause you do."

"I got nothing."

"Just prostitutes."

"Exactly."

"And drugs," Jake said.

Guo shrugged in a placid non-response affirmation.

"God. You guys are a piece of work," Jake said. Without warning, Jake gripped each side of Guo's collar. Scrunching the fabric tightly with his fists, he pulled Guo out of his chair and pushed him against the glass mirror behind him. "Tell me where I can buy a fucking cell phone jammer down here! Now!"

"I don't sell that! I don't know!" Guo replied, raising his voice back.

"Goddammit." Jake expelled all the pressure inside by slamming Guo against the mirror. The mirror cracked, and pieces of it began to fall down to the floor. Guo collapsed back down to the floor.

"You happy?" Guo asked him.

Jake stared at his reflection against the mirror. He thought he knew who he was, but the pieces were still splintering around him. He'd spent his whole life trying to keep the mirror from changing, but he couldn't stop it. That's how everyone is. By the time they've seen their reflection, they've already become someone else.

Then Jake heard a small whimper. He looked down. It wasn't Guo, whose body had suddenly metamorphosed into a rock-solid state of panic.

"What was that?" Jake asked.

Guo started to stand up. "Huh? You need to get out of here. I'm going to tell Sunny."

"No. The noise . . ."

"No noise. Maybe my mirror crashing."

Jake heard it again. It sounded like a sob—or a rat trying to scrape against the back of the mirror. Or both. He pushed Guo out of the way and placed his ear to the wall. He heard it again. He knocked with his hand. He heard another knock back. Jake pulled his gun and aimed it directly at Guo. "Sit down," Jake commanded Guo, who followed his orders, a miserable look cast upon his face.

Jake examined the wall. He realized that it was framed in by external two-by-fours. The construction was strange, as if the wall was missing half its wallboard. Still holding his gun, Jake let out an enormous scream. He lifted his leg and slammed it as hard as he could into the interior wall, which shuddered back a few inches. Jake could tell that something was hidden back there. After another kick, the fake wall swung open to the inside. Jake suddenly stared into the eyes of twenty extremely filthy, illegal Chinese immigrants stored in a room about the size of a walk-in closet.

▪

A few hours later, Guo's massage shop was swimming with cops. Villalon stood outside with Jake. They'd just finished loading Guo into an NYPD paddy wagon idling on the street.

"It's a huge bust," Tony said.

"Not what we were looking for," Jake replied.

"Makes you look good."

"This whole thing is turning into a stupid wild-goose chase. I'm starting to believe we're not going to find anything down here," Jake said.

"Don't trust your instinct?" Tony asked.

Jake grinned at him. Villalon had grown up perfectly middle class and had never broken the speed limit. The guy didn't know his instinct from his elbow, but he was a solid cop. "Keep searching the internet for me, Tony. Buy as many of those pieces of crap as you can on eBay or wherever you can find them, and let's pray that one of them looks like ours."

"Will do. We're also searching every home improvement store in seven states for the steel cutter."

"All right," Jake said. He turned and then glanced back at Tony. "We're too on the nose. There's something I'm missing—and it's everything. It's the critical element."

"On the nose breaks cases," Villalon replied with a shrug.

"No—just mirrors," Jake retorted.

As Jake leaned over to check his motorcycle, he heard commotion down the street. He looked up and was blessed with the rare sight of

Sunny's five hundred lumbering pounds standing outside Palace. Jake had never even seen Sunny standing up before. Five of Guo's employees had materialized from the various businesses of the street. All young men in their late teens and twenties, they kneeled in a line on the sidewalk in front of Sunny. Jake was fascinated. He couldn't take his eyes off the genuflecting ritual. Sunny focused directly on Jake, who kept his eyeline locked. Sunny wound up and slapped one of the men, like a windmill to the face. The man collapsed to the ground. Sunny stepped left and hit the next one. In quick succession, he smacked the crap out of each of his henchmen. They didn't fight back. They didn't look up. They remained on the wet cement underneath Sunny like a pack of whipping boys, which was exactly what they were. He stared directly at Jake. Then Sunny opened his mouth and spoke. "Get out of here, Mr. New York."

Jake did just that. He jetted the hell out of the belly of the beast in search of a song more beautiful.

■

At the very same moment, David Belov was blowing chow all over a drain on the side of the road in Brooklyn. Vlad waited for him patiently by the car.

"You see, my peach? Bankers," Vlad said with a grin.

David looked as though he was going to be sick again.

"You okay?"

David nodded, but his face was white.

"You can handle this. I know you can. And if you can't? I don't know what to tell you. I warned ya," Vlad said.

"I need to see my family," David said.

"I get that you're pissed. But your cell phones, your landline, computer, e-mail . . . The police will have bugged it all," Vlad said.

"I wasn't asking, Vlad. I have to see Marina. I have to talk to her, tell her that I'm okay, and promise her that we're figuring this out," David replied.

"I'll do something to get you guys together. But you gotta give me a little time, ya? And while I'm on that, it's time to get to work on that villain's Blackberry."

■

Back in Konstantin's safe house studio apartment, David reached for Tyler's Blackberry. He sat down at the small desk, where a laptop had been set up for him. He hooked up Tyler's phone via a USB cord to another device laying on the desk—a PIN hacker. David was very familiar with the device, having developed a similar one in college for his CS 201 class. The PIN hacker was about the size of a pack of cards, with two inputs and a power cord. One input entered the Blackberry device. The other was attached to David's computer, where he ran a command-and-control application. The first thing the PIN hacker did was circumvent the BIOS, the phone chip's operating system. It tricked the system into disregarding its self-destruct mechanism following the entry of ten incorrect passwords. This prevented the phone from erasing itself. Then the PIN hacker began to parse through billions of possible numeric unlocking combinations, anywhere from four to ten digits long. Tens of thousands of options processed through the phone every second. Although the numbering choices were statistically chosen, with the most common combinations first, David still had no way of knowing when he'd break through Tyler's encryption. The breakthrough could occur in thirty seconds, or it could take a few days.

David stood. As the application hustled along, he shuffled to the small bathroom sink. He washed his face while staring at himself in the mirror. He imagined how Marina would feel if she saw him like this. Boiling with hate, most likely. And what about Mikey? David couldn't even bear contemplating the notion. He abruptly stepped away from the bathroom. He didn't want to see himself anymore. He paced back and forth across the room. After a while, he looked at the laptop—still nothing. David finally lay down on the tiny bed with its minimal thread count. Stiff as a board,

David stared up. The off-white surface of the ceiling was illuminated only by the listless digital glow of the workhorse computer to his left. The blurry numbers filtering above taunted him. He was deadly tired, having not slept in two days. He was also completely unable to sleep.

SIXTEEN

Fifteen Years Prior

BY THE TIME THEY were sophomores at New Utrecht High School, David and Vlad rarely hung out. They'd still chat whenever they passed one another in the halls, or if Vlad needed an injection of knowledge regarding European history. But their interests had diverged to the point where they weren't even in the same hallways any longer.

The municipal funding regime had financed a new computer lab down in the basement and had filled it with ten brand-spanking-new computers that none of the students used. They sat in all their boring glory like expensive paperweights. Not a single kid at New Utrecht would be caught dead there. Social media didn't exist, and internet browsing was in its infancy. Encouraged by his math teacher, David Belov had been the only student interested in the lab. He loved getting lost in the programming software that was preloaded onto the computers. He found the positive feedback loop of inputting instructions and receiving immediate results to be very addictive. Besides the fact that David wasn't interested in miscreant activity any longer, the computers held most of his attention and were the main reason that he didn't cross paths with Vlad. As one might imagine, Vlad would never have volunteered to sit in front of a CRT monitor for hours. But David loved it. He found himself exploring the inner workings of the machine as he used to explore Gravesend and Coney Island. He'd watch tutorials on CD-ROM relentlessly, trying to replicate the coding described until his shoulders ached. At first he had to follow directions, but eventually David became fluent in the programming languages he was learning. He started with tiny little text programs. Then he created calculators for various types of math problems. Eventually he coded an algorithm that would allow anyone to calculate the area underneath a curve, and another that rendered 3-D boxes complete with lighting effects. And that was all within the first year.

▪

On the other hand, the only element of school that still held any of Vlad's interest was basketball. He was a pretty good shot. More importantly, he was a consistent and skillful bruiser. The varsity basketball team's coach loved him for it. But even the coach couldn't overlook the preseason afternoon when Vlad shaved an incoming freshman's head and tried to stuff the poor kid into a locker room. Vlad was relieved of his duty as a player on the team by the school's principal, and his future in team sports ended.

When one door closes, another opens. Around the same time as Vlad's unceremonious departure from the basketball team, he had begun to refine his natural boxing skills. Vlad had developed his fighting acumen in the wild, as it were. But having perfected his ability to rumble like an animal, he began to channel his energy towards a more professional version of the same pursuit. If basketball wasn't going to save him, then a nascent boxing career certainly might.

It helped that his father owned the boxing gym on Cropsey. Vlad began to spend the majority of his time there. Each afternoon he would walk over after school, followed without fail by his growing crew of scalawags. Vlad's crew had grown past the amiable Baranowski to include the brothers Roschin and Petrov. His dad's gym was a business, but it was also a de facto clubhouse for Arseni and his "people" to hang out. This was especially true after Arseni built a sauna in the back of the building. The older men spent a little time boxing and a lot of time bullshitting. It didn't go unnoticed to Arseni's colleagues that all of their sons and sons' friends considered Vlad their leader. They'd seen what boys like Vlad grew up and became. They didn't have to look any further than Arseni for this inspiration. Like father, like son.

Vlad's high school years were actually the most peaceful of his life. After a year or two in the gym, it was established that he was a boxing prodigy. He was regularly destroying eighteen and nineteen-year-olds and turning all of Arseni's other top prospects on their heads. Only greatness lay ahead. That's when Vlad was first gripped by the power of the dream. Maybe he could work incredibly hard in order to get himself in a position to be incredibly lucky. Maybe he'd be able to make the jump. Vlad could be the kid who got out of Bensonhurst—the one people would talk about forever—the bear cub that made it in the world. And the boxing ring was going to be the arena in which he would make that happen.

▪

In the early spring of his junior year, David had perfected his abilities with the most advanced programming language he'd tried his hand at: C+ +. But he was becoming bored. He was tired of writing little sideshow programs that even his teachers were no longer able to debug. He was also starting to look forward in life. He wanted to figure out how he could use his skills in the future—in the real world. While browsing Wired magazine's first version of an internet presence, David read an article about robots that were being developed by researchers in Japan. He found a computer-controlled robot kit on Amazon and begged his physics teacher to purchase it for the school. A few weeks later, David's request was granted.

Thus started New Utrecht's first robotics club. David was the inaugural and only member at the time, although he was eventually able to scrape up a few of the other techies in the place and force them to pay attention. They were a motley crew. There weren't many and they weren't particularly polished. One of the kids in the club forgot to wear underwear to school multiple times a year. They weren't even talented engineers—but they were nerds with passion, and that counted for a lot. Although it took them until almost the end of the semester, the robotics club eventually assembled a slightly humanoid robot that would respond to digital commands from a controller. Their machine could accomplish simple tasks for its human masters, like holding up a book and turning the pages or opening a root beer bottle. Even though it was far more efficient for David to open his own soda pop, he was thrilled with the club's accomplishments. And for the first time in his life, he was the leader of the pack.

There was one final propitious event that occurred during the second half of the school year. David's physics teacher was under pressure from the school administration to justify the four-thousand-dollar cost of the robotics kit and signed the club up for a science fair in Atlantic City. The event was scheduled to take place during the last week of the school year. Putting aside the fact that their machine was at the developmental age of toddler, David and his team were pumped. With its bottle-opening skill already hard coded, the club decided that a "couch potato" theme would be entertaining. They spent three more weeks using code to cajole the robot into pressing a television remote and then moved on to sandwich preparation. They succeeded in training their robot to make a full sandwich, albeit a dry one. No matter how delicately they calibrated the machine, they simply weren't successful in making their robot squeeze out mustard or ketchup in a reasonable manner.

▪

Emotional moments achieve permanence in one's memory banks. The first notable moment at the fair was the New Utrecht Robotics Club's arrival on the floor of the giant arched-ceiling convention center in Atlantic City, New Jersey. Everyone on the team proudly donned their admission lanyards and matching blue polo shirts that they'd scrounged up through school bake sales. Even Veronika had gotten off her butt and made some Rice Krispies treats for David to sell. David felt quite official in his new duds. As the team walked into the massive convention center space, they truly felt that they'd arrived. It was only after they'd set up the robot that David took a breather to look around at the other clubs and began to realize how completely outmatched they were. A handful of clubs were using the exact same robot kit as theirs. But most of the machines on the floor were completely custom built, some to the tune of hundreds of thousands of dollars. David's competitors were far past bake sales. Even the robots that were based off his kit were incredibly advanced. They put his to shame. The machines were powered by solar panels on their shoulders. They could walk to a bicycle, saddle up, and cycle around the convention center without colliding into anyone. They didn't require a wired connection. A handful of them were designed to utilize artificial intelligence strategies. One of the robots had actually been jury-rigged into a helicopter drone that flew around the rafters of the convention center and fed live video to a public website.

David was stunned. At first he thought he had simply failed—that he wasn't smart enough to compete with the big boys. But eventually he came to understand that sometimes brainpower isn't enough. He was proud of his polo shirt, but some of the teams had entire sets of matching apparel down to their duffel bags. He was precious when it came to his robot. The majority of the groups possessed multiple builds of the same cyborg, just in case their primary model began to malfunction. David presumed that he was just as smart as some of these kids from the green suburbs of New Jersey and the Upper West Side of Manhattan, but he didn't have his hands on nearly as many resources as they did. That made all the difference. That's why the New Utes didn't win any medals in Atlantic City. In the end it didn't come down to skill or math. David realized in this moment that in order to get what he wanted from life, it wasn't about how he played the game. It all depended on his ability to tip the playing field in his favor.

▪

However powerful this realization was, and however lasting, it was not the most important thing that happened to David at the science fair. A few days beforehand, David had learned that his club would be traveling with another group from a different high school in Bensonhurst. The two teachers had put their heads together and concluded that they could save money by renting one school bus for both teams to share. That meant that David and his nerdy handful of robotics experts were on a bus to and from New Jersey with a group of five girls from Lafayette High School.

The girls' presentation was about biology, with an esoteric subject matter regarding the power of moss in the jungle. On the bus, one of them rabidly explained how easy it was to classify the mammal taxonomy of a forest area based on the moss within that environment. Most of the spiel was lost on David, because he didn't care nearly as much about animals as he did about numbers. The girls from Lafayette also found themselves equally outmatched by their competition in Atlantic City and, although they might not have readily admitted it, equally disheartened.

As excited as both groups had been beforehand, it wasn't the most auspicious performance for either school. But the ride home was interesting, and not because the teachers decided to stop at Wendy's afterwards. David had noticed one of the girls in the beginning of the day —the one who didn't say much but seemed just as engrossed by the topic she was presenting as David was with his robot. David was not a ladies' man. He left that skill to Vlad, who would boast about his exploits on a daily basis in the lunchroom. The sociological wave of adolescence and flirtation had already passed by the time David was in junior year, and he was positioned at the back end of it. Although he was late to the game, at least David had started to realize that the opposite sex existed. What that really meant was that even though he wanted a girlfriend, David had no idea how to accomplish that feat. He leaned over to her when they were both waiting for their hamburger orders and muttered, "Do you like ketchup?"

"Huh?"

"Ketchup?"

"No thanks," she answered. And those were the first words that David Belov said to Marina Duranichev, the young lady who would eventually become his wife.

At least Marina was a good sport about it. They chatted about inconsequential subjects on the way back home. David may have bent the truth a little when it came to his hobbies, because he didn't really have any. He presumed that his true interest, computer programming, would horrify her. But after a run-through of their favorite movies and best places for funnel cakes on Coney Island, a funny thing started to happen. The whole group started talking, just a little bit. It began with baby steps—laughs across the aisle. But they had all spent the day saying nothing and only glancing at one another, so this was an improvement. Marina quickly realized that David was their leader. She found out that David had located the robot, convinced their school to buy it, and was in charge. It was easy to recognize that the rest of the robot club revered David. The bus eventually stopped at Lafayette, and the girls departed. As Marina was getting off the bus, David made his last valiant attempt.

"Do you want to hang out again?" he asked.

"Sure," she said while walking down the aisle of the bus.

"Can I have your number?"

"I don't have a phone," she said.

"Your house?"

"That won't work. Here."

He looked down. Marina had passed him a folded note.

"Bye, David," she said.

After she had stepped off the bus, David opened the note. It was a cartoon drawing of a sheep and a lion—holding hands. Marina had written both of their names at the top of the page. Hers was positioned above the lion, David's over the sheep. A conversation bubble emerged from the lion's head.

"I work at the ice cream parlor. Surf Ave. Every weekend. Come see me?" the lion said.

"Your wish is my command," the sheep responded.

■

Promptly the next weekend, David told Veronika that he had a meeting at school with his college counselor. He jumped on the subway and headed down to Coney Island. He found Marina at the ice cream shop on Surf Avenue, just as she had instructed. Unfortunately she wasn't at the cash register when he ordered his cookies and cream. He could see her through a door to the back kitchen. He didn't say anything. He sat down outside and tried his best to lick slowly, instead of snarfing the treat down. He lasted about twenty-seven minutes in the hot sun before his ice cream turned into sludge and he was forced to ingest it all or lose it forever.

David sauntered back into the shop and felt his heartbeat rise when he saw her again. This time she was at the register. He stood in line. Unfortunately, a woman in front of him started complaining about her bill, and Marina motioned for her to step aside. As Marina dealt with the wretched lady, a pimpled teenage boy popped into David's view. This was not going according to plan. David was forced to ask Marina's pimpled co-worker for a water. He grabbed the water and walked back outside. He paced up and down the boardwalk for a few minutes before deciding to check out the back of the building. He found an alley behind the ice cream shop, with a gate on the other side that led towards the Gravesend train lot. As he was staring through the fence at the trains, he heard a voice behind him.

"What are you doing?" she asked.

He turned. Marina. He lost all his words right then and there. Actually, he thought he emoted something, but no words actually came out.

"Did you come to see me?"

"Uh . . ." he replied.

"You're not doing a great job of it. You can just say 'Hello' you know," she said.

"I'm sorry. I am. I, uh, was . . . Uh . . . Do you have to work?"

"I took my break."

"How come?"

"So we could hang out. Isn't that what you wanted?"

David's face broke into a huge smile. "That's exactly right. Can I buy you an ice cream?" She frowned, and he realized that was the wrong question to ask. "You have enough ice cream. Right. A funnel cake and soda?"

"Sure." She smiled. "That sounds nice."

They walked along the Coney boardwalk towards Brighton Beach. At the end of the wood-paneled boardwalk, David bought her a funnel cake and soda as promised. They turned back and headed towards the parlor. Once she was done with the cake, she started pulling off pieces of it with her fingers and throwing them towards the packs of seagulls and crows that crowded the beach.

"Is that good for them?" David asked.

"Maybe it's not as natural as God intended. But they like it. And we're part of the ecosystem, aren't we?" she said. "Everyone needs a little leeway in life."

"Right. I agree," David concluded.

At the end of the walk, they found themselves standing in the alley by the back door. David tried to keep chatting her up, but he knew that precious time was ticking away. He was grasping at straws.

"What's up there?" David asked her, pointing to a fire escape leading up to the roof of the boardwalk buildings.

"The roof, silly."

"Have you been up?"

"No . . ."

"Do you want to?" David asked.

"Maybe next time," she said as she glanced at her watch, and then rotated nervously. "My break's over."

"Thanks for hanging out with me," David said. He leaned in. He was thinking about the kiss, but he wasn't committing. She didn't seem particularly receptive. He chickened out, turning his face into her shoulder for a hug.

"It's okay," she said.

"What?" he asked.

"You know . . ."

"I don't."

"Then that's your own fault," she said. Her face turned slightly sour as she stepped back through the door.

"Wait!" David practically yelled. She turned. He raced towards her in the portico. He reached for her face and he kissed her right then and there. It was David's first date and his first kiss. He would never kiss another woman again.

▪

Their relationship grew slowly. Neither David nor Marina was particularly good at communicating feelings, and they were both young grasshoppers. To them, what they felt was difficult to recognize. But they persevered throughout the summer and into senior year. David eventually concluded that he didn't have to visit the ice cream shop every time he wanted to talk to her. He could chat with her using instant messaging. Her father was very patriarchal and refused to allow Marina to date, but he'd permitted her to have a computer in her room to do homework. So David gave Marina a program called ICQ, with a plugin that allowed them to speak to each other using their computer's microphones. They spoke every day. They also started to meet up surreptitiously.

After six months, and in parallel to a dedicated campaign by Marina's mother, David was finally allowed to call the house phone. He displayed enough etiquette and poise to jump over the barrier that was Marina's father, and they brought their relationship into the public eye. Marina found herself increasingly interested in David's quiet intensity and his obvious intellect. She was smart herself, planning on becoming a veterinarian when she grew up, and she admired David's work ethic. Unlike most of the boys she knew, he was driven to make something of himself outside the bubble.

Once David and Marina officially pronounced themselves boyfriend and girlfriend, the first problem developed. It wasn't either of their faults— it was Abe. Abe Newman was also a senior at Lafayette, and he'd held a long-burning torch for her. Abe became hopping mad when he heard word of their relationship, but David knew nothing about it. Marina had hid the other boy's affections from David because she didn't care about Abe. But he was obsessed, and truth be known, she'd committed one small mistake—Marina had made out with Abe at a dance a few weeks before she met David. What was David's first kiss wasn't hers. It was actually her third.

▪

One morning David woke up to the sound of his mother screaming like a banshee. He ran down the stairs to find Veronika standing in her robe on their front porch, mouth agape, staring back up at the house. David followed and realized that his mother's car, all her plants, and the entire front of their house had been splattered with orange paintballs. They spelled out a sinister romantic message in terrible grammar: "STAY AWAY MARINA!"

The warning freaked David out. Marina begged him to just forget about it, but he couldn't. Even if he wanted to, Abe was calling his house and hanging up a few times every evening. David knew exactly who the anonymous caller was, because he had reverse dialed the number and a woman whom he later learned was Abe's mom had answered. David pretended to be a representative of the water company. He inquired as to whether she'd received her last bill. She had. She confirmed her last name —Newman. David was destined to be an engineer, but he would forever remember the significant power of social engineering. After David discovered that Abe was indeed behind the recent intimidation, he wasn't sure exactly what to do about it. But he definitely had a friend who could help.

▪

David located Vlad a few days later, walking along the sidewalk to the gym.

"Hey, my peach," Vlad greeted David.

"Hey, buddy."

"How you doing?"

"Honestly? Not so good," David revealed to Vlad. The floodgates opened. David told him everything. He wasn't sure where Vlad's opinion would fall. Vlad could be very black and white. Maybe he would think that David needed to man up. But to David's relief, Vlad flew into a parallel rage directed at Abe. No one was going to fuck with David if Vlad had anything to say about it. They devised a plan. Vlad knew a third party at Lafayette—a boy named Konstantin who was a recent émigré and had been spending most of his time at the gym. Konstantin was willing to leave a message for Abe on David's behalf, indicating that David was ready to settle this once and for all, just the two of them, at the southwest corner of the Washington Cemetery on Twentieth Avenue. Konstantin delivered the message, and Abe confirmed his participation.

▪

On the day of the fight, David appeared at the correct time and place. But Abe wasn't there. David sauntered around, watching as yellow school buses from the nearby high school passed. Just when he was about to leave, Abe appeared at the other end of Twentieth Avenue. He had six bruisers from the Lafayette wrestling team with him, flexing their muscles and pounding tight fists into their palms. David screamed down the street, "That's not fair! Not what we agreed to!"

"Life ain't fair, you puss," Abe retorted. David knew Abe had a point. The lesson would be relentless. Abe and his boys charged David with no abandon. When they were about twenty feet from David, about to beset upon him with juvenile testosterone and all the violence and lack of mental foresight it provides, Vlad popped out from behind the cemetery walls. He was holding a massive pipe and twirling it like a whirling dervish. Then Baranowski and Konstantin stood up from behind a grave, and Roschin and Petrov from another. Unlike Abe's crew, they were armed with all manner of blunt objects and knives. They'd been waiting.

Vlad and his crew turned that street into mincemeat. They showed no mercy. One of Abe's crew had to be picked up by an ambulance after being discovered unconscious down the block later that night. Abe and the captain of the wrestling team both ended up in the hospital with multiple stab wounds. When the police pressed Abe for what had happened, he told them nothing.

If Vlad's reputation had been in the foundational stage before the fight, it was cemented after it. Abe would never mess with Vlad or, by extension, David ever again. And neither would anyone else who heard about what had happened, which was practically everyone who called shots in the entire borough.

▪

A few months later, David, Marina, and Vlad graduated. The whole community came together for the ceremony, making banners and showing up in their most festive outfits. Veronika was dressed to the nines, wearing her one set of pearls and incredibly proud of her salutatorian son. After exchanging pleasantries, taking photographs, and going out to an early supper with their respective parents, the party started.

David brought Marina. Vlad brought the vodka and taught David how to play quarters for the first time. One of David's classmates who considered himself a disc jockey, and who would later spend years humping around the Meatpacking in search of fame, pumped techno music mixed with hip-hop. The crowd got crazy, groovy, and weird. It was high school in the heart of Brooklyn, and the vibe of their culture pulsed through the night. The party was aggressive—full of Goldschläger shots and strobes and maybe even a spliff or two. David let go and actually enjoyed himself. Vlad caught David dancing with Marina out of the corner of his eye and gave him a thumbs up, but he quickly turned back to the girl in front of him who had been eyeing him lasciviously and grinding all over his body. Vlad was in heaven. David was happy. The party was incredible.

The graduation party changed Vlad. His night started out on top and ended at the bottom. He made out with four girls in a row, each one happy to be next, and the last two at the same time. And then around one in the morning, Vlad received a phone call from the hospital. He learned that his father had been admitted. Arseni had been helping Vlad train for an upcoming fight in Connecticut, Vlad's first professional match on the IBF tour after turning nineteen years old. In the weeks leading up to graduation, Vlad had started to notice his dad coughing. Arseni had visited the doctor, come back with antibiotics, and seemed to be on the mend. But then the hacking had returned in earnest. It was two weeks from the graduation party to the day that Arseni passed away from lung cancer. And even though Vlad had a few amateur wins under his belt, his first major fight to compete in, and a whole chunk of momentum behind him, nothing would ever fill the hole that Arseni's death created.

The party was momentous for one more reason—David had rented a room at the Holiday Inn in Brighton for the evening. Both David and

Marina had engaged in the time-honored tradition of telling their parents that they were staying with friends for the night. Whether Veronika believed David or not, it didn't matter. She'd never been able to control her men anyways and David was clearly becoming one. David and Marina left the graduation party early. They walked hand in hand to the hotel. They fell into the bed together and had the best night of their young adult lives.

SEVENTEEN

Wednesday

JAKE RIVETT RIPPED HIS Ducati down the quiet and boutiqued-out streets of SOHO. The rain had finally stopped when he departed Chinatown, but a shroud of low fog remained on the island. This type of night made the city feel like an oil painting. Dying light flowed serenely over the cobblestones. Gotham was always precise and becoming more so, but nights like this reminded Jake that it also remained mysterious. The storefronts were turned down, their bare bulbs low, casting lovely shades across the grey, purple, and black planes of the environment. There were no people in sight. Jake loved the city at times like these.

He'd always loved it. Well before he'd witnessed Manhattan, he'd heard about it. To the rest of the world, New York represented freedom. It was the same for Jake but on a truly personal level. He'd been able to finally escape from his restrained childhood to the Oz-like metropolis. The city had always been the beacon that he'd been actively aiming for since he was old enough to know he should. But his feelings were about more than what the city provided him. His feelings were about *now*. He loved the spirit of the place. The city was an animal. Jake knew that he could never rule this urban landscape, but at least he could wrestle with it. Just like mankind, just like Jake himself, the creature was both stunningly sublime and exceedingly rough at the same time. Its perfect marble façades, luxurious fountains, and floor-to-ceiling luxury glass boxes were all evenly matched by its aggressive elements. No matter how far one's wealth allowed for themselves to be removed from the streets, one was never fully removed from the steam vents and the trash heaps, the pure volume of cars with their gaseous fumes, the pedestrians going in every direction, and the serpentine tunnels sharply carved out of previously undisturbed bedrock. Just as humans shape the environment around them, the environment shaped the humans. The city made men and women in its own image. Their lives were geometric, refined, and tailored. But often if you dug down through the spreadsheets and formality to the core of what they were doing, their essences were as elemental and primitive as the building blocks of the place itself. They were selling—they were buying. They were stealing and loving and fucking and conniving and crying. Jake happened to know this—not only because he could sense it, but also because it was literally his job. He parked his bike next to a small recording studio and walked into the entrance.

▪

A loud, cacophonic wail crashed through the space. Jake was on the microphone in the studio, his eyes closed. He was swaying back and forth as he screamed. Or was that singing?

No. It was screaming. Everyone has his or her own personal anxiety release valve. Some choose the drink, others go harder or stranger. There are people who choose to relax by throwing themselves off the top of mountains with parachutes on their backs. Jake's therapy was screaming. There was something about a long, sustained yell that succeeded in taking him far away from reality.

▪

It had begun when he was a child, with the screaming in his house. His father was also named Jake. Jake was actually Jake Rivett, Junior. But he'd dropped the nod to his family tree when he'd moved to New York City. Even though Jake shared the man's name, he wanted nothing to do with him. The word "Junior" placed him squarely in a stack with a man whom he hated. The moniker jammed him right back in the living room in Albany, where Jake Senior was screaming at the television in between swigs of whiskey. Most of the dads on Jake's block would use any downtime to play catch with their kids, do yardwork, or hustle up a home-improvement project. Jake Senior would spend his time in front of the television, watching sports. And the drinking—oh, the drinking. The only time that Senior would leave the house during the weekend was to get more alcohol or pal around with his friends at the bar on Main Street a half mile away. While Jake's mother was out in the yard mowing the grass, Senior would stumble past her without a word. Jake would watch from the window and then go outside himself. He'd have to ask his mother to throw a baseball with him. And she would do that, but she would never speak ill of her husband or tell Jake how disrespected she felt. She wasn't an apologist. She just didn't say anything. Her policy was silence, and muted depression her sentence.

Jake Senior was a functioning alcoholic. Ironically he was also a high-ranking police officer who would later become the chief of police, until it all came crashing down. Senior stopped himself from drinking when he was in the office or out on a shift. But the rest of the time was spent with the bottle. It wasn't a huge problem during the week. That's not to say it wasn't extremely evident. Senior would arrive home a few minutes before six. And just as the old grandfather clock in the dining room started to ring, the first beer would be open. By the time it was ten or eleven, he would be asleep, surrounded by a Stonehenge of bottles and glasses.

The weekends were worse, because he could start as early as he liked.

By the time the evening came along, Senior would always have found something to get mad about—something that Jake's mom hadn't done right, or a tidbit he'd heard in the news, or the tragedy of his favorite team losing. He'd turn that perceived slight into a tirade. He'd stand up and he'd beat his chest, and he'd rap his knuckles across the dinner table. He'd smash glasses. He'd rage at Jake's mother for hours. She was so stupid. He didn't want to eat chicken again. He wanted a goddamn hamburger. Men like red meat. How did she not know? Why didn't she understand what he was thinking? He was sorry. No, he wasn't. He was under pressure at work, and none of them realized how hard it was. He was supporting all of them. What the fuck didn't she understand about that? It wasn't his fault. She brought the anger out in him. It was her fault—and society's. It was all the criminals running around the place those days. The country was going to hell in a handbasket and had been since the New Deal. Racial tension was on the rise because of Bill Clinton. We'd lost so much culture because we couldn't sing in blackface any more. If the Yankees lost again, Joe Torre would have to be taken outside and shot.

Jake would hide in his room. He'd cup his hands around his head so that he couldn't hear the rages, but the sound waves would still work their way through his fingers. He'd talk to himself. Sometimes he'd pretend that he was a spy, or a soldier, or a detective. He was solving the case. He was beating the Germans. He was catching the terrorist. He would walk around the room, only allowing the verbose and maximized volume rants from the living room to seep into the edges of his stories. When he was a little older, he'd started singing. And the songs that Jake sang were not fun, rhythmic pop songs or romantic ballads. He would scream and he would do it in unison with his father's tantrums.

One evening while he was in the middle of screaming, his father opened the door.

"What the hell are you doing in here?" Senior asked with manic, bloodshot eyes.

"Same thing you are," Jake replied defiantly.

Senior pushed his way in. Jake could see his mother standing in the living room, watching quietly.

"You'll never speak like that to me again. You think this life is a right? Ain't nothing like that! Living in this house is a privilege," Senior raged.

"Whatever . . ." Jake retorted.

"What?"

"Nothing."

"You little bastard. Everything you've got—all those CD's, that CD player—I paid for it. You don't want it? That's what you're telling me?" Senior asked.

"Who cares? I don't! Take it!" Jake screamed right back. He was angry. He'd never talked back to his father like this, but the rage was spilling out of him unabated. He couldn't hold it in any longer. "Fuck you!"

Senior bounded at him and with one heavy swipe slammed Jake to the ground. He reared up with his knee and fired down on Jake on the ground like a piston, kicking him—once, twice, a third time—as Jake rolled into the fetal position on the floor. Senior stomped out of the room.

The next day Senior went to work as though nothing had happened. Jake's mother said nothing, as per usual. But when Jake came home from school, he noticed that she had poured out all of the beer. There were thirty empty cans in the kitchen trash bin. She had also hidden all of Senior's liquor.

When Senior returned that evening and saw what had happened, the savage beast emerged. He quickly located the beer cans in the trash, but he didn't believe she would have had the audacity to pour out his liquor. So he broke the whole house down looking for it while Jake and his mother sat at the dining room table nervously. He ripped through all the cabinets in the kitchen. He clawed underneath the bed in the master bedroom, and then proceeded to yank out each and every drawer from the dressers. About an hour later, Jake heard the chime of seven o'clock on the grandfather clock.

But the tone was off. Senior approached the clock like a bull in a china shop. He flipped open the door and spied a pile of liquor bottles inside. He'd located the hiding spot. Senior couldn't quite reach to the bottom, so he simply grabbed the metal chord inside the grandfather clock and ripped it out with his bare hands. He turned to the two of them, who were still watching silently.

"I hate this goddamn clock," Senior snarled, holding the chords in his hand. "Your father gave it to us. He was a prick. It's a hand-me-down."

"It's an antique," Jake's mother replied calmly.

"Well, soon, it's gonna be trash," Senior replied. He yanked out the four bottles of liquor that she'd stored inside. He placed them on the table one by one. He picked up a bottle of vodka and slowly unscrewed the cap. He poured a quarter of the clear liquid down his throat while staring at the two of them. He burped. Then Senior kicked the grandfather clock as hard as he could. It started to teeter, and he charged it like an offensive lineman. The clock tipped and fell onto the floor. Senior jumped on it, pitting his two hundred pounds of cop muscle against a few screws and glue. He smashed the wood, splintering the grandfather clock completely. He shattered the glass clock face, ruining the timepiece, and yanked out the spindle columns holding the fine workmanship together.

Jake Rivett Jr., age fifteen, couldn't bear to watch anymore. He took one more glance at his mother before he ran out of the house and down the street, screaming his head off. He didn't go home that night. He snuck onto the Amtrak train to New York City. And after he disembarked, he wandered his way to Chinatown.

■

The actual name of the music was "screamo," Jake's preferred musical genre. He opened his eyes as he finished singing. Schaub, the drummer, stood up from behind the drum set. He walked around and plopped down on a couch across from Jake.

"Something on your mind?" Schaub asked.

"It's been a rough few days," Jake said.

"Still can't believe you're a fuckin' cop," Schaub said.

"Yeah? Well I still can't believe you're alive."

"Well, I am. Know why?" Schaub asked as he opened a small decorated wooden box on the table. "'Cuz I take my medicine." There were a few rolled marijuana joints in the box. Schaub picked one up and lit it. "You're not gonna, like, arrest me, right?" Schaub asked.

"Expect a civil citation in the mail," Jake joked.

Schaub closed his eyes and took a huge hit from the jay. He exhaled a smoky mass into the center of the room. Marco, one of the sound engineers working the booth, stepped in from the other room and asked, "Can I get a hit, bro?"

"No, you cannot. This here man is a police officer," Schaub replied.

Marco glanced at Jake. Jake shrugged in the affirmative. Marco turned around and hightailed it out of there.

"They got you working that gold robbery that's on the news, don't they?" Schaub asked.

"I can't talk about it. You know that," Jake replied.

Schaub took another puff from the joint. "You should smoke more weed," Schaub said.

"I don't smoke any," Jake replied.

"I know why you sing, Jake. The whole black-leather thing, the hair . . ." Schaub said.

"I'd love to hear your opinion."

"'Cuz deep down inside you're still a schoolboy from Great Neck revolting against your mama who dressed you until you were twelve and your papa who absolutely, definitely worked for the government," Schaub guessed.

"It was Albany," Jake finally replied.

Schaub smiled. He extended his fist. Jake fist bumped it.

"Ready to go again?" Jake said. "Now that you've had your meds?"

"Sure. But hold on. I brought a little . . . inspiration," Schaub replied.

Schaub ducked into a side hallway. The band got ready to record again. Jake fiddled with the settings on a nearby amp.

"Who's ready to rawwkkk?" Schaub suddenly screamed. Jake turned to notice that Schaub had re-entered the room wearing leather chaps and a leather bra. But that wasn't all. Over his face and shoulders, Schaub had placed a completely lifelike prosthetic woman's face. Like some macabre nightmare from a Gene Simmons dream, Schaub's frozen-in-time prosthetic face belied expression.

"You are demented," Jake said as he chuckled.

"That's harsh. Does my appearance change what you think of me?" Schaub asked. "Why can't I be whoever I want to be—man or woman? Isn't that the dream?"

A thought flashed across Jake's brain. It started out far away and deep, only tapping the sonar of his synapses briefly. And then it began to multiply rapidly until it was the only thing Jake could think about. The rest of the room laughed while Schaub spun around and pirouetted—except for Jake. Jake sprinted out of the room without notice.

"Fuck. I'm stoned. Should I have waxed? Is that why he left? What did I say? Was it something I said?" Schaub asked.

EIGHTEEN

MEANWHILE, AN AMBULANCE DROVE up to the Belovs' house in Bensonhurst. The back door of the ambulance opened and Marina helped Mikey out. A paramedic lifted the IV pole down and Marina taught Mikey how to push the IV into the house.

■

Once inside, Marina cleaned Mikey's portable intravenous insulin pump and the injection zone on his thigh.

"I'll be okay, Mummy. Know why?" Mikey announced positively as Marina held the needle just above his skin.

"Why, honey?"

"Because I'm a brave little man," Mikey said.

At this moment, Marina caught sight of a person stepping into the doorway of Mikey's room. Startled, she dropped the needle haphazardly on the floor. She peered up to find Jake Rivett standing there and holding his helmet. She rose and angrily pushed Jake out of the room.

"What are you doing in my house?" Marina demanded.

Jake held up his cell phone. An official document was displayed with a circuit court seal on it. "This is a digitally signed search warrant, executed five minutes ago by Judge Nichols. So basically, to answer your question,

I'm in your house because I have the power of the law behind me, and you don't have one ounce of choice in the matter," Jake said.

Marina realized that in addition to Jake, Villalon and four more crime-scene investigators stood in the foyer. "Are you serious? You're going to do this to us again?"

"Where is he?" Jake asked Marina.

"I have no idea. I don't know what David got himself wrapped up into. I don't know why any of this happened, and honestly, what you're asking me is exactly the same thing I've been asking myself—over and over again. If I had that answer, I'd be a much happier woman right now and so would my son."

Jake listened to Marina's response carefully, attempting to calibrate her words. What shook him the most was how honest she sounded. Of course, he remained wary. He'd already made the mistake of believing a witness who seemed truthful, only to get stung when the case shifted like a boomerang and flew right back into the cuckoo's nest itself. But he was still a man, and a human, and he relied on his intuition to survive. In this case, what he heard from the wife seemed like the truth. The conclusion didn't comfort him. The paradox was that most husbands and wives tell their partners everything, even the ones who hate each other for the ninety-five percent of the time that they aren't having sex. But the Belov family seemed to have a real bond with one another, which would imply that they would share their plans. And if that was the case, then why didn't she know where her husband was?

▪

Jake huddled his team together in the hallway. "You know what we're looking for. They just came back from the hospital, so let's do this quick. And if you mess with the kid, I'll mess with you."

Tony Villalon and the CSI team moved to the basement, where they set up folding lights. They conducted an itemized search of piled-up plastic storage bins and the rest of the basement. They opened a bin to reveal various cheap Halloween costumes.

▪

In Marina and David's bedroom, Jake carefully picked through the items in Marina's closet. Marina watched him from the corner of the bedroom, her arms folded defiantly across her chest.

"What didn't you find last time—that you won't find now?" Marina asked.

"Any other costumes in the house? Cosmetic items? Wigs or masks?" Jake questioned.

"Is it Halloween?" Marina retorted.

"Answer my question, please."

"No—just what's in the basement."

Jake rose, seemingly satisfied. "So you haven't heard from him?"

"Oh my god," Marina exclaimed. "You're impossible. Are you done yet?"

Jake took in Marina's contempt. "I read the report about what happened to you and Mikey," he said. "I know what went down. I saw the pictures they sent. I'm really sorry about that. I am. The truth is that I know it was all too real for you, and that's what makes it real for me. But I can't leave any stone unturned. It wouldn't be right. If you think about it, that wouldn't do justice to you, either. You're a victim. I know that. But your husband? I don't know what he is. I need the truth. My old man was a jerk, but he taught me one thing I've always held with me: What separates humanity from chaos is the difference between right and wrong. Okay? I want to be right."

"They scared the living daylights out of Mikey."

"I'm sorry."

"But they didn't really touch me—not like that." Marina looked up and met Jake in the eyes. "They could have. They could have done anything. I had to accept that I was going to die. And all you can do is come in here in the middle of the night, harass me, and frighten my son—instead of getting your ass on your motorcycle and going out there and finding the cocksuckers that did this to us," she said. A heavy tension rested in the air between them. "I have to put Mikey to bed," she announced as she turned towards the door.

"Mrs. Belov?" Jake asked. She turned back. "The truth is that your husband's a fugitive. If he hasn't got anything to hide, why's he running? I don't know why you'd want to protect the person who did this," he said.

"David did not do this," Marina said sharply.

"He was involved," Jake replied.

"No. I know my husband. I know everything about him, and I know his heart. He would never knowingly put me or Mikey in danger—not in a million years. Something else is going on. You better figure out what that is," Marina replied.

Jake wasn't sure how to respond. It was rare that the push and pull was so powerful. On one hand, he wanted to slap handcuffs on her for impeding the investigation. But on the other, he knew that she was completely right. He needed to figure this out.

"Good night, Mrs. Belov," he finally said.

■

Outside the house, Jake conferred with Villalon on the steps.

"Get the Stingray," Jake ordered.

"There's procedure for that. Need a national security letter, which I don't think we'll get—"

"Tony. When you look at me, what part of me do you think cares about procedure?"

■

Marina watched Jake and his team exit the yard. Her face twisted as she walked along the landing and entered Mikey's room. But she was blocked by a wall of wooden building blocks. She stepped over it and found Mikey sitting on the floor.

"What are you doing?" Marina asked.

"I wanted to build a fort."

"I see that, honey. You need to rest."

"Who else is going to protect us if I don't?" Mikey said.

"We'll be fine. I promise." Marina comforted him. She grabbed Mikey underneath his arms and pulled him up onto the bed. It was only then that she noticed he was holding the green Froggie Finger device in his little hands. "Why do you have Froggie? I know where you are, silly."

"I thought if I pressed its nose enough times, then . . ."

"Then what?"

"Daddy might come back," Mikey said.

This hit Marina in the gut. She stuffed Froggie into her pocket and pulled the covers over Mikey.

"Is it true what the policeman says about Daddy?" Mikey asked. He was very serious.

She pulled Mikey in for a warm embrace. "No, honey. Not true. It's not true at all." She looked over his shoulder so he couldn't see the tears running down her face. "It's okay. It's going to be okay . . ."

NINETEEN

Thursday

HE'D DONE EVERYTHING RIGHT. He'd jumped over all of life's hurdles in sequence with only a momentary quiver or two, but David's path had inexplicably brought him right back to the start. Was that the truth about fate? Was it stronger than both intense desire and flawless execution combined? David didn't deserve any of this. In fact, he'd done everything he could to avoid the situation at hand. But life had still reared its ugly head and slapped him silly.

He played the scenarios out in his head endlessly. The first person he thought about was Howard Bergensen. The impossible was turning real and what Tyler had said in the van didn't make him feel better at all. Tyler's information had turned all expectation on its head and provided a horrible premonition of what was to come. If the people whom one aspired to become were just as bad as those one desired to move on from, then what was the point of the journey in the first place? That's all David could think about. He couldn't believe that Howard would have this inside him. It pissed him off—somewhat because of what it appeared to be, but more so because of what it meant he didn't know. The unknown scared him. It also had a worse effect—it popped his bubble. What does one really gain from a place where they'd do this to you? This wasn't the narrative of the American dream. It was the opposite. David was sleeping inside a nightmare—or trying to. More like lying on a bed with his eyes wide open waiting for his computer to process through Tyler's Blackberry. He hadn't been able to catch a wink, and the sun was coming up on a new day. The haze lifted as David finally heard a series of confirming dings emanating from his computer. He sat up, moved to his laptop, and checked.

The PIN had been cracked—*finally*.

David opened the phone and started going through Tyler's correspondence and files. It wasn't hard to find what he was looking for. He simply searched for "Tsunami," and the results piled up. It didn't surprise David that Tyler wasn't technical, but it did shock him that Stanton hadn't even tried to cover his tracks—not that deleting any of the emails would have made any difference. David had an app for that. He browsed through shipping container-manifests, rental agreements, and digital photographs of shipping containers. He pulled up GPS coordinates of the various containers, trying to get a feel for the flow of money and commodities. What was Tsunami doing? The truth was that most of it looked on the up and up.

A few outliers piqued David's interest. Tsunami owned approximately two hundred shipping containers. Ninety-five percent of them were located outside of the United States. Of the ten on U.S. soil, five were positioned in the same warehouse adjacent to Port Newark. David pulled up the address of the warehouse on a map. It was operated by a large commercial logistics concern. What was most interesting about these five containers was not only their location and proximity to one another and New York, but they were also the only vacant containers of the entire fleet. They weren't currently being rented out to third parties. They were just sitting there in New Jersey, in an anonymous building with load-in and load-out privileges.

David stood. Vlad would be thrilled to hear the results of the hacking. But first he had to make sure that Vlad was going to uphold his side of the bargain. He needed to talk to Marina.

▪

Marina brewed coffee and mixed eggs in her kitchen. She stared through the kitchen window at two unmarked police cars parked obviously at the end of her driveway. She sighed.

Then she spotted Cat Zhadanov and her daughter walking up the sidewalk with a set of animal balloons blown into cartoonish characters of a sheep, a lion, and a crocodile. Marina smiled.

A few minutes later, Mikey and Cat's daughter Alina played with the balloons at one end of the living room while Marina sat with Cat on the couch.

"Honey," Cat leaned in and whispered conspiratorially to Marina, "go into the bathroom. Turn on the water. You only have a minute." Cat held out a mobile phone. She tossed it into Marina's lap, almost disturbing her cup of coffee. A call was already on. "It's David," Cat said quietly.

Marina cradled the phone and rushed for the bathroom. She would take Cat up on her offer. Screw Jake Rivett. Once she was in the bathroom, Marina asked, "Baby?"

"Hey Mair. It's okay. It's okay . . . It's me. Are you alright?" David asked.

"The cops are staked out here," she said.

"I know."

"They searched the house—again," she told him.

"For what?"

"No idea. Wigs, or masks or something . . ."

"Wigs?" he asked.

"That's what I said. Didn't make any sense. What are you doing?" she insisted.

"I'm close to figuring it out. I'm going to find out who hurt us. They won't be able to get away with this . . ."

"But what's it going to do to you?" she asked.

Marina could only sigh as she listened to David respond on the phone. As hard as he tried to explain his mindset, she didn't think he was making a lot of sense. He thought that somehow he could break this thing wide open all by himself. That was the thing about David. The contrasting force to his raw intelligence was an often stunning naïveté regarding the ways of the world. Or maybe one could call it relentless optimism. The result of such unhedged optimism was that he would succeed in leaps and bounds, but always take steps back—always. It wasn't entirely his fault. He was the product of his ambition mixed with his origin. Marina and David were the same in that way, and that's part of the reason why they loved each other.

■

The mark of a calmly gentrifying neighborhood, a non-descript cable installation van sat down the street from the Belovs' house. Inside of this van, however, was a device that Marina would never know she needed to worry about: a Stingray. The military and intelligence communities seemed especially adept at finding aggressive animal names to label their latest devices. The Stingray was just a black box the size of a desktop computer. But when used correctly, its power was shocking. The Stingray could scoop up any cell phone conversation within a given radius. It would essentially cut in between the phone and the network without the person talking knowing they were being spoofed. When someone connects to a Wi-Fi signal, such as at a coffee shop, he or she must actively select that network. But that's not true for a phone connection. Phones simply indicate "Verizon" or "AT&T" at the top of the screen, and users take their cell connectivity completely for granted. The Stingray was its own cell phone tower. Any phone within the Stingray's radius would automatically connect to it first, instead of whatever carrier the phone normally connected to. The Stingray would then forward the phone to their default carrier. The target would still be able to make phone calls, send emails, and send texts. But without the user knowing, everything he or she did was being recorded.

In this case, the Stingray's target was Marina. Villalon operated it inside the van while Jake sat next to him, monitoring the feed. David and Marina's conversation fed through the system and out a small speaker.

"I'm going to figure everything out, baby. You have to trust me," David said.

"Baby . . . I have to know," Marina asked, "Did you do this?"

"Absolutely not. Never! If you know me then you absolutely know that's the truth," David paused for a moment, then continued. "Do you remember where we went for our second date. Summer after junior year?"

"Yes. Of course."

"Meet me there tonight—at one. Go through the garage window in the back. Take the Petrolitos' car. She leaves the key on her left tire, remember?"

Inside the van, Jake and Tony exchanged the look of two hungry coyotes at the end of a hunt. Sometimes law enforcement was too easy. That's sort of why Jake enjoyed it. Most of the targets he was set off against were halfway oblivious like Marina, taking piecemeal protective measures but not nearly enough. Or his perps were dumb enough to be career criminals, which meant their lack of critical thinking would eventually cause their own demise. And because Jake liked it, he was good at it. He continued to listen.

"Where are you, baby?" Marina asked.

The detectives listened with bated breath for David's response.

TWENTY

DAVID WAS IN FACT standing on a raised parking lot about a mile from Port Newark, watching cranes unloading shipping vessels like dystopian animals pacing across a multicolor container city. This was the raw underbelly of industry, and not just for New York. Port Newark represented the entire Eastern Seaboard's mouth, ready and open for consumption.

While David spoke to Marina, Vlad made a "finish it up" motion with hands. David noticed.

"The minute's up. I gotta go, honey," he said without revealing his location. He hung up. He wasn't exactly thrilled, but he was hopeful. At least he had been able to speak to the woman he loved and make her certain that he was alive and well.

David observed Vlad and Baranowski as they stared across the warehouse district with their binoculars. Even though Marina hadn't said it outright, it was clear to David that she didn't approve of what he was doing. Eventually he'd find out if she was right. A gnawing feeling had slowly begun to nibble at his soul. Perhaps there was another way than Vlad's. The problem was that he couldn't see it clearly yet. No road is without forks, and David knew that there were certainly options along the path ahead. One option was Jake Rivett. Jake wasn't quite an olive branch, but he was more than nothing. Could David tell Jake about Tsunami? Would it matter? It wasn't entirely clear. David had been waiting to find the right time to approach Jake again, even though their first encounter had gone so badly. But David was an optimistic man. Jake would understand—eventually. He had to, especially if David could show him hard proof.

"I have a good feeling about this. How 'bout you?" Vlad asked David.

"Never thought I'd be breaking and entering . . ." David pondered.

"The ends justify the means. You want your proof? It'll be in there."

As David stared out over the city of storage containers, he realized that he might only be a few miles away from the smoking gun he'd been searching for all this time.

▪

After the sun set, a Ford Bronco rumbled down a street parallel to the razor-wire fence protecting the series of storage warehouses from the public. The Bronco parked on the shoulder, outside the gates. Baranowski's face was illuminated through the windshield by the small flame of a lighter for a brief second, as if he was lighting a cigarette. Then Baranowski jumped out of the Bronco and briskly walked away down the street. He fell into a shadow and disappeared. A few seconds later, the Bronco began to burn from the inside. The combustion was swift. Within moments the car metamorphosed into a massive bonfire, and finally, after the heat had sufficiently expanded various internal oils, the truck exploded into a fiery supernova of glass and shrapnel. An abandoned vehicle, susceptible to arson by a wandering transient—that's how the local news would categorize the incident on the airwaves later. But unknown to them, it was also something else. It was a diversion.

David and Vlad observed the flames from the other side of the facility. Three security SUVs raced across the massive yard towards the ball of fire half a mile away. The coast was clear. Vlad and David pulled on black balaclavas and scrambled towards the fence. Vlad grabbed a pair of wire cutters from a large internal backpack strapped to his back. *Snip. Snip. Snip.*

Vlad and David crept towards their target warehouse and crouched behind a pile of fencing supplies. They checked the building's perimeter—no visible windows. Each storage bay consisted of a reinforced rolling steel door with Series 2000-brand locks that could easily withstand a bullet round or sledgehammer.

"You have the torch cutter, right? Should we just go around the locks?" David asked.

"It'll take too long. And there's five doors to get through," Vlad said while he scanned the warehouse. "They have cameras on the loading bays. So I got a better idea: We go in the back door," Vlad said. He pointed towards a small side door that permitted staff access to the inside of the warehouse.

"See the alarm box next to it?" David asked. He had noticed two small grey pipes emerging from the ground and entering the side of the building.

"Ya. Shit," Vlad said.

"If we snip the circuit, power stops running. It'll have a built-in stopgap. Alarm goes off when it stops receiving power," David said. Then David noticed an outdoor electrical outlet. "Screwdriver?" he said. Vlad handed the tool to him. "Ready?"

"You got this? You're sure?"

"Alarms are real low on the totem pole," David said as he grinned.

"That's funny, coming out of your mouth."

"Desperate times can change a man," David replied.

"Well, let's do it, pal."

David and Vlad scampered towards the warehouse's side entrance. David went to work on the outlet. He got the plate off and pulled out the outlet housing. He finally found what he was looking for: A small circuit board with an electrolytic capacitor. "I'll splice the alarm back into this circuit. Then cut the wire. The power will still flow into the alarm, so it won't trigger. But it will be unable to communicate that it's been snipped," he said.

"You always were the best," Vlad said, observing David with respect.

David stripped the wires, prepared the transistor, connected one to the other, and then powered the circuit. He snipped the alarm wire and nothing happened.

"Thank gawd," Vlad grinned as he pulled out a portable drill. He spun out the hinges of the industrial door. Within a few seconds, the last hinge was freed. David and Vlad eased the freestanding door down slowly.

Inside the warehouse, they quietly paced past numerous bays before reaching their intended targets: five red containers in a row. The containers' doors did not face them. They were oriented towards the loading bay for obvious reasons. Vlad pulled his backpack off and placed it on the ground. He pulled out an acetylene cutting torch with two tanks of gas.

"Help me up," Vlad commanded. David hunched down. Vlad stepped on his back and placed the torch on top of the container. Then he climbed up. Situated above the container, Vlad engaged the torch. After a few minutes, he cut a two-foot hole in the top of the container, making sure to prevent the loose steel piece from falling through. He ignited his flashlight and peered into the container. "Empty," Vlad announced sullenly. He passed the torch down to David.

"Gimme the welder," Vlad said.

David reached into Vlad's backpack. He tossed a welding iron and large protective mask up to Vlad, who proceeded to quickly weld the hole shut. The repair wouldn't stand up to massive scrutiny, but a cursory or uninformed inspection would miss Vlad's handiwork for months to come.

They repeated the process for the next two containers, but both were empty as well.

"You think we're kicked?" David asked.

"Don't lose hope, my peach."

Vlad cut a hole in the top of the fourth container and shined his flashlight through. "David," he announced, "get into my belly."

David climbed up the side of the container. He and Vlad carefully hung from the sides of the hole before dropping gently into the container. They each turned on flashlights.

The two of them were greeted by an enormous industrial machine. The machine filled two thirds of the container and was sided with Japanese lettering. It was befuddling to Vlad and David, and certainly not the smoking gun that either of them had been looking for. This was one of those moments when the pieces of the puzzle begin to fill themselves in and the picture that's being drawn on top isn't what anyone had expected to see.

"What the shit is this thing? Fuckin' useless," Vlad said. He angrily pounded the side of the machine with his fist.

"It's in Japanese . . ."

"Ya. I can appreciate the letters on it too, but ya know what? I don't actually read Japanese. And more importantly, it's not gold," Vlad said.

David investigated the rest of the container. "Okay. Well, first of all, there isn't supposed to be anything inside this box," David said, which was true, but also irrelevant to Vlad.

"So what?" Vlad asked.

"So they're hiding it. Shine over here."

Vlad complied with his flashlight: Two portable power generators, an abandoned laptop, and a scale were scattered nearby. Waste bins surrounded the area, filled with fast food remains.

"Someone's been holed up in here," Vlad said.

David inspected the machine further. "Have you ever made Jell-O before?" David asked. "I have a feeling that's what this does. It's a die caster. Pour gold into one end and out of the other . . ." David reached for a panel at the end of the machine. He flipped a handle and pulled up on the panel to reveal ten gold bars lined up in racks inside the machine.

"New bars. With new serial numbers."

"Wow. There she is. But where's the rest of it?"

David shrugged. Vlad flashed the corners of the garage with his flashlight, and then brought it back to the bars.

All of a sudden, they both heard a noise at the end of the container that was exposed to the loading bay outside. Vlad extinguished his flashlight just as the back door to the container opened. He and David shimmied around the side of the hulking machine, climbed up the back end, and quietly exited the container.

After replacing the warehouse door and its hinges in the dark, Vlad and David scrambled along the side of the building. They crept a few hundred yards away to see a black van parked outside the loading bay. The fourth red container had been unlocked and was open. A few men stood inside it, pulling gold bars out of the smelting machine. After a while, a large, heavy black case was lowered to the ground and subsequently loaded into the black van by the mysterious men. After a few more seconds of conversation, the men secured the container and jumped into the black van. The van departed from the logistics facility.

"Where do you think they're headed?" David asked.

"I dunno. But wherever that is, we're going along for the ride," Vlad replied.

■

The van raced northeast, over the Newark Bay Bridge, and then up the New Jersey Turnpike. Vlad and David followed in Vlad's black Mercedes, making sure to keep a safe trailing distance of no less than three or four cars at all times. They expected to end up somewhere near Jersey City or New Rochelle. But the black van passed through New Jersey. It actually seemed to be headed towards the Holland Tunnel. This was unexpected. One would not naturally figure that the best place to bring hot gold was back towards the jurisdiction it had been stolen from. But then again, nothing about this heist had been normal.

"No way. The city?" David asked.

"Sure as shit," Vlad replied succinctly.

They followed the black van under the tunnel and into Manhattan. It continued to maintain a course south before finally reaching the Financial District. They turned down Cherry Street as they followed it.

"Uh . . ." David muttered. The black van's blinker was on. It turned right towards the delivery entrance of a large building ahead. The steel mesh gate at the base of the building's loading zone grinded up, and the van disappeared into the depths of the building.

"Where are we exactly?" Vlad asked. David had a pale-white look on his face. Vlad noticed immediately. "Spit it out, my peach," he commanded.

"That's the bank . . ."

"The bank?" Vlad asked.

"My bank," David replied. He pointed to the glowing words of the Montgomery Noyes nameplate atop the main atrium entrance and both of their jaws dropped simultaneously.

TWENTY-ONE

LATE THAT EVENING, DAVID sat at a large table in the gym's office amidst Vlad, Baranowski, Konstantin, and the brothers Roschin and Petrov.

"Howard Bergensen is sitting on a couple tons of stolen gold." Vlad was steaming mad. He twirled the tip of a large hunting knife on his finger as he spoke. "And we are going to take it." Vlad slid the knife across the desk, sanding off a tiny layer, before flipping it up in the air and catching it.

"Impossible," David replied.

"Anything is possible. I become the President is possible—but less so," Vlad said flippantly. "It's not a coincidence that the bars went right back into the place they were stolen from. It's not a fluke that Howard Bergensen controls a company that shipped a smelting machine from Japan over to Port Newark, just in time for the robbery. Old bars with old serial numbers go in. New ones come out that are completely different. None of it's random. It is, however, one of the most amazing and brazen plans I have ever come across. Gives me a lil' more respect for your kind, David."

"I didn't mean *that*. We will never get into that building, so I'd stop thinking about it. The vault is three basements deep. I've only seen it once

—on an employee tour. The whole thing is air-locked and guarded by cameras, people, and sensors. It's designed so that you literally can't even walk into it. There's these series of robots inside that do all the commodity moving from command-line prompts," David said.

"Ya, ya . . . Not a problem," Vlad said.

"How is that not a problem?"

Vlad flipped the knife again. It rotated four times before he expertly caught it by the handle. "Because the guy who stole this stuff can't complain if it gets stolen again. 'Cause then he'll go down. This is what everyone in my business looks for. It's the perfect crime. How can your man Howard do anything if the gold gets stolen? He can't, and he won't."

"We still don't know that Howard is aware the gold's back in the vault," David retorted.

Vlad simply began to laugh. "Sometimes your naïveté obeys no bounds, my peach. Everything—all of this—it all comes back to Howard Bergensen. I know that when there's smoke, there's fire. You talk about edges all the time, and now you're staring one directly in the face. And this isn't just for me. This is for you." Vlad pointed the knife directly at David. "This saves your life. You know how you're going to protect Mikey?"

"How?"

"Money. With money, my friend, you can move out of New York and pay for Mikey's medical bills without a blink. Be set up for the rest of your life. Shit. Live in Costa Rica and meet me in Bermuda so the kids can hang out again, ya know?"

"What if there's another way?" David asked.

"And what might that be?"

"We take what we know and we tell the police. I don't want to be a fugitive all my life," David said.

"And what exactly are you going to tell your friend Mr. Rivett? That you assaulted your co-worker with a taser, stole his possessions, and burgled a warehouse in Port Newark? You became convinced that Howard

Bergensen, at the very tip-top of one of the biggest investment banks in the country, orchestrated a physical gold robbery? He'll laugh you out of his office with just enough time to arrest you in the hallway." Vlad paused to collect himself. "I told you exactly what was going to happen when this started. I said that people were going to die over this. Maybe they still will. I just don't want that person to be you, pal. You're with me now. There's only one course of action that will work for everyone, and it's mine," Vlad said.

"We were lucky at the container warehouse, but the vault . . . You won't succeed," David said, steaming up inside.

"David, we've both changed a lot."

"What does that mean?"

"Let me explain a couple things. You know this gym doesn't make a lot of money, right?"

David nodded and said, "Yeah."

"I don't have a job. It's been a bunch of years since I was in jail, but I haven't sustained even a scratch from law enforcement since—"

"I don't need to know what you do, Vlad. I'm well aware of your proclivities," David retorted.

"Don't assume. You think that all we do is cart drugs around and store prostitutes in safe houses. But I've changed—just like you, David. All of us have." Vlad gestured to the crew around him. "We're different now. We're sophisticated. The reason I was so confused about who took out the gold carriage . . . Normally that would be me. You are looking at the best crew of second-story men that exist on the face of this Earth. Maybe Montgomery's vault is impossible to get into. But if there is anyone who will try—and who can succeed—it's us."

"I'm going out—for a walk," David replied. "I need to think about this." He stepped towards the door.

"No. Sit down and hang out with your friends. We have a lot of planning to do," Vlad replied sharply. David stopped at the door, and then turned, eye to eye with Vlad. Vlad jacked the knife blade deep into the wood table. "Sit the hell down!"

But David did not sit. He left the building and slammed the door behind him. He needed time to think. But more importantly, he had a date.

TWENTY-TWO

Ten Years Prior

AFTER A MONTH OF grieving for his father, Vlad received a christening in the realities of self-sufficiency. In addition to preparing for his upcoming fight without Arseni by his side, Vlad and his mother had begun to contend with major financial stress. The boxing gym had a significant amount of bills to pay. None of the fellas who did business with Arseni seemed to know if, or where, any of his money was. Vlad found their apparent sudden amnesia to be quite suspicious. He'd been thrown into the deep end of the pool at nineteen years old, suddenly and without warning, only to realize that it was treacherous water filled with sharks.

There was only seven thousand dollars in the family bank account, which didn't make sense, considering the thousands of dollars of rent Arseni had been paying for the boxing gym and their house combined. Before he passed away, Arseni had handed Vlad a list of people who either owed or were holding money for him, along with the amounts owed. It was close to half a million dollars—a fortune in Vlad's eyes, more than he could ever imagine his father being worth. Vlad needed to get his hands on that cash soon. Rent was coming due, and there were many other expenses to pay, including his transportation and lodging at the match up in Stamford.

Vlad's life was still not preordained. Even though Arseni's colleagues weren't being very forthcoming regarding their debts, Vlad did his best to push the list out of his mind. He had bigger fish to fry. He had a future. He would win eighty thousand dollars if he won the IBF fight. He'd worry about the financial obligations when he got back, or he'd win and he wouldn't have to worry about anything at all. Vlad did his best to train hard. Roschin's uncle Axel took the reins of preparation. Axel was much less refined than Arseni, but he had done and seen it all. They both knew they had a lot of work ahead of them. Vlad's opponent was a black kid named Cameron North, from Florida, who looked like an absolute monster on all the videos that Vlad had managed to scrounge up.

▪

The match was hard fought. Vlad kept up with Cam. Neither man had knocked the other out when the fifth round came along. Vlad hadn't lost, but he certainly wasn't winning. Cam's pressure was constant, his attacks relentless, and his blows just shy of crushing. Vlad spent his time backing up, on the ropes, defending himself. In the middle of the fifth round, Cam tapped Vlad with a right jab to the head. Vlad spun to his right, into the ropes. He turned and saw the second shot coming from the left side. It was a mean hook, launched with all the power of Cam's shoulders and rotating core. Cam's eyes peered far past Vlad, aiming into the stands for maximum devastating impact. Amazingly, Vlad was able to duck the punch. He parried down and away from the blow, his head missing the kid's fist by just a hair. Cam's boxing glove impacted squarely with Vlad's shoulder, and that's when Vlad heard the tearing of cartilage and bone. He began screaming. He dropped to the ground, his shoulder unhinged from its joint. The referee jumped in between them immediately as Vlad writhed in agony on the floor. Axel and two emergency medical technicians came running to help him. They popped his shoulder back into the joint while Vlad bellowed in excruciating pain. He could barely hear the EMTs speaking.

"We need you in the ambulance and to the hospital if you ever want to use your arm again," the EMT droned. Vlad had just enough capacity on the gurney to watch Cam's hand being raised in the center of the ring. Vlad had lost. Orthopedic surgery was required on his shoulder, and he would have a year of major rehabilitation and therapy ahead. Vlad was told in no uncertain terms that the match in Connecticut was the last professional boxing match that he would ever participate in.

▪

After he returned home from the hospital, Vlad bought his first gun. The gym had fallen into disarray with Axel running the show, and the building's landlord began to pressure Vlad for two months of back rent. Vlad didn't have the money. Neither he nor his mother knew how to extricate themselves from the financial whirlpool they had fallen into. Vlad's mother had done her part, and Vlad had followed up, by paying visits to the characters who owed their family money. Then they had placed kind reminder phone calls. Nothing was working. They had received just a few thousand dollars. It seemed as if Bensonhurst had dried up like a desert around them. The town had altered itself following Arseni's untimely death. He had been the last local big man who had competed with the major international crime syndicates. But after his death, his competitors were more than happy for Vlad and his family to head straight down the tubes. Cash is king, and Vlad was a fallen prince headed towards pauper.

But Vlad wasn't done fighting and he wasn't afraid of it either. There was always another way. Vlad decided to go ballistic. He showed his gun to Baranowski first and provided a slight preview of what he was planning.

"I'll go anywhere with you, partner," Baranowski announced.

▪

And they did. They went to every single person on the list and did their best to inject the fear of God into them. Vlad and Baranowski would pound their victims into bloody pulp anywhere—while they were out at the park with their terrified families, leaving a local barbershop, or walking through a parking lot. They started with the easy marks—Arseni's clients. The pawn counters, butcher shops and convenience stores that he used to provide protection for. That crowd quickly succumbed. And as soon as Vlad received the money he was owed, he made a very intelligent move. He would pivot back to the friendliest guy in the room. He'd pitch them on his gang's services: "Now we're going to protect *you*. Just like my dad did. Better, actually. I'm the new breed."

There were still a few holdouts. Vlad smartly didn't mess with the real power brokers. For example, Joe Raffaeli supposedly owed Arseni forty thousand dollars. Vlad wouldn't mess with Joe. It was unspoken. He cleared Joe's debt as a favor, knowing it could come in handy later. But the second echelon of the criminal class was completely fair game. They were generally an unruly bunch—miscreants with drug addictions, short tempers, and careers in crime. Vlad and Baranowski had to refine their techniques when dealing with that lot. Axel taught Vlad many tricks of the trade that he'd learned in the motherland. Soon enough, Vlad was well versed in the power of the taser, the balaclava, and the printing of fake license plates for plausible deniability. Vlad increased the size of his crew, formally bringing in Roschin, Petrov, Konstantin and a few other interlopers whom he felt he could trust.

The biggest debt of the B-squadders on Arseni's list was a local cocaine dealer named Justin Thompson. After a gun was stuffed three inches inside Justin's mouth, he was still swearing up and down that he had no way to get the twenty-five thousand dollars he'd borrowed from Arseni. Thompson's story was that he'd bought product with the money, sold it for a hundred-percent markup, and then been robbed at random.

All of the cash was gone, and so were the drugs. But Justin did have something Vlad might be interested in. He had a lead on a way for Vlad to make three hundred thousand dollars in one evening. Justin's cousin was a security guard. During a late-night poker session a few weeks prior, Thompson's cousin had informed Justin that a particular payday loan business, Cash & Loan Xpress in Brighton Beach, was emptied every two weeks. Due to the schedule, the cash load inside the store would rise significantly in the days before the armored car pickup. And the night before, there would be hundreds of thousands of dollars sitting in a room in the back. The further Vlad pressed Justin, the more legit the information seemed. He had the armed guards' routines. He had the employees' schedules. For some reason, Cash & Loan Xpress didn't have a proper vault. The cash room was secured with multiple locks, but those measures could be circumvented. One could burrow in, around or above it and gain access. The main issue was the alarm system. Justin's cousin had a daytime code for use during business hours, but he didn't possess the nighttime master.

"So all that's stopping you is an alarm system?" Vlad asked, a lightbulb erupting in his head.

▪

At the very same time, Marina and David were moving in together. Their new apartment was on the west side of Bensonhurst. Marina was studying biology at the local community college in the hopes of eventually transferring to a four-year university and then veterinary school. David was taking a semester off while he prepared to apply to Stony Brook. Neither he nor Veronika had enough money to send him to college immediately after high school. He was working back at New Utrecht as one of the school's IT administrators. But due to Marina's insistence, he'd started to research grant programs and had taken a campus tour. David just had to figure out where he was going to find the forty thousand dollars required to attend college for the next four years. It wasn't growing on the few trees that split the cement wasteland of their neighborhood. But although life was tough, they had each other. They were happy. And that was extremely important, because it was only a few months later when David and Marina found out that they were pregnant.

A few days after the positive test, David arrived at the gym. He knew he had an open invitation from Vlad to work out at any time. And he had a lot on his mind. When he needed to blow off steam, the punching bag was a fantastic therapist. And it was cheap. He flew through twenty minutes on the treadmill and then started slamming the bag. Vlad approached David towards the end of his workout.

"Hey, my peach. How you doin'?"

"A lot's going on," David replied. He told Vlad about Marina's pregnancy. He was excited but equally petrified. They only had one part-time job between the two of them, and he wanted to go to college. Vlad smiled.

"Maybe we can help each other," Vlad said. "You need employment, and I got a job that needs filling."

"Huh?" David perked up.

"I'm talking about an alarm system. Can you hack them?"

"What's your definition of 'hack'? I hope you're talking about a system that you own . . ." David inquired as he stopped the bag and focused on Vlad.

"Mine? I don't know . . . Not technically," Vlad answered coyly. "When there's a box on a pole, and you're doing electrical work nearby, and you happen to cut through a few wires accidentally . . . Is that considered illegal?"

"Yes. It is. I can't get into that with you. No way, Vlad."

Vlad's head wobbled slightly, as it normally did when he heard something he disagreed with. "Well, there's always a way, my peach," Vlad answered. "Let's just say we're talking hypothetically, then."

"Okay . . ."

"An alarm controller. Any idea how those boards work?"

"Sure. They're simplistic—continuous-circuit signaling conduits, expandable zones, PGM outlets . . ."

"I have no idea what you're saying, and it's exactly what I wanted to hear. And how hard would it be to circumvent a system like that? I want no sound—no alert sent to the alarm company."

David thought for a moment. He responded succinctly. "Not."

"Good. You help me, and I'll tell you what I'll do for ya."

"Didn't you hear what I said?" David asked.

"I did. But I saved your life, David. Remember Abe? You think you weren't going to the hospital that night if it weren't for me? I did that for free. Maybe now you help me, but for money. You still get the better side of the trade. You won't get in trouble. You're never inside the building. You don't even need to know what the target is. It ain't important. But I'll pay you twenty thousand dollars. That's gotta help a bit, right?"

"You might think I should know this already, but, yeah . . . I really did think you helped me out of the kindness of your heart . . ." David trailed off.

"Hey. The heart palpitates. Change is constant." Vlad held up his fist in a slightly threatening gesture. He pounded the bag next to David's head. "Wouldn't want to be in the way when it does."

David stepped away and stared at Vlad. "If I'm gonna do this, I want to know," David announced.

"Know what?" Vlad asked.

"The target. What is it?" David inquired.

"I tell you? Then you're in."

David said nothing.

"A money-transfer business," Vlad said. "Cash & Loan Xpress. Down by the boardwalk."

TWENTY-THREE

Friday

MARINA PACED DOWN THE empty boardwalk aside the Coney Island's amusement park. She glanced up at the familiar sign for the defunct "Surf Ave. Ice Cream Parlor" as she hurried through the night. She continued past the glowing yellow letters of Cash & Loan Xpress and various shuttered boutiques before turning down a dark alley. It was very late, way past twelve. There was no legitimate reason to be there unless one was a fifteen-year-old kid looking to make out with his girlfriend, or a forty-five-year-old drug addict with nowhere else to go. Marina was definitely neither of those. But she was determined to keep her family together, and that required talking some sense into her husband.

That's why she had done exactly as David had suggested and crept out the back gate of her house, into their next-door neighbor's garage, and "borrowed" their car for a few hours. She presumed that she knew David better than anyone, but she was starting to have doubts. Or maybe they weren't doubts. Maybe she had created a version of her husband in her own mind that was simply a lovely veneer strung atop reality. Everyone was guilty of doing that at some point. Either way, she was going to get to the bottom of it—*tonight*.

She turned a corner and found the lowered fire escape. As she climbed up, the memories piled on. Once she was standing on the roof of the old ice cream parlor, Marina gazed over the expansive view—the Ferris Wheel, the Cyclone, the old Parachute Jump tower. Tacky neon fluorescents accented the edges of the place. Thirties glitz mixed with nineties malaise rendered the beach city a sad spectacle. The playground of their childhood was no longer exciting, but it wasn't boring either. As Marina took in the panorama, she heard the clanging of the fire escape being pulled up, and then footsteps. It was David.

"I'm so sorry this happened. But, please, whatever you do, don't forget how much I love you." David immediately wrapped his arms around her. "Is Mikey okay?"

"He's eating. I'm trying to keep him to his diet. But everything has too much starch. And there's sodium in all the meat at the stores, and the doctors told me that he shouldn't have more than five hundred milligrams, and . . . That's the first question you're going to ask me?"

"Honey, you need to relax," David said.

"Relax?" Marina pulled away from David. "I'm scared for my life, and for my son. When I close my eyes at night, what I feel is . . . fear. And all you can say is to relax?"

"That was the wrong word. I'm sorry."

"I don't care if you're sorry. Mikey thinks he has to defend the house because his Daddy is nowhere to be seen," Marina said as she gazed out over Coney Island, suddenly unable to look her husband in the eyes for the fear that she would completely burst into tears. "But the sad thing is . . . maybe he's right."

"Darling . . ."

"Because what the hell are you doing for us? I want to know. Tell me," she exhorted.

"I've figured most of it out," David replied. He reached into his pocket and handed Marina a note he'd written earlier. "I need you to do something for me—one favor. Give this to the detective—Rivett. It's a location of a storage container in Port Newark. Okay? Make sure the police go there and bust it. They'll find physical evidence. Tell them to track the owner of the box. Tell them to check out all the video footage, and figure out who picked the gold up. The gold was there, and the container's full of evidence."

Marina glanced at the note. She thought about it. "What evidence?" she asked.

"If the detective follows my directions, he's going to be able to crack this wide open. That's what matters," David half answered.

Marina glanced back down at the note David had just handed her. "I know that whatever you found, you didn't do it by yourself. You're with him—Vlad. Aren't you?"

David said nothing.

"You think I'm dumb? If you won't tell me, Cat will."

"He's all I have," David said after a long pause.

"No. You don't get it. You have me. You have Mikey. That's the point. That's the only important thing. We spent our whole life knowing that. Now it seems like you forgot. Look." Marina pointed to the yellow fluorescent lights of the Cash & Loan Xpress storefront across the street. "Even though I was nineteen years old, I remember every detail of that day. Don't you? Mikey was coming in six months. We were so scared. I had to quit school. You took me out to ice cream. I thought it was the cutest thing—made me feel better. We climbed up here to our favorite spot. Then you told me why we were really here. We were looking directly at that yellow logo across the street, and you told me what Vlad was planning. You told me there was a couple hundred thousand dollars in there—that Vlad needed you to break the alarms. And you didn't want to. You wanted out, but you were scared of him. Remember?"

David nodded.

"It's ironic, isn't it? The reason I love you all comes down to that moment—because of what you chose. You bailed and the police got Vlad. And I got you. The man who made the right choice, a long time ago . . . That's the man that I love. That's who you need to be now."

"I figured it out," David said.

"I know," she said.

"That's what I do. Why don't you think I will this time?"

Suddenly there was a faint whooping noise in the distance.

"Did you hear that?" David asked.

"No. Do you hear me?"

David pulled Marina in for an embrace. "You have to trust me. I know what I'm doing . . ."

"He's a scorpion."

"What?" David asked as he scanned the horizon, searching for the source of the mystery vibration.

"Your mom's favorite story. I'm sure you remember. A frog needs to get across a river, and there's a scorpion sitting there at the riverbank. The scorpion helpfully offers to carry the frog on his back. So the frog says to him, 'Well you're a scorpion. Why should I trust you? How do I know you won't just sting me?' And the scorpion answers, 'Because you have my word. I promise that I won't bite you.' So the frog takes the ride. And just as the two of them are about to reach the safety of the other shore, the scorpion suddenly stings the frog. As poison runs through his body and he lays there dying, the frog asks the scorpion one final question: 'Why'd you do it?' And the scorpion says, 'Because I'm a scorpion.' Vlad's stung you before. And he'll sting you again."

All of a sudden, a huge spotlight ignited the night sky. A helicopter ripped off the water's horizon and was approaching their position on the roof. David pulled Marina away from the edge of the building and towards the back wall. He peered over. A SWAT team advanced down the alley, tossing a grappling hook to the bottom rung of the fire escape in an attempt to lower it. David hustled Marina along the roofs of the buildings, all built flush with one another, as the heavily armed SWAT team piled out onto the top of the building. SWAT was screaming, "Drop to your knees!" David and Marina reached the last roof. Tears ran down Marina's face.

"Cooperate with them. Okay? Give him the letter," David said. Marina nodded. David kissed her. "I love you," he said as he took off running towards the edge.

▪

Jake Rivett stood in the alley. He did a double take as he saw a black shape silhouetted against the dark sky above him. It was David, jumping from the second story of the building and over a fence.

David landed on the raised subway tracks on the other side. A train approached. He sprinted down the tracks. Glancing over his shoulder, he spotted Jake climbing the fence behind him. David locked eyes with Jake, who pulled his pistol. David lay down, and the train peacefully glided over his prone body, kicking up a small spray of debris. Squinting to prevent the dust and small pebbles from entering his eyes, David turned his head to the side, attempting to time the train's wheels. He established a rhythm and rolled out. He found himself inside Gravesend, in Coney Island's overhaul yard, home to the gargantuan machine shop that serviced all of the MTA's trains.

Helicopter lights splashed over David as he raced across the large gravel surface that lay between the iron tracks in the overhaul yard. He reached a small control station and tried the handle. It was unlocked. He pulled himself inside and then ducked down. The helicopter lights searched above the glass, reflecting all around but missing him—then moving on.

Still in pursuit, Jake waited for the train to pass. He finally crossed the commuter tracks and followed David into Gravesend. The lone control station stood in the middle of the tracks. Jake approached cautiously. "David?" Jake screamed.

David huddled in the control station, observing the fifty levers in front of him. Each was tied to a track ahead. David pulled down all of the levers, one by one.

Jake approached the booth, which was about a hundred feet away. He tried to see what was inside but couldn't make David out. He slowly moved forward. He lifted his gun, the sights taking the entire booth into frame. Jake was about to squeeze the trigger and let off a warning shot, when a series of linked subway cars glided in front of Jake and stymied him yet again.

David had released the entire overhaul yard, causing many of the cars to roll with the force of gravity down the hill between Jake and David. David sprinted out of the booth. He ran with a passing car, then jumped onto the connector between two cars. He rode it for a brief moment before jumping off. He navigated the moving cars like salmon up a river. David finally reached the other side of the tracks and sprinted into a mechanic's office.

Unable to work up the nerve to attempt David's technique, Jake waited while Markle and the SWAT team caught up with him in the overhaul yard. The group finally reached the mechanic's shop. All was silent.

Farther down the blacktop outside the garages, a large roll-up door opened and two headlights shined out from within. SWAT formed a semicircle around the garage door as an MTA bus accelerated out of the shop. Jake and SWAT unloaded their weapons into the bus. Windshields shattered. Tires turned to goo. But the bus didn't stop. Jake dove out of the way as the bus slammed into a cement wall across the street. He pulled himself up and boarded the pockmarked bus warily. But David wasn't inside. Jake found only a large cinderblock placed on the bus's accelerator pad.

▪

A half mile away, David splashed through a drainage pipe. He emerged adjacent to the Marlboro Housing Projects. He turned to the sky and watched the police helicopter circling a mile behind him, casting long lines of light down upon Gravesend. David took a few deep breaths. He dusted himself off and walked out of the project's main courtyard and onto the street. He padded down the sidewalk, moving farther away from the authorities. He headed back through his neighborhood. He walked past the park and New Utrecht. He crossed in front of his childhood home, where he saw the amber light shining from the TV room. Veronika was sure to be watching her stories late into the night. A few blocks later, he bit his tongue as he passed by his own street. He tilted his head to the right, spotting the omnipresent unmarked car and cable installation van parked in front of his house. He only allowed himself a few seconds of gaze before he kept going.

TWENTY-FOUR

AS THE SUN BROKE from the east over the low-slung borough, David returned to Vlad's gym. He walked in the door and five sets of menacing eyes stared at him. Vlad snickered, his mouth wide as a Cheshire cat's. He stood up and walked towards David.

"I'm in," David said, somewhat unexpectedly.

"You walk out on me?" Vlad asked.

"I needed to be alone—to think."

"That's not your prerogative any more, my peach," Vlad said. He stood up and stretched his hulking body. Then in one sudden and brutal step forward, Vlad whipped his arm down and brutally smacked David in the face.

David doubled over. Trying to regain composure, he felt blood dripping from the inside of his mouth as Vlad continued to yell at him.

"Ya see, you can't unwind the knot you've tied. Life doesn't work like that. Whether you like it or not, we're all in on this together now—you and me. Partners. Just like the old days," Vlad said.

∎

Jake Rivett led a column of police cars through the storage terminals and towards the warehouse that David had identified. He ground to a stop in front of the red container. With a nod from a manager, a warehouse employee lifted up a diamond-tipped circular saw to the heavy padlock securing the red container's door. Jake tore the padlock off and peered into the container.

But there was nothing there. It was completely spotless.

"The quant's leading us on a wild-goose chase," Jake opined.

"What do you think this was all about?" Tony Villalon asked.

"Hell if I know . . ." Jake started looking around.

"Logistics company that rents these bays out said it's been inactive for two months—all five of 'em," Tony nodded to the other four containers down the line. They had all been opened and were just as empty as the first. "They're registered to a Greek shipping company domiciled in the Seychelles."

"That's weird, right?"

"Not really." Tony shrugged. "International shipping becomes very murky at the operational level. More important is the fact that there's nothing in here."

"It's a big problem," Jake said as he nodded. "He's chumped us a couple times now." What Jake didn't say was that people who tried to play him usually ended up in a state of severe hurt. He was beginning to imagine the creative ways in which he could pay David back for the injustice.

Jake slowly paced around the outside of the warehouse itself, inspecting the location for clues. He motioned to the warehouse supervisor on scene.

"Tell me about your process here," Jake said.

"Well, these here are open-access twenty-four-seven bays. We give our account holders passcards. There's a slide at the main gate and another against the garage door itself." The manager nodded towards a small card slider installed next to a nearby door. "So the card will give access to the lot and open our door. Beyond those two levels of security, the client is welcome to use their own padlocks for a third measure of protection."

"And you have cameras?"

"Yes, sir," the manager answered.

"Where?"

"There's a two-hundred-forty-degree rotating camera above each loading bay, plus a number of moveable cameras on our perimeter and at each gate."

"I need to see them," Jake ordered.

"No problem. But I should mention something. Last night, most of them were aimed at the fire."

"The fire?" Jake's eyebrow raised.

▪

Inside the office, Jake stood with the manager as they played through the tapes.

"So your gate cameras were rotated away from the gate itself?" Jake asked incredulously as he observed footage of a Ford Bronco burning by the side of the complex, with the entry gate only visible as a fragment at the bottom of the screen.

"Yes—unfortunately."

"And the loading bay camera?"

"Coming right up," the manager said as he loaded up the feed from the camera above the door. It slowly rotated over the top of each bay, but the image was pixelated and lacked any contrast in the dark.

"No infrared, huh?" Jake asked. Besides the general shadows of shapes of trucks moving in and out, this footage would give him nothing. He couldn't make out vehicle models, license plates or faces at all.

"Not in this section. The more the client wants to pay, the more we provide. You have to understand—it's a step up from your average storage facility, but these are considered low-security bays. If you have something that could get stolen, you wouldn't put it in here."

"But if you wanted less cameras, not more, and the ability to get in and out any time of the day . . ." Jake thought out loud.

"Right," the manager agreed nervously.

Jake turned and beat it out of the office, slamming a door angrily behind him. He happened upon Tony standing outside.

"Not good?"

"Worse. This place is a joke," Jake replied. "Figure out who owns those things."

"Things?"

"The shipping containers—the company in the Seychelles—whatever. You're going to have to work with those morons. I can't stand 'em. Get all their paperwork and get into it."

Tony nodded and scurried back into the security office.

TWENTY-FIVE

VLAD STOOD COURT IN front of David and the rest of his crew inside an old cherry-manufacturing plant a few blocks from the gym.

"David wasn't wrong," Vlad announced. "The Montgomery commodity vault is impossible to break into. To access the building conventionally, there's a security booth in the front. An RFID card is required for that."

"Which I could probably fake," said David.

"Right," replied Vlad.

"But never the visual. That's the second line of defense. They know who each person is, and all guests are escorted."

"In the back," Vlad continued, "we have a few loading bays. There's also RFID access as well as sign-in access. Now, once you've gotten through the elevator or down the stairs, both also only scannable or through escort by a security guard, then we arrive at the vault entrance. It's protected by multiple armed security guards. Outside of the personnel, this vault is not human accessible. There's the usual—redundant electricity, off-site surveillance, passcard access, eighteen inches of steel, pressure-sensitive glass—and the unusual. There are vibration sensors built into all sides of the vault. You simply cannot drill or blow your way into this place." Vlad glanced around to make sure they were still with him. "Now how do I know all of this?" Vlad asked rhetorically. "Because David has seen it himself. And Baranowski works for the Sandhog's union. Which means that we have blueprints."

David grinned. Vlad truly did have his fingers everywhere. Sandhog was the moniker of the group of construction workers that toiled in the tunnels and cisterns underneath New York City, specializing in building drainage pipes and drilling huge tunnels for future public-transportation projects. Vlad unrolled a massive schematic of the bank's vault, basement, and the underlying subway and sewer. He turned to David. "Will you do the honors?"

"These plans might look like chaos to you," David said as he traced his finger along the plumbing systems, "but what I see is a complex industrial system just begging and pleading to be hacked." David continued to pitch the assembled crew.

What David did not present to the group was his inner turmoil. He had spent the morning conferring with Vlad. The two of them were a potent combination. David provided the significant technical factor, but Vlad was downright ingenious. Vlad had figured out the one, and perhaps only, possible way to break into Montgomery's vault. It was a solution so far out of the box that David wouldn't have contemplated the scenario in his wildest fantasies. That said, the approach only had a small chance of succeeding. But if anyone could accomplish this heist of heists, it would be Vlad. David also knew that he didn't have a choice. His options had dwindled down to nothing. If luck is the residue of design, then David had done a fairly poor job of constructing his life.

David had spent the previous night expecting a police spotlight to suddenly appear outside his window, followed by a battering ram and the sly face of Detective Rivett whispering snide obscenities. It might have been a relief. When it didn't happen, he had dreamt about it instead. Except in David's dreams—the faces of authority were those of his own family. His wife was the judge. Mikey and Veronika were in the jury. The court case went on forever, as dreams often do, ebbing and flowing through conversation and dramatic action but never getting anywhere. It was the trial of the day, the week, the century. When he was finally sentenced to the jail of infinity, the cell blocks repeated themselves ad infinitum. He could walk between the cells, but always found himself in a new one. And although each cell was made of concrete and iron, they looked like the rooms and offices and corridors of Montgomery Noyes.

He'd woken up in a cold sweat, as though an ice pack had been wrapped around the back of his neck. Then he'd remembered that he was still David. Even though he could be naive at times, and his shrimp-like physicality notwithstanding, David was a winner. He solved his own problems with the power of his brain. He reached his goals, even when they seemed impossible. Those successes had defined his life. The triumph was not dead. It would return. He just had to trust himself. What happened from then on out would define his place in the world once and for all. Driven by his own sense of self-preservation, he'd make sure that he came out ahead in the end. He was sure of it.

▪

That afternoon, Petrov took the train ten miles east of Bensonhurst until he didn't recognize a soul, which wasn't saying much, because he rarely traveled more than five miles from the hospital where he was born and had never been on a plane. Petrov exited the train, packed a huge dab of dip, and jammed it into his cheek. He crossed the street towards a blue van. He looked left and right before stabbing a thin metal slim jim lockout tool into the window well. He fiddled for just a moment before the door unlocked. Petrov glanced around. A few men sat on a stoop a block down the street. They were staring at him, but doing nothing—par for the course. Petrov jumped into the van and began to work on the steering wheel with a screwdriver. After a moment, he had successfully hot-wired the van. He drove away while the stoopsters finally rose. They applauded him.

■

Still ensconced in the old cherry factory while Petrov and Roschin took care of necessities, David studied the vault's underground systems from the schematics that Vlad had provided.

Vlad stood on the other side of the warehouse, using a jigsaw to cut a long PVC pipe in half. He fit a joint onto the piping, attaching the new joint to a series of other custom-cut PVC structures. David glanced at the plans again, comparing them with the web of PVC in front of him.

"Can you raise that one by two inches?" David asked.

Vlad did as instructed. David double-checked the measurement again.

"Perfect," David concluded. "Now let's keep going with the last set."

Vlad continued to attach pieces of PVC piping, creating a massive gridwork of hundreds of PVC pipes on the floor of the warehouse. David supervised.

After another hour, David and Vlad stood back over their creation with grins on their faces. They'd managed to replicate a scaled model of the underground sewer system extending out from underneath Montgomery Noyes' vault.

"We ready to test her out?" Vlad asked.

"That's an affirmative," David responded.

Vlad connected a hose to a water valve he'd inserted in the piping. He turned the hand valve to the open position. Water began to surge through their rickety plumbing system. David held a ping-pong ball. He placed it inside a hole atop one of the central PVC pipes. The two men watched with anticipation as the ping-pong ball disappeared. David ran excitedly along the PVC piping, guessing the path of the ball with his finger. Water began to pour out from the various open ends of PVC pipe on all sides of the warehouse.

"Round and round and round it goes. Where it stops, nobody knows," Vlad orated poetically as David sprinted towards one particular pipe opening. As if by command, the ping-pong ball popped out into David's expecting hand. He raised the ball for Vlad to see. "But we do," Vlad said, grinning.

▪

Roschin entered a convenience store in Brooklyn.

"You're two days early!" the shopkeeper exclaimed when he saw him.

But Roschin wasn't interested in the man behind the desk. Instead, he admired the soda machine set up against the wall of the store. He finally turned back to the shopkeeper.

"I will take it," Roschin said.

"A Coke?" the shopkeeper asked.

"No. The whole machine." Roschin gazed through the back of the store to a parking lot filled with white rental vans—the proprietor's other business. "And one of those vans. For a week. I'll pay for that one," Roschin said. He placed a credit card down on the desk and stared directly at the shopkeeper. "You know my face?"

"Of course."

"You know my name?"

"Uh . . . No. I don't think so. Vlad's boy, right?"

Roschin shook his head defiantly. "You do not know. You will not use Vlad's name in anyone's presence—ever. You do and this place burns to the ground, but not before your house on Hendrix Street. Understood?"

"I . . . Yes. Of course. Sir . . . Then who are you?" the shopkeeper stammered nervously, not wanting to make any verbal missteps in front of Roschin's stony face.

Roschin tapped the credit card sitting on the counter between them. "This is who I am. This is the only name you know," he commanded menacingly.

▪

Petrov drove the stolen blue van through a roll-up door and into the cherry factory. He guided it onto a mechanic's lift set up in a dusty side of the warehouse. Vlad quickly checked the van out and nodded his approval. Konstantin pulled a lever and lifted the van up. He and Petrov quickly began dismantling the main axle of the vehicle and then pulled away wiring and insulation from the bottom of the van. After they were finished, Baranowski held a steel-cutting circular saw to the floor of the van. Sparks flew as he cut a large square out of the van's bottom, about four feet long by four feet wide. After a few more measurements, Konstantin welded two super-sized hinges to the new piece of metal. They screwed the hinges back into the bottom of the van, creating a trap door. The steel panel rotated perfectly down on the new hinges and dropped into place as the floor of the van, practically imperceptible from both inside and out of the vehicle.

TWENTY-SIX

One Week Later

JAKE SAT IN HIS rarely utilized office, inside the major crimes division on the second floor of the One Police Plaza building in the center of Manhattan. He stared at the wall. Even though the entire space was jam-packed with information, pinned photos, taped e-mails and marked maps, it felt blank. None of the leads were worth anything. They didn't have legs. Close to two weeks after the gold had disappeared, it was safe to say that this was the most profitable and successful theft that had ever occurred in New York City.

Jake had hunted down each piece of evidence like a hound after truffles in the forests of Lake Garda, but found himself smacking headfirst into stone walls with each attempted sprint. Everything that he'd turned up had suggested a diabolical set of thieves. It wasn't just the gold—it was the operation. The sheer amount of heavy equipment involved stunned Jake. Either the criminals had been planning this heist for years, or they happened to possess a huge cache of identity-backstopped machinery available for use any time they wished. Neither option seemed very realistic.

The flatbed truck had been easy to locate records for. When Jake had found the truck in New Rochelle, it still had Connecticut plates that hadn't been registered for seven and a half years. Through the DMV, Jake had quickly discovered that the flatbed had gone missing eight years before. It had been stolen from an equipment yard in New Haven. Based on eyewitness testimony, a nineteen-year-old kid had been arrested, tried, and convicted for the theft. Apparently the thief told the police he'd sold the truck to an auto-body distributer in New Jersey and the Connecticut troopers were never actually able to locate the vehicle. There weren't any other records available for Jake, and the perp had long served his time and was no longer in jail. Jake knew that even if he tracked that guy down, it was an extreme longshot that the effort would reveal anything of substance. The flatbed had obviously been processed through multiple links of the criminal ecosystem throughout the years.

The magnetic crane that had been secured to the top of the flatbed was stolen more recently from a construction site in upstate New York. Jake had reviewed the security footage from the one camera at the location, and had been unable to catch more than a dark silhouette wearing a mask and rushing past the blurry lens.

The torch that had been used to cut open the armored car had been sold as a cash transaction out of a hardware store in Wilmington, Delaware. That lead had excited Jake and Tony for about thirty-six hours, until they learned that the establishment didn't possess security cameras or, apparently, memories. And of course Jake had still not been able to locate the source of the most unique tool they'd found lying inside the crime scene: the cell phone jammer. The evidence was scant, clean as a hospital ward, and none of that was the worst part.

What was driving Jake batty was that David Belov was still out there. Jake was sure that if he could find David, the whole case would open up like an orchid from eve to sunrise. He knew that David was scared, afraid, and desperate. David needed him, and he, David. But for some reason the entire metropolitan police force couldn't find one dorknut on the run. If anything, this conundrum fit part and parcel into Jake's worldview that the nerds were taking over the Earth and there was nothing the strong could do about it. The thought actually made him happy, because it was a just progression—a moral evolution. And Jake was sort of a nerd himself. Eventually he had become tougher than everyone else around him because he didn't want to feel any pain. But he knew how it felt. The anguish was still there. It was simply hidden behind the façade. Maybe it was impossible to avoid the pain of life, whether you were David or Goliath.

Jake plugged in his earphones, swiped across his phone, and looked for some music to play. He found the comforting tunes of AFI and kicked his booted feet onto his desk. He stared out into the empty abyss of reason that was the world. He'd accepted that both the city and life itself were too big to make sense of for one man. All he could do was point his boat in the direction he wanted to go, paddle like hell, and hope for the best. And just moments after Jake had finally zoned out, Tony Villalon came pounding into his office.

"The container—I got it," Tony said.

"Got . . . what?" Jake's eyes creaked back open.

"Figured out the registration."

"What do you have?"

"Honestly? Doesn't seem like a lot—sort of like the empty container itself," Tony said.

"Fine. Except, why would the quant go to the trouble? He gets all the way to his wife and that's the one message he leaves?"

"To push us off track," Tony replied simply.

"Sure. Where's he pushing us from? Or to? It's not like we can't chase him and also send someone to examine the container."

"Curious to know what I've learned, at least?"

"Hit me."

"The containers were registered to an LLC called Tsunami in the Seychelles, which we knew. A lawyer down there signed their documents, but it just so happens that one of our money-laundering guys has a friend in the registrar general's office, who gave me the inside slip. Tsunami's actual hundred-percent shareholder is the lawyer's client—another LLC called Forest Park. They have U.S. bank accounts and were registered domestically by a turnkey solution-type place out of Nevada called Incorporation Services."

"Of course," Jake said.

"So I got the federal ADA to hit up Judge Arsht last night and force Incorporation Services to turn over their books related to the account. It pings right back here."

"Good stuff. To where?"

"Queens. A man named Stefano Dubbiono. We've got his signature and his social on the Forest Park incorporation documents, and wire transfers in and out of Tsunami LLC's bank account."

"And who's Stefano?" Jake asked.

"That's where it gets a lil' screwy. He's a driver," said Villalon.

"Huh?"

"A limo driver," Villalon replied, "who checks out so far. Works for one of those black car services. Office says he's never had any trouble. Hard worker. But they'll yank him off duty and we can go chat anytime we want. What do you think?"

Jake stared at his empty board and replied, "I'll race you to Queens."

"You know we can just go together, right?"

"Tony, do I ever ask you why you have a wedding ring on, but no pictures of a spouse on your desk like the rest of the stiffs here, and never talk about her?"

"No . . ."

"Then don't ask me about me and my bike. No one gets in the way of us. And by the way, I don't care. But neither should you. Some things are personal."

▪

Their interview with Dubbiono did not provide clarity, at least not right away. Jake and Tony met the driver in a small conference room at the dispatch headquarters of his employer, one of many luxury chauffeur and black car services that operated in the city. A hefty and broad-shouldered man whose black shirt exhibited permanent sweat stains underneath the arms, Dubbiono smoked ten cigarettes throughout their hour-long interview. He had slightly long, greasy hair, which he combed severely over his head, and he was always turning his left ear towards the detectives due to the unilateral deafness he'd picked up in a bar fight in his twenties. Dubbiono was nervous, but open and honest.

The detectives began with his past. It was a good way to achieve an understanding of a man, and also to disarm any anxiety and gain the upper hand. Dubbiono had been a gambler when he was young. That's why it had taken him so long to get a regular job. But he'd been driving for the same black car service for eight years. Before that, he'd driven a limo independently. His work phone kept track of his schedule, and he referenced it many times. Not only did Dubbiono claim to be working the night of the robbery, but at most other instances throughout the timeline of the gold carriage job, he was with his family. The dots of his alibi connected, and not in a way that helped Jake and Villalon. But something about Dubbiono's messy demeanor, mixed with the exactitude of his records, still bothered Jake. It reminded him of the perfection of the rest of the heist. The only issue was that Jake was so far leveraged down the branch of logic that he wasn't sure if he could even balance any longer. They were pursuing a lead given to them by their main target, after all. Maybe Jake was just batting at a red herring on a tee. But still, there was the matter of the signatures. Towards the end of the interview, Jake pushed a piece of paper across the table towards Dubbiono. "Can you write your signature, please? Right there," he said.

"How come?" Dubbiono asked.

"Because I asked you to?" Jake said with a shrug.

"Sure. Like I said, I wanna cooperate. I have done absolutely nuttin' wrong, sir." Dubbiono leaned over the paper and signed his name quickly. He pushed the signature back towards Jake and Tony, who examined it silently. Dubbiono's John Hancock was an exact match to the scrawl on the corporation documents. There was a long pause. Jake decided to pounce.

"You told me earlier that you'd never heard of a Forest Green LLC, or Tsunami LLC. Right?"

"Not once in my life."

"Then why am I looking at the exact same signature that created Forest Green LLC approximately eight months ago—with not only your signature, but also your social security number and your home address?"

"Can I see it?"

"No," Jake replied.

Dubbiono lit up his eleventh cigarette. He took a long pull. "I have no idea. I get a W-2. I don't open businesses. I just drive businessmen around."

"Want to think about that answer? We'll give you one more chance," Villalon prodded.

"There's nothing to think about."

Tony kept going, trying to channel Jake as best he could. "Lying to us. That's aiding and abetting. Maybe you didn't do this, but you still know something about it. You tell us—you tell us everything—it'll release your soul. You can get on with your life. We're your way out. We're a lifeline. Why don't you grab it while you can?"

Dubbiono's eyes were clouding over from the questioning. He had nothing else to say, but especially nothing else to give. Jake remained glued to the driver. Something about Dubbiono told Jake that he was on the right track. He could feel it tingling through the pores of his skin, unless that was just the cigarette smoke. He could smell the path ahead, but he definitely couldn't see it yet.

▪

On the way out, Jake stopped in the manager's office to verify what Dubbiono had told them. Not only did Dubbiono's alibi seem legitimate, it was actually backed up by data. It turned out that the company attached a GPS to each one of its vehicles. The detectives were able to double-check Dubbiono's story against data from the GPS company's central server. It all matched. When Dubbiono said he was working, there were paid invoices for the jobs. When he said he was at home with his family, his car was parked outside his house.

Jake stood outside the office and examined the passenger lists and trips that Dubbiono had gone on over the last six months. As he flipped through the pages, he became extremely excited. Dubbiono had a regular client—a man whom Jake was well acquainted with. A few times a month, Dubbiono picked up none other than Howard Bergensen and drove him for two hours out to the Hamptons.

"Do you see this?" Jake pointed out the series of pickups to Tony. "He drives Howard Bergensen."

"Unbelievable," said Villalon.

"This isn't random. That's our connection. Maybe the quant is actually onto something."

"But what, exactly? There was nothing in Port Newark. Fuckin' zilch. We need a chain of evidence . . ."

"You're very right, my lovely Anthony. And I'm not quite sure about that part. But I'm telling you that Stefano Dubbiono knows a lot more than he's saying. He knows he started that company. He knows Howard Bergensen. He lied to our faces, point blank—even after he'd signed his name. That's risky. What's he thinking?"

TWENTY-SEVEN

BUILT IN THE NINETEEN twenties, Howard Bergensen's weekend house was one of the rare homes along the elite five-mile Meadow Lane in Southampton that hadn't been completely razed and replaced with a megamansion. That placed it squarely at a ten-million-dollar value instead of forty. Having been built during the roaring years, the house had been updated and expanded and remodeled many times, to the point where it didn't reflect its ancestor in any way. However, the mansion still maintained its original gate columns, re-mortared, through which one was led down a long lane of towering purple bougainvillea into the grand driveway and motor court in front of the house. Inscribed into the stone in the driveway was the house's original name: Windswept. When Howard had purchased the property, the seller's real estate agent had told him that the name was meant to be an oxymoron. For years Howard had relished in the fact that absolutely nothing could blow the manor and its bedrock foundations away. No amount of wind, water, or other natural cause had managed to do so yet. But Howard was starting to realize that the house might outlast him. He wasn't feeling as powerful as Windswept any longer. As he sat in his grand office and listened to an irate voicemail, he gazed through a floor-to-ceiling bay window towards the infinite horizon of the

Atlantic Ocean.

"Do you realize the position this guy's in? He's taken two hundred million of our money, Howard, and he still says he can't finish the remodel. It was supposed to be open for guests next weekend. But he's going to need another year and sixty million more dollars in debt with, like, ten in equity. I'm not going to be on the hook for that shit," the voice on the speakerphone blasted out. The angry man was one of Howard's partners in the Taos hotel deal, a money and time suck that no one had any more money or time for. The investor continued, "I called up your commercial property guy, like you said. Mackenzie? Right? He tells me that Montgomery will give us a loan at LIBOR plus seven. Seven! I may as well kill myself, sell all my organs to Planned Parenthood, and then auction my soul to the devil for that. We can't make money at L plus seven. We can't make money at two and a half! But that's not even the worst damn part! Mackenzie ran a background check on the guy back in Minnesota, which I guess your counsel forgot to do. Our proprietor has thirty moving violations in the last four years. Who the hell gets thirty speeding tickets? Who is this guy, Howard? I trusted you and I'm fucking pissed. The home office wants my head on a platter. You got me into this. Now you gotta get us out. You need to—"

Beep. Howard stopped the voicemail. It was stressing him out and he couldn't listen to a second more. He'd call his lawyer tomorrow and threaten to sue the shit out of them for the background-check mishap. Then he'd talk to Mackenzie next week—get a lower rate. This would pass in time. Time was all he needed to solve his problems. Real estate was going up. They could offload the whole project and leave someone else high and dry when the ball dropped again. He didn't like to think about work when he was at Windswept, anyway. Windswept was for his family. The majority of them were back for Thanksgiving, and he was ready to sit down and enjoy his damn meal.

▪

Howard's son Sebastian sat in the living room engrossed in his phone. Sebastian also lived in the city. He was nineteen years old and a first year at Columbia, but they only saw each other at Windswept. Even though he was a freshman in college, this wasn't his first year of freedom. Sebastian had been doing whatever he wanted since he was fifteen years old. As much as they loved each other, they didn't want to waste their time hanging out. A meal with his father would take Sebastian away from whatever social event was around the corner. At this point in his life, he could go to any lounge or club in the entire city with a five minutes' notice via text to one of ten rotating club promoters in his cell phone. That's not to mention the stunning babes that he was involved with—sourced from school and Tinder and stepping at the club—or the drugs, or the lack of schoolwork that was getting done.

Howard knew what Sebastian's life was like because his own had been similar, minus all the technology. But he knew that Sebastian would figure it out. They'd set him up to succeed, and he was doing that, wasn't he? Ivy League ain't too shabby. With the politically correct ideals of meritocracy that were creeping into high society, Ivy wasn't even a guarantee any longer. Howard had some friends at the bank, SVPs even, whose kids were going to places like Hobart and Trinity. Not that there was anything wrong with those schools—not at all. But Columbia looked good on the résumé. Maybe Sebastian didn't take life as seriously as he should, but he wasn't falling behind. He was failing upwards.

"Hey bud," Howard started up.

"Pops . . . What's up?" Sebastian responded.

"Not much. What're you doing?"

"Browsing."

"You're being careful with that social media stuff, right?"

"How come?" Sebastian asked.

"We've been through this. The Rich Kids of Instagram . . . I don't need my face on the top of Daily Mail at any point. You saw that RBS guy who got fired for it . . ."

"There's a new world order, Dad. Visibility is everything. I don't expect you to understand."

"Don't be an ingrate. The life you live isn't a right. It's a privilege," Howard replied hastily.

"Are you pissed, Dad? What's wrong?"

"No."

"Business?"

"Business is wonderful. Thanks," Howard said.

"I heard that call in there. What's up with Taos?"

"Why don't you go swipe for mail-order brides or something," Howard said as he hurried out of the living room and into the kitchen.

"Thanks. I thought so," Sebastian said.

▪

Marjorie pulled the turkey out of the oven with the stuffing already inside. Howard had heard the old wives' tale saying it was a little risky to do that, but he didn't care. He loved the way it tasted, and he'd lived long enough on the edge. He could smell the wonderful aroma of Thanksgiving all around him, punctuated by the excited chatter of his oldest daughter from his first marriage—Caroline. He wasn't great at saying no to his family, but Caroline was the one who really had Howard wrapped around her finger. She sat at the island, going over plans for a kitchen remodel at her new house outside of Chicago.

"Can you look at these, Daddy?" she implored.

Howard quickly scanned the diagrams, not quite sure what he was seeing. He wasn't an engineer and didn't have much skill when it came to aesthetics. He generally left that to the women in his life. But he knew that she wasn't really asking him to decide if the plans looked good or not. "Great. What do you think? And Richard . . . He's onboard?" Howard said.

"Richard does what I want. You know that. And yes, I love it. We had to make room for the Aga in the island. You know Aga?"

"No." Howard shook his head as he sat down on a stool.

"Well, they're the best ovens you can possibly buy. They stay on twenty-four seven, with eight different heat sources—three stoves, four burners, and a hot plate. It just makes sense, you know? They're only a few thousand more than a Viking, but you always taught me that you need to spend money to make money." Caroline dipped her head back down to the plans, studiously examining a tile pattern.

Howard knew it was his time to speak. "So how much are we talking for the remodel now?"

"I don't know, exactly. Our designer is still putting the number together. But you know how I said two hundred before?"

"Yes . . ."

"I mean, we might be closer to four or four-fifty. Would that be okay, Daddy?"

"Money doesn't grow on trees," Howard said.

"I know that."

"But it's no problem, honey," Howard said. "Just tell me when you need the check."

Behind Howard, Marjorie picked up a small bell that sat on the counter in the kitchen. She stepped towards the foyer and rang the bell vigorously. At the sound of the cattle call, the thundering herd of Bergensen family members began to echo throughout the enormous house. A dozen sets of feet pounded down the elegant, three-story staircase in the center of the house, pulled from the ten bedrooms and multiple living spaces of the place. The complicated lives of the Bergensens collided in the dining room. And just as the turkey hit the eighteenth-century French table and its elaborate inlaid gold patterns, the front doorbell to Windswept rang out loudly.

▪

Howard answered the door to find Jake Rivett and Tony Villalon standing on his front steps.

"Hello, Mr. Bergensen. Really sorry to bother you. Can you chat for a few?" Jake asked.

"It's Thanksgiving."

"I . . . didn't realize that. But we need to shine a light on something," Jake replied.

"Food just hit the table. Don't you guys have families?" Howard asked as he glanced back into the dining room. Everyone inside was staring at him.

"My turkey doesn't come out till six," Tony replied.

Howard ducked back out onto the front steps, closing the door behind him. "Okay. What's up?" he asked.

"How many times has Stefano Dubbiono driven you?" Jake asked.

"Who's that?" Howard replied.

"Your chauffeur for the Hamptons hauls—Stefano Dubbiono."

"You mean Steve?" Howard said incredulously.

"Is that what he goes by?"

"Are we talking about Steve? Honestly? He's driven me hundreds of times. He's one of my favorites. Guy has stories for days . . ."

"When you're taking those rides, do you talk about business in the car?" Jake inquired.

"Not with him. But on the phone? Absolutely. That's the whole point," Howard said. "What's this all about? What did Steve do?"

"We think that he—" Villalon started up but was interrupted by Jake.

"We're not sure yet. Just pursuing a lead. Could Steve have reasonably known about Montgomery's gold position because of what he overheard while driving you?"

"I guess it's possible, sure . . . I still say very unlikely. There's a reason he's a driver. Right?"

"What about the vault? Would you have talked about that?"

"Again, it's possible. It's not a secret. But I wouldn't . . ." Howard trailed off and then concluded, "There is so little likelihood that Steve could have picked that up from me."

"What about Belov? Any connection there?" Jake asked.

"You mean between Steve and David?"

"Yep."

"How would I know?" Howard shrugged.

"Anything else you can tell me?" Jake asked.

"Just about as much as you're telling me, detective, which is zero. I'd appreciate knowing what this is about. My neck's the one on the line right now. You can't imagine what the last two weeks have been like."

"We've just drawn some connections. Dubbiono was doing something shady. He knows you. He might know David. I gotta play it out. What else can you tell me about him?" Jake said.

"Look. Steve's a good guy—family man, I think. He tells me stories. I like that stuff. I like hearing about his world. It's so different from what I know. He used to run with a rough crowd. He's . . . loquacious. I mean he'd rattle off for the whole two-hour trip about the days when he was a bookie if I didn't stop him. Who knows? Maybe he does that about me, in reverse, to all his buddies. Maybe the wrong guy heard him. Could be. You know my policy, Jake. If you think Steve knows anything at all about this disaster, I'll do anything I can to nail him to a fucking cross."

"Okay, great. Thanks, Howard," Jake said. "We'll be in touch."

"Fine. But maybe next time you can schedule it with my assistant," Howard replied.

"Will do. And sorry to disrupt your Thanksgiving," Tony added.

"That too," Jake said.

▪

While feasting, Howard couldn't help but think of famine. Luckily his family's joy masked the tension, and their unspoken fractures kept serious personal discussions from the dinner table. After the meal was over, they all spread back out across the house. Howard sat at the table while Marjorie cleared his plate. Sebastian sat at the other end of the table as well, face glowing from the screen in front of him. Howard realized that in a few hours, all of his progeny would creep back across the nation to their own lives. That's the way he had designed it, the way he normally liked it, but this evening he felt something new: a pang of guilt. As Sebastian stood up, Howard rose with him. He caught up to his son and put his arm over Sebastian's shoulder.

"Want to go outside and shoot some bows and arrows?"

"What?" Sebastian asked, startled.

"Remember when we used to do that? You loved archery."

"I was like, eleven."

"I got you all the good stuff—the equipment. Hoyt bows. Easton arrows. Remember? We'd drive up and down the East Coast, go to competitions . . ." Howard reminisced.

"Yeah. I know, Dad. I remember."

"I was just thinking about that. I think we still have at least one of those bows out in the pool house. And we never use the lawn for anything anymore . . ."

"You're serious?" Sebastian asked.

"Sure. Why not?" Howard said.

"Dad, I can't."

"How come?"

"Isabelle's picking me up in twenty minutes. There's a concert tonight —in the city. We've got tickets already," Sebastian said and then added, "Sorry."

"It's okay. I just . . . I loved those times. Sorry if there wasn't enough of them. I want you to know that. I love you, too, son," Howard said.

Sebastian stared back at his father strangely. "Love you too, Pops."

TWENTY-EIGHT

Sunday

VLAD ZHADANOV AND DAVID Belov drove out to the edge of Staten Island's Silver Lake Reservoir, six miles south of Manhattan's southern tip and Wall Street. Rolling through the industrial wasteland, they followed a prompt on Vlad's phone towards a set of coordinates. Once they had reached their destination, David and Vlad parked underneath a highway overhang built against the side of the reservoir.

"It's completely bare of humanity," David said.

"Perfect," Vlad concluded.

David contemplated a set of city plans. He pointed ahead, and Vlad climbed over a small chain-link fence to reach the concrete tiers around the edge of the reservoir. David followed. Directly underneath the bridge and built into the side of the reservoir, David found a steel grate in front of a sewer output pipe. It was rusted shut.

They sprayed WD-40 on the bolt and with a little elbow grease, the bolt loosened. Vlad and David took turns to finish loosening all of the bolts on the sewer output pipe, but they didn't open the grate.

As Vlad was wrapping up his tools and placing them into the back of his Mercedes, he noticed David standing at the water's edge, gazing over towards Manhattan and the glowing Montgomery Noyes building far in the distance.

"I always knew they were never going to look at me like an equal. But I was loyal. I thought it meant something," David said.

"Loyalty is nothing to them—not like it is with us. People like Howard Bergensen sit in that black tower and dictate their sense of right and wrong to the masses, calling themselves bankers and the people they work for clients? Please. That's just a tower of thieves. It'll crumble down to rubble and destroy half of civilization no matter what you do. The job of a real capitalist is to make sure you're there to pick over the pieces of debris on the way out," Vlad said.

"Right. I know that now."

"Now, let's get out of here, my peach."

▪

The entire team assembled in Vlad's office for their final meeting. Vlad went through the upcoming robbery for the hundredth time, including the post-heist plan of attack.

"Baranowski will put the stuff on a truck to Florida. They'll melt it and sell it in bulk to our Cali fences," Vlad directed. "David. I got you a gift."

"I don't want a gun," David replied once he saw the black case Vlad was holding in his hands.

"It's not exactly a gun. At least read the instruction manual. A little offense can come in handy," Vlad said. He opened the case to reveal the neon yellow taser gun that had been used to great effect on Tyler Stanton. David accepted and pocketed the taser.

"Help the twins with the burner, why don't ya?" Vlad suggested. "Cleanup is one of the most important parts of any job, and we are not going to leave a single clue for the pigs to slurp up. I want your clothes in there too. Then we scrub this whole place with mineral spirits before we leave."

David followed Roschin and Petrov towards an incinerator that was installed in a dark corner of the warehouse. Although long forgotten for its original purpose of destroying soiled food stock, it was still in working order with a gas connection. Roschin and Petrov lit the pilot light. David opened the heavy feed door and peered inside. It had been used relatively recently. The ashes of a previous burn were evident in a pile at the bottom of the furnace. But something was stuck on the inside hinge of the incinerator, not having been completely burnt through: a piece of charred rubber. David grabbed the mushy plastic with his hands. He noticed that it was the remains of a prosthetic facial mask. He couldn't make out any of the features except for an ear. It was rubber. Was it a Halloween costume? An uneasy feeling crept across David.

"You just gonna stand there like a deer in the headlights, my peach?" Vlad said, suddenly appearing behind David.

David dropped the plastic mess back into the incinerator as Vlad and Konstantin loaded sections of PVC pipe into it for destruction. The crew took turns loading up the incinerator, cranking it on, and shoveling out the ash debris into plastic garbage bags every hour or so.

After almost everything in the old cherry factory, including their tools, had been incinerated, Vlad brought the group together again. The six men stood in a small circle, stripped down to boxers and disposable flip-flops.

"Tomorrow we'll do the most amazing thing we've ever done. It will be life changing for each and every one of you. The most important rule afterwards is that you live the same life you do now. No one spends anything. And the only person that leaves town is David, after we deliver him to our vanish man in Pennsylvania. Every single day that passes from tomorrow is a good day, because the chance of our busting up falls exponentially. I'm not going to be a statistic. I'm going to be an outlier. Or maybe I got those terms wrong. David? Either way—you get the point. You stick with me—you listen to me—you'll be all right. I won't let you down. That's what I promise you. Give the same back to me, and all of us are going to glide into the sunset together—rich as hell, smooth as butter, baby." Vlad grinned while the rest of the group cheered.

David's situation had pushed him down the hill, and the momentum was turning into an outright landslide. He just hoped he could hold on long enough to land on two feet at the end of it all. He pulled Vlad aside as they left the building.

"I'm not hiding, Vlad," David said.

"What?"

"I can't run. I need to be with Marina and Mikey."

"During visitation in prison?"

"Listen, I appreciate your offer. But I can't do it. I can't just disappear. I'll turn myself in. I won't blow your scene. You know I never would. You hold my share—take care of my family. I'll do my time, whatever that is. Then when I get out? I'm solid. I'm on the up and up."

Vlad stared at David against the sunset for quite a while. Then he nodded his agreement. "I understand. That could be a tough road, David. But I get it. That's fine. Ya. Do it that way," Vlad said.

▪

It was midnight at the beautiful brownstone built on bonus money. Tyler Stanton descended a spiral staircase into his basement. *Beep. Beep.* About to head out for a late-night errand, or perhaps a rendezvous, Tyler opened the door to his Porsche in the garage. Then he heard a man's gravelly voice.

"Tyler," the man said.

Tyler turned quickly, shocked by the presence of someone in the shadows of his garage.

Bang. One precise shot to the forehead echoed through the chamber. Tyler Stanton died instantly. He fell to the floor like a sack. His assassin calmly stepped over him and exited the garage without even checking his handiwork, apparently confident in a job well done.

▪

The assassin dropped the pistol from his gloved hands into a drain in the alley outside Tyler's house. He walked through the alley and out the other end, whistling a bit as he did and pulling his hat down farther over his head. He stepped onto Amsterdam Avenue and disappeared into the night.

But after the assassin departed the alley, an apparent lump sitting next to a large dumpster started to move. But it wasn't a lump. She was a destitute homeless woman. She emerged from her sleeping position behind the dumpster and skittered towards the gun. She gazed into the drain, her eyes wide with fright.

▪

In Konstantin's safe house apartment that evening, David paced back and forth nervously. He finally grabbed a jacket and exited the room.

▪

David walked past his house in Bensonhurst. He ducked across a neighbor's lawn when he spied the unmarked police car at the driveway. Hiding within a grove of trees across the street, David gazed at a glowing light emerging from Mikey's bedroom. David rotated slightly around the tree. He could finally make out Mikey sitting on his bed, a reflection of a Samurai Cat cartoon playing across Mikey's face. David smiled.

▪

Marina sat in the kitchen. She suddenly heard a suspicious light thud emanate from the other side of the house, breaking up the peaceful night. Slightly alarmed, Marina stood and walked through the kitchen. She passed the Froggie Finder still sitting on the countertop. She hadn't touched it in two weeks, because she would never allow Mikey out of her sight again.

She entered David's office, where she could have sworn she'd just heard the noise. But nothing was amiss in the sunporch. She glanced out the windows. Then she walked to the back door. She tried the handle. It was unlocked. Marina opened the door and gazed into the night.

"Hello?" Marina asked. But there was no response. After a beat, she closed the door and locked it. She walked back through the kitchen to where she'd started. She sat down, pondering the state of the back door. She was sure she'd left it locked. There was no reason for it to be open. She was confident of that fact. But then again, she was having trouble putting any chain of logic together recently. She had trusted David when she'd seen him in Brighton Beach, believing what he'd said. As much as her brain was screaming at her to disagree with him, she couldn't help it. She loved him. But then Jake had informed her that the containers were a bust—nothing there. She was furious that David had misled the police, but she was apoplectic that he had lied to her. Her rock-solid judgment was at stake. As the days went on, she realized that her entire life was shifting underneath her feet. Her and Mikey's future might look nothing like the one she'd been picturing for years. And for the first time in her life, she had no idea what to do.

Perhaps if Marina hadn't been spending so much time doubting herself, she would have noticed that an element of the kitchen had changed. She would have seen that the Froggie Finder was no longer sitting on the counter. It had vanished.

▪

Upstairs in his bedroom, Mikey sat and watched his cartoons. Then he heard a knocking on his window pane. Mikey's head curiously darted in the direction of the glass. He hopped off his bed and reached the window. He looked outside. There was something sitting on the sill. He opened the window for a better look. A hand-drawn picture of Samurai Cat stared back at him. Mikey pulled it inside and smiled broadly. He looked around to see if anyone was watching. Then he hid the drawing under his pillow without telling his mother.

▪

Early the next morning, Tyler Stanton's body lay in his garage, covered by a white sheet. Police officers guarded the scene. Jake watched as Villalon ran a small electronic fingerprint scanner across the gun that had been retrieved in the alleyway. Tony checked a connected laptop database and confirmed a successful pull. It was only seconds before a match appeared: David Belov.

"Unbelievable," Jake said. "Where did his prints come from?"

"He got picked up when he was a kid for shoplifting. So you think the quant shot Mr. Stanton?"

"Sure looks that way," Jake said, nodding, "This guy is digging himself a hole in a lake of quicksand, and I don't think he can ever get out." Jake glanced into the alleyway. The homeless woman was being interrogated by another officer.

Interested in what she was saying, Jake stepped towards them both. "You saw the shooter?" he jumped in and asked. She nodded her head affirmatively. Jake pulled out his cell phone and cycled through a series of photos. He held out the phone towards her. She inspected the photo Jake was showing her.

"Is this him?" Jake asked.

"Yesiree. No doubt about it—not one bit. That's the guy."

Jake turned his phone around. He'd pulled up the old photo of David and Marina and the other couple that Jake had encountered and snapped a frame of in David's office during his initial search. Jake placed his finger on David's face. "This man. Right?" he confirmed.

"No," she said and shook her head defiantly. The homeless woman was suddenly confused by Jake's action.

"You're not sure?"

"I'm sure that it wasn't. It was the other guy—this one. He was the killer," she said. The woman pointed to the photograph. She was pointing at the other man in the picture.

"And who the hell are you?" Jake asked as he stared at Vlad Zhadanov's face on the screen.

TWENTY-NINE

Monday

THE MONTGOMERY NOYES SKYSCRAPER rose into the sky like an imperial obelisk. But today it was a target. The city began to buzz as David walked down the street in a suit, circulating amidst the urban lemmings. It was another Monday morning, only two weeks after the flash crash. It was a return to familiarity for David—and the habits fit nicely. It was also a sorrowful moment—the last time he'd set foot in the city for the foreseeable future. This time around, he appreciated the place drastically more. Every cloud of acrid sewer stench that he passed through brought a smile to his face—not because his senses enjoyed it, but because of the memories.

He thought back on the evening he'd finally saved up enough money to take Marina out on the town. It had been dinner at Morimoto's followed by the Les Misérables show. Every little detail was etched into his mind. He'd worked so hard for it. He didn't even like Broadway, but he hadn't known that ahead of time. He had just known what he wanted. He wanted to sit down amongst the elite and watch the lights dim with his lady by his side in her sequined dress. He would never forget the moment when he waited for her to use the restroom during intermission. When Marina emerged at the top of the flight of stairs, he couldn't take his eyes off her. She set his heart on fire. Words could not express the sensation—they were below his feelings. He had ordered drinks at the bar—martinis—one for each of them. And they sipped the drinks quietly, watching the rest of high society filter throughout. They didn't say much to each other in that moment, because they both felt exactly the same. This was the definition of living, and it was theirs that day. He finally had it all.

With the last gust of smoke from a hot dog stand, and a last glance upwards at the perfectly blue sky with only a sliver of cloud in sight, David cocked his head down to avoid surveillance cameras and stepped through the rotating doors of Montgomery Noyes.

▪

David entered the main atrium of his old building but made sure to not walk towards the security desk in the back. Instead, he entered the coffee shop spanning the front of the lobby and ordered an espresso. He sat looking out the window and sipped on his drink as he watched the throngs of humanity pace past.

"Hey, brother," a man's voice rumbled.

David glanced up to see Hank, Montgomery's sandwich guy. David reached into his pocket and pulled out a silver sticker and an electrical-outlet extender.

"You're sure that this won't come back on me?" Hank asked as he glanced at the items.

David handed Hank an envelope. It was stuffed with cash. "You'll be fine. Even if they see you on the cameras, they won't—"

"I didn't ask you to sell me," Hank interrupted him. "Like I told you on the phone, I just wanted your word. You need this for your family, right?"

David nodded.

"Then all I need is a handshake," Hank said. They shook hands. That settled their transaction. Hank grabbed the items and walked away. David took a final sip of his coffee and exited the building.

▪

David was minding his own business as he stepped down a side street and away from his old headquarters, until a suited man suddenly stopped him.

"David? What the fuck! Aren't you like . . . wanted?" It was Rick Stanfield. What a terrible coincidence. David picked up his pace in an attempt to escape him, but Rick ran after David. Rick was holding a large file box in his hands, stuffed with personal items. He jammed David against the side of the building.

"What's up, man?" Rick asked again.

David didn't respond, staring at the box in Rick's hand, unsure of his intentions, or if this meant the whole setup was busted before they'd even begun. But Rick didn't seem perturbed at all. He actually seemed excited to see David.

"I got fired this morning. I guess they don't condone helicoptering prostitutes into the company ski retreat. Whatever," Rick said.

"Hope you land on your feet, Rick," David replied, jumping back into a normal act for the time being.

"I'm money. Already got a new gig doing the exact same shit."

David twisted away and continued to pace down the sidewalk, but Rick followed him.

"I can't believe one of those high-frequency, automated trading outfits hasn't snapped you up yet. That's where the real money is nowadays—not with us old dinosaurs," Rick said.

"I'm not exactly hirable material," David replied.

"Yeah. But fuck man . . . Honestly, it doesn't matter."

"Why?"

"'Cause you're a legend now. The street will never forget your name.

And no one can ever take that away from you," Rick said. He put his hand on David's chest. "Hey. Did you hear about Tyler?" Rick asked.

"No. What about him?"

"He died last night," Rick finally said.

"Are you serious?"

"Murder. Google it," Rick replied. "Well, I guess I should go. Great to see you, David. It really is. And don't worry—I won't call the police. I'm too busy, and I don't like kicking people when they're down. Except if I can make money off it. Can't make a buck off you, now, can I?" Rick finally turned and walked away, and for once, David believed him.

■

David paced towards his originally intended direction—a white rental box truck parked legally on the street beside Montgomery Noyes with the words "Soda Supply, Inc." freshly painted on the sides. David jumped into the truck to encounter Petrov and Roschin in the back. They nodded at him as they fiddled with a large piece of machinery in the rear of the rental.

David pulled out his laptop and connected it to the internet through a mobile card. He quickly searched for "Tyler Stanton." David read a small news article about the murder. Rick hadn't been lying. David confirmed that Tyler had been shot dead a night earlier, in his garage, in what was described as a carjack attempt gone wrong. The revelation ripped through David's body like an earthquake. Tyler's death couldn't be random. He looked up. Petrov and Roschin stared at him coldly. He smiled nervously.

"Did you guys know about this?" he asked. "Tyler Stanton got killed?"

Petrov shrugged as if he couldn't care less.

"I don't know anything," Roschin said.

"Yeah, you do. That's what you say when you do."

"Believe me or not, David," Roschin replied, seemingly disinterested. "We got work to do here."

David nodded. He nonchalantly placed his hand in his pocket.

Without the brothers noticing, he pulled out the Froggie Finder. He glanced down and tapped the Froggie's nose. The device activated. He stuffed it back into his pocket.

▪

Roger O'Neill rushed down a hallway in the basement level of Montgomery, popping open a can of Sunkist as he did. Roger loved Sunkist. He'd recently noticed that he was one of a dying breed. His daughter had moved to Ojai, California, a few years ago. Like all O'Neills, she had no fear. But the last time he was there, he hadn't seen a single Sunkist can in any of the soda machines. It made him a little upset, but then again, it also made him a little bit more thankful for New York. She was perfect for California. She was a vegan who disapproved of carbonated beverages—very brave indeed. But he was meant to live and die in New York, and Sunkist would remain his private little vice. Roger nodded as he passed by the familiar sight of Hank pushing the sandwich cart towards the small bank of snack machines, where the soda machine was located.

Hank reached the soda machine that Roger had just utilized. He inserted a dollar and selected a drink. The can fell. Hank leaned down to grab it, but as he did, he surreptitiously affixed a small sticker to the bottom corner of the machine. Hank looked around. Roger had turned the corner and disappeared. There was no one around, and even if there was, they probably wouldn't have noticed Hank fiddling with a snack machine. He didn't mess with the trader's spreadsheets, and they didn't touch his soda machine. This was his domain. Hank threw the first soda into a trash can. He walked around to the other side of the machine. He quickly reached down and unplugged it. He attached the outlet extender that David had handed him a few minutes before, and then he nonchalantly plugged the machine back in. The refrigerated box began to hum again as it started up.

"What's wrong with it?" Hank heard someone ask. He stood up to greet a young Montgomery Noyes intern, hands on hips, wondering earnestly.

"Havin' a little trouble with my soda. But I think she'll run now," Hank said.

"I have a better way," the intern said as he violently slammed the front of the machine with both of his fists. Noticing Hank's reaction, the intern added, "It works in the dorm." Then the intern wrapped both arms around the machine and tried to pick the whole thing up, as if he was carrying on some sort of football drill. Hank stifled a chuckle. The method was not effective, and not just because the kid was such a shrimp. Hank watched the barely twenty-year-old child and realized that the effort expended wasn't about the machine at all. It didn't take a mind reader to realize that this intern was blowing off steam from the pressure cooker upstairs. Luckily for both of them, the machine turned back on within a moment, just as Hank knew it would—except that no soda came out.

"Ah, darn. I don't need it anyways," Hank said as he shrugged sheepishly.

"I got an extra dollar if you want one," the intern offered.

"Nah, it's cool. But thanks." Hank pushed his cart away from the machine and continued on his way.

■

Inside the rental truck, David glanced at the brothers as he tapped away on his laptop. They were both waiting for his word. He noticed a red dialogue box turn green.

"We're connected. What's your least favorite soda?" David asked them.

"I only drink Sprite reg. That's regular—not Diet. I don't want to die," Petrov replied.

"And dip. He also drinks dip," Roschin added.

"Diet Sprite it is," David said. He continued to type rapidly on his computer screen. The application he was running contained a schematic that looked roughly like a soda machine. David fiddled with a few of the settings, and then hit enter.

"But why not reg?" Petrov pondered out loud.

▪

As the intern walked away from the soda dispenser in Montgomery Noyes' hallway with his Coke in hand, he had no clue that what was happening inside the refrigerated device was the first in a long set of dominos.

The unit began to grumble. Gears turned inside its chassis, slowly at first. Then the machine's velocity grew, until its insides were rotating with vigorous speed. The receptacle-release mechanism underneath a column of Diet Sprites opened. But due to David's programming prowess, the mechanism didn't close. The lever lifted a can of Diet Sprite, then dropped it into the discharge section. The soda rolled down a small ramp, sticking inside the open machine slot. Since the receptacle release was permanently stuck open, another Diet Sprite dropped—then another—and another.

In the basement hallway, the machine finally expelled the first Diet Sprite due to the pressure of all those behind it. After the third can fell, the first can rolled over the lip and onto the floor. A secretary nearby finally noticed a handful of sodas rolling past her office door, each separated by about five seconds. She stood up, curious. She gazed down the hallway and noticed the soda machine, apparently unattended, spitting sodas out. She picked one up from the ground by her feet and opened it—big mistake. It exploded and coated her with carbonated beverage. She screamed.

▪

Vlad sat in the front seat of the large blue van with the retrofitted floor. He heard David announce the status of the soda machine over the radio.

"Malfunction complete," David said.

"Thank you, my peach," Vlad dipped his face towards the radio and said, "Buckle up, boys. This ain't no test run. It's the master class."

Vlad turned off the radio. He made sure the van was locked from the inside. He turned and climbed through the two front seats of the vehicle towards the back, pulling down a black curtain to block any pedestrian viewpoints into the van. The floor had been rotated up by its newly soldered hinges and secured in the open position. The street was visible underneath the van. A large portable generator situated in the back of the van ran cables through the hole in the bottom and into an open sewer hole on the city street beneath. The waterproof cables flowed into the hole and out of sight. Vlad grabbed a large backpack hanging in the van and slowly climbed down through the hole in the bottom of the floor and into the sewer. He carefully held onto the edge of the sewer with both hands, and then finally lowered himself and disappeared into the dark depths beneath the city.

THIRTY

MARINA APPROACHED THE ZHADANOVS' house. Her face was stiff with purpose but also buffered by a distinct sadness. A few moments after Marina rang the doorbell, Cat answered. She noticed Marina's dour expression immediately.

"Hey, babe! What's wrong?" Cat asked.

"I'm sorry. I don't want it to be like this—but it is," Marina said solemnly.

Cat glanced behind Marina to see Jake Rivett climbing the hill up to the house. A large pile of police officers followed him. Jake pushed past Marina and Cat and stepped into the Zhadanovs' house.

"Where's Vladimir?" Jake asked. Cat noticed that Jake was holding his trusty crowbar in his hands.

"Who are you?" Cat retorted.

"The fuckin' cops. Where is he?"

"I . . . I don't know," Cat finally stuttered.

"You don't know where your husband is?"

"No. Why should I?" Cat said and then turned to Marina, "You brought them here?"

"This has nothing to do with her," Jake said. "It's a damn shame that you don't know where Vlad is, because he's wanted for murder. Maybe he's actually here, and he's hiding?" Jake asked as he eyed a tall closet in Cat's kitchen. Jake leaned back and placed two hands on the crowbar. With a fluid leap, he used all his might to swing the crowbar and crush the cabinet's wooden surface. He ripped the door open and stood back as the remnants flew everywhere. But there was nothing inside. "I guess we'll have to look everywhere for him," Jake said.

"You asshole! You can't do that!" Cat flailed towards Jake.

"I was afraid for my life," Jake replied.

Cat tensed. She was about to explode, but Villalon jumped in and pulled her away. Tony handed Cat over to another police officer, who escorted her out onto the porch.

▪

Cat huddled on a chair. Marina placed her purse on a small side table and sat down next to Cat, attempting to comfort her.

"Do you know where they are?" Marina asked Cat. "This isn't right, honey. Whatever they're doing . . . It has to end."

Cat accepted Marina's embrace but didn't answer her question. Instead she buried her face into Marina's arm and cried. Marina sighed.

Due to the loud torrent of tears emoting from Cat, Marina couldn't hear her phone buzzing in her purse. It was on vibrate. But deep inside the bag, a notification popped up on her device. Froggie Finder was sending her a message: "Mikey" had checked in—in Manhattan—just a few blocks away from Montgomery Noyes.

▪

A Montgomery Noyes maintenance man levered a wrench into the guts of the soda machine in an attempt to fix the unit, to no avail. Not sure what to do next, he noticed a small silver sticker on the bottom corner of the machine: "SERVICED BY AAA+ VENDING: 212-444-2 . . ." The maintenance man pulled his phone and dialed the number for service.

▪

Inside the soda supply truck, Roschin watched as his phone started to vibrate. He grinned and picked up.

"Soda," Roschin said. He listened before replying, "Yes, yes. No problem. Thirty minutes or less. That's our guarantee."

▪

Using his flashlight to navigate, Vlad carefully splashed through the two feet of fast-running water inside a large main located underneath Montgomery Noyes. Below the depths of New York City existed a world unto itself, consisting of ancient aqueducts, catacombs, and a bird's nest of municipal and private plumbing systems. With David's help, Vlad had spent the last week studying these systems, to the point where he knew them like the back of his hand. He followed the electrical cables around a corner to reveal a "base camp" set up for his operation. A platform had been built over the running water. Baranowski stood guard over a collection of boxes and equipment they'd hauled down earlier in the day. Konstantin was kneeling over a bulging pile of folded synthetic cloth, carefully unspooling the various ends while referring to printed directions. They both heard Vlad's footsteps and turned.

"Is it ready?" Vlad asked.

"I think so," Baranowski replied. "Did they get the call for the soda machine?"

"Ya. We're at twenty-six minutes. Do it," Vlad said.

Konstantin pressed a button and activated an air pump charged by the power cables strung down the tunnel. The motor in the pump revved up. It was connected to the mass of fabric sitting on the platform. Soon the material began to inflate. Its sides slipped out of their folded patterns and the fabric began to expand like a wobbly bubble. As the bubble became larger, the men pushed the contraption off the platform and into the running water. They secured it with a rope so it wouldn't float down the tunnel. It soon became clear what the item itself was: a high-pressure tunnel plug. Consisting of three interwoven layers of Vectran, a manufactured fiber spun from liquid-crystal polymers, the tunnel plug continued to grow in size.

After ten minutes, the plug became large enough to completely block the sewer pipe the three men were standing in. After a few more minutes, the power of friction would make the plug completely unyielding. As the plug closed off the pipe, the running water had nowhere to go. It began to rise. Similar to jamming a stopper into a tub's drain, Vlad had plugged the sewer system underneath Montgomery. The water molecules' path of least resistance became vertical. Baranowski quickly set up a ladder inside the pipe. Wielding an acetylene torch, he climbed up and began to cut a hole into the top of the water main. Behind him, Vlad and Konstantin opened the boxes of supplies they'd prepared and began changing into wetsuits and pulling out air tanks.

▪

Wearing "AAA+ Vending" uniforms, Petrov and Roschin guided a new soda machine down a ramp into the shipping-and-receiving bay of Montgomery's headquarters. The guard at the gate looked up to see the huge soda machine in front of him. Roschin handed the guard a purchase order, but the guard didn't want to read it.

"I thought you were just coming to fix it?"

"It's broken," Petrov said succinctly.

"I know, but . . . Never mind. Here, I'll show you where it goes."

▪

Following the guard on the way to the small kitchenette with the soda machines, Petrov and Roschin couldn't help but glance down the various hallways of the bank's back office like a pair of salivating dogs being led down a hallway lined with red meat. They eventually reached the malfunctioning unit. It was completely out of stock. All of the offending sodas had been helpfully piled up against the wall. After Petrov and Roschin unplugged the broken machine and moved it out of the way, they rolled the new one into its place next to the other snack units. They plugged it in. In seemingly perfect working order, the new machine's light illuminated the Coke logo on front. Roschin pressed a series of buttons and selected a soda. After a light rumble, a Sunkist fell out of the slot at the bottom.

"Test complete," Petrov said.

"You gonna put those Sprites back in?" the guard asked.

"No," Roschin answered. "Is already full."

"So what're we supposed to do with them?"

"It's your soda. Drink it," Roschin said.

"Excellent point," the guard replied.

▪

Jake Rivett stepped out onto the Zhadanovs' porch and addressed Cat. "How long have you lived in the house?" he asked.

"Twelve years."

"Do you love it?"

"It's where my children grew up. It's full of love," she answered.

"What does that mean?" Jake asked. Although she perceived his comment as facetious, he was seriously wondering. But before she could open her mouth to reply, he proceeded. "I'm going to go back in there and treat this place like the mosh pit at a headbanger's ball."

"But I told you everything." Cat began to tear up.

"Too bad that everything provided nothing. Guess I'll have to look even harder."

▪

Jake entered the house, dragging his crowbar on the floor with him. The steel scraped along the wood floor with horrible premonition, like a rabid predator waiting to strike. Marina and Cat watched in horror through the porch windows as Jake moved through the house and proceeded to methodically destroy everything in his sight.

He was a leviathan of destruction. He was doom incarnate. He was his rat-bastard father. He shattered a row of glass cabinets in the kitchen. He saw an antique buffet table in a hallway and gave it three harsh hits. The table cracked down the middle. Broken china fragmented everywhere. Jake moved into the living room. After yanking the pillow off, he flipped each couch and chair over. He dissected the furniture with his crowbar, and then went for the pillows. Feathers and foam erupted. Jake caught sight of something out of the corner of his eye. It was a grandfather clock, sitting in a corner of the living room. He stepped towards it, but instead of swinging the crowbar, he stopped. He stared at the clock, and his expression grew darker and denser.

"I fucking hate you," he said to no one in particular. His shoulders heaved backwards, about to punish the grandfather clock with a heavy-laden swing of the crowbar. Just as he was about to destroy it, he heard Cat screaming bloody murder from the porch.

"Stop! Stop! Stop it!"

▪

Marina was screaming too, but at Cat. "Just tell them!"

Jake emerged back onto the porch. "Did you want to say something? This is your last chance," he said.

"It's . . . He's . . . They're . . ." Cat tried to say the words between tears, "They're at the bank—David's bank."

The revelation washed over Jake's face as if he were waking from a long night of terrible dreams.

THIRTY-ONE

IN THE VAULT'S CONTROL room, Roger O'Neill sipped his Sunkist and gazed through the massive window that framed the commodity vault. Even for a man such as Roger, who overlooked the vault five days a week, it was impossible to not be occasionally dazzled by the sheer buying power of the commodities stored within—the gold, the platinum, the silver, the bullion, the currency. In addition to O'Neill, a handful of technicians sat inside the control room and kept track of the various mechanical, electrical, and computer systems running the vault.

"Gotta hit the head," Roger said as he finished his pop. With a nod to one of the operators, he headed back outside the control room.

■

Howard Bergensen sat in silence while Dubbiono drove him into the city. Although he'd kept Steve on at the police's request, he would be lying if he said it hadn't been a bit awkward during the morning pickup. Dubbiono wasn't talking much this morning either, and neither was Howard. He was staring at the urban jungle whipping past the window and thinking about the nature of meritocracy.

A woman in Montgomery's human resources department, with whom Howard had managed to conduct a two-year affair and emerge unscathed, had just sent him a cartoon about standardized testing. An elephant, a dolphin, a bird, a monkey, and a giraffe stood in a line. A docent was informing the collection of animals that he would be conducting a standardized test.

"The task is: tree climbing. Go climb a tree. And to make sure this is fair, everyone will climb the same tree," the docent said.

The competition was fair and square, except that it simultaneously wasn't. Sometimes it's nice to be a bird or a monkey. The irony rang true in Howard's mind because he knew full well that merit was a sham. He hadn't succeeded by obeying the rules of the system. He'd made it in life by figuring out where they could be bent or broken without blowback hitting him in the face. But maybe he wasn't as good at dodging debris as he used to be. In the middle of this thought, Howard's cell phone rang. He picked up and listened. His face drained white.

"Tyler Stanton? Are you sure? Get me Roger," Howard commanded his underling. While waiting to be connected, he thought long and hard about all that was happening to him. He had experienced a long career full of bold, impressive action, tailwinded by powerful common interests. But nobody had taught a predator like Howard what to do when one suddenly found oneself the prey. The cartoonist had a point. Howard was the dolphin. He was the elephant. He could no longer strike back in the way he was accustomed, because the rules of the game had changed. He was sure that there were only two actions he could take.

First, he could use the force of his own will to move the goalposts back to a comfortable position. Or second, and seemingly more appealing, drop the mic and quit the game. It was clear that Howard wasn't a quitter. He was a winner. But he didn't want to be the one who drove himself over the cliff with his eyes wide open. If he was going over any cliff, someone else was going to have to do all the legwork.

▪

Roger sat on the toilet and absorbed *Page Six*. Midway through a fascinating dissertation on Upper East Side daycare price inflation, he observed a small line of water running across the tile grout in his stall. Moving quite slowly, the liquid parted ways with itself at each intersection, forming a bizarre aqua crossword puzzle. Roger put down the magazine. He flushed, stood up and followed the water throughout the bathroom. The path led to a supply closet. He opened the door and looked down. The drain was completely backed up and gurgling underneath him, about an inch of water filling the bottom of the closet.

▪

Roger exited the bathroom at haste and proceeded directly for the service stairs. He opened the door and took the first flight of stairs down towards the second sub-basement, but water rushed up the bottom steps below. Roger could make out sparks crackling from the generators and industrial machinery in the lowest basement level, which was alarmingly now submerged in a foot of water.

"Water," Roger said succinctly, which sounded incredibly distinctive in his old Irish accent and similar to "Wooder."

▪

Roger burst back into the vault's control room, his face weighted by dread.

"Call DEP and Con Ed—water and power. Get upstairs on the line. We need to shut off power and evacuate the entire building, immediately!" he exclaimed to the vault operators around him. Two of them picked up phones and gave the order to the uniformed security in the lobby.

"What about us?" a technician asked.

"Keep the vault's auxiliary power on—for now. If we have to we'll turn that off too. I don't want to have water short the systems out," Roger replied. "But get on the phone to the city. They need to be here!"

"Hey, uh, Roger? Howard called," another technician said, nervously letting Roger know that his master was looking for him.

▪

In Montgomery's lobby upstairs, sirens screamed and the building lights flashed and then dimmed to signify to the rest of the complex that an honest-to-goodness emergency was taking place. A stream of businessmen and businesswomen emerged from the stairs and the elevators. Lit by only the glow of emergency lighting, security guards ushered them out the front door of the building.

▪

All of the lights in the kitchenette near Roger's office were darkened. The new soda machine hummed along in the hallway before suddenly shutting down with a mechanical whirring noise. Its bright face dimmed slightly and then extinguished completely, a sign that the main power supply had been shut off in the building.

After a few seconds, a faint noise began to emanate from the inside of the machine. Suddenly the front panel of the unit rotated open on its hinges, and David Belov tentatively stepped out from the inside of the machine, where he had been hiding for the last hour.

David surveyed his surroundings. Due to the evacuation, the entire floor was deserted. The alarm continued to ring, and small emergency flashers at each exit sparkled. David padded down the hallway. A few steps from the kitchenette, Roger's personal office door was open. His computer displayed a screensaver.

David entered Roger's office and shut the door behind him. Just to be safe, he locked it. He ducked underneath Roger's desk. He located an ethernet cord and used crimping pliers to splice the cable. He cut himself into the network through an ethernet splitter. He pulled his small laptop from a bag and hooked it into Montgomery's network. He began to explore the intranet while speaking into his microphone to Vlad and the rest of the crew.

"I'm trying to find the stacking machine's executable and the vault's storage index. They're somewhere in the Box, I think. I'll have access from here under Roger's credentials," David said as he scanned through the various computer systems that comprised the building's network ecosystem. First, he located the database containing the vault's indexing information. This was essentially a record of exactly who or what organization owned which shelves inside the vault at any given point in time. But Tsunami wasn't on the list.

"Okay, I'm in the index. But there's no shelves tied to Tsunami. Hold on . . ." Instead of searching by the owner's name, David chose chronological order. He narrowed the results to the same night that he and Vlad had witnessed the gold delivery back into Montgomery's vault. Bingo. There was only one movement initiated from a new account and logged in at two o'clock in the morning of that same day.

"Found our gold," David whispered excitedly. He closed the location index and browsed through Roger's network to the server that contained the Stacker's operating executable. "And the Stacker is mine," David said into the little microphone attached to his shirt.

David ran the Stacker's program inside a virtual machine on his laptop, tricking the robot into believing it was receiving commands directly from the control room. The program provided its operator with full control of the Stacker's physical movement. This included the ability to program directional coordinates, import automated moves, and even control the Stacker in a live condition, like a video game. David selected a few options from within the user interface of the algorithm and started to use his directional keys to control the Stacker inside the vault.

▪

The Stacker was essentially an automated yellow bookshelf loader on steroids. It sashayed vertically and horizontally across the facility along a series of gridded track paths that had been constructed to allow the Stacker to access virtually every square foot of the vault. Under David's control, the robot continued to operate. First it headed deep into the back of the facility. It identified a lone, physically unmarked shelf full of gold. It picked the gold pallet up and ran ahead towards the front of the vault.

▪

In the control room, an operator watched the Stacker operating seemingly by itself.

"Who told the Stacker to move?" the technician asked. No one responded. They all turned to watch the Stacker bow down and lower the pile of gold directly in front of the window, as if a peace offering to the Gods.

"Not me, dawg," another technician said. "Electronics must be getting funky because of the leak. I'm getting all sorts of crazy input reads over here."

"Con Ed better get here soon. They got no time to dodder around," Roger said after he hung up with Howard.

What a complete shitstorm of a day. With a dead employee and a flooded building, Roger could look forward to much more police involvement in his life. That sucked. The primary focus of Roger's job was to make sure that situations involving the authorities cropped up as rarely as possible. Tyler Stanton's unusual death aside, the water issue was massive but not unprecedented. The sub-basement had been flooded during Hurricane Sandy. The vault wasn't impermeable, but it was designed to be highly water resistant, even on the occasion of a flood. During Sandy, the space had done its job and stayed high and dry. Roger hoped this time would be no different. At least in the case of the hurricane, the cause of the water had been clear. This time around, Roger couldn't be sure, and the sheer speed of the water level's rise was alarming. He hadn't yet been able to discern if the issue originated within Montgomery's own piping infrastructure or if it was a municipal malfunction. By the volume of the water, it clearly seemed like the city's problem. That was worse, because the city could be slow, and at the given moment Roger was watching water inch underneath the control room's door and spill into the room itself. That meant the second sub-basement was completely flooded and the first sub-basement and all of the building's and vault's auxiliary power systems were next in line for shut down.

▪

Still crouching in Roger's darkened office, David's fingers dashed frantically across his computer keys. He continued to control the Stacker's operation from his laptop, knowing that the water level was rising and soon the Stacker wouldn't be able to move any longer. There was one final task remaining.

▪

After the Stacker finished moving the entire shelf of illicit gold into a pile in front of the control room, it suddenly rose until it was staring directly at Roger. Without hesitation, the Stacker jolted forward aggressively. Its lifting arms collided with pneumatic force into the Gorilla Glass of the control room window—a grudge match of offensive velocity versus defensive might. After a few hits, the Stacker caused the glass to splinter. A hairline crack appeared in the control booth's window, and the technicians inside began to scream.

They were trying to gain back control from the Stacker, but something was going wrong with their systems. Each time they loaded the Stacker's executable from the server, their screens froze up or became corrupted.

"What the hell is it doing?" Roger exclaimed incredulously.

"Shorted," one operator said.

"The whole system's dead, boss," another technician announced with melancholy. All of the men in the control room could do nothing as they watched the Stacker line up for a fourth hit. The robot launched forward, impacting the glass. The window splintered further, speeding beyond a hairline and into an earthquake. Its tendrils grew wider and deeper inside the window like roots of a tree expanding in hyper-fast-forward. Roger became aware that his shoes were soaked. He looked down. The water in the control room had reached his ankles. He made a decision.

"Turn off all the power—even the auxiliary," Roger said. "We'll evacuate—one level up."

The technicians started shutting down various systems. Since many of the computers were no longer responding electronically, they resorted to pulling out power cords and physically disabling the machines. Amidst this, the whole room watched as the Stacker wound up for another hit. The booth shook when the Stacker pummeled the glass again. Although the window appeared to have gone through a righteous hailstorm, the glass still stood, having not yet lost its structural integrity. The Stacker backed up once again. As the robot screamed forward for the sixth time, sparks flew from its track below. The machine suddenly stopped directly in its tracks, inches from the window—full power failure.

▪

Roger sprinted through the center aisle of the HVAC and power room, shutting down the twenty massive emergency-power generators that had turned on when the building's external power had been extinguished. He reached the last generator and slammed down a lever, causing all of the remaining power in the building to disappear. It was pitch black. Roger pulled out his cell phone and used it to navigate back out of the power room. He found his technicians and they headed for the stairs, the water rushing up to their hips.

▪

One floor up in the basement, David tried to control the Stacker to no avail. He noticed that Roger's computer had shut down. He leaned into the radio.

"They shut off all the power. I'm out of the Stacker," he whispered into the radio.

"Did you break the window?" Vlad's filtered voice responded.

"I . . . I don't know," David finally said. "I got at least five good hits in."

"Proceed, my peach."

David nodded. He unplugged his laptop from the spliced ethernet cable and raced out of Roger's office. He sprinted down the hallway, past the kitchenette and back towards their Trojan horse of a soda machine.

David opened the dispenser's door to reveal a full set of scuba gear hanging inside. He pulled out tanks, a BCD, and a full-face mask and began to outfit himself.

▪

Roger and the other guards ran up the service stairs from the sub-basement level, emerging at the level of their offices in the basement. The water was nipping at their heels. Roger raced past his office and the soda machine, but David was no longer there. Nothing was disturbed. Roger and his security staff rounded a corner and passed an elevator bank on the way towards another set of stairs. They began to climb up to the surface level.

▪

On the other side of the elevator door, David balanced on the inside edge of the elevator shaft. Outfitted from head to toe in scuba gear, he was about to dive into the water when he cocked his head up. He could hear something. He pulled off his mask to listen. He could clearly make out a metallic, echoing noise emanating from above him. He looked up and saw an elevator stuck midway up the shaft above him. The cab was no longer moving due to the lack of power, and the people trapped inside were banging for help. Putting it out of his mind for a moment, David looked down. There was only dark, dirty water below. He jumped in.

David swam down the shaft and into the first sub-basement level. The door to the control room was wide open, but he couldn't spot anyone. All at once, bright lights exploded around him. Having already arrived in the vault's control room and also suited up themselves, Vlad, Baranowski and Konstantin shined their underwater spotlights at David. Vlad gave David the universal thumbs-up sign. Everything was on track.

They swam into the control room and addressed the window separating them from the vault's floor. The four of them floated in front of the splintered frame and examined its condition. The Stacker had punctured the glass but had not quite caused structural collapse. The water had finally made its way into the vault, and the Stacker was completely submerged with its circuits shorted out. Vlad put his hand to the glass and pushed. Nothing happened.

"This is bad," David said over the radio.

"Truth. But we don't let bad stop us," Vlad replied.

"I don't know 'bout you, but I got two missiles on my back," Baranowski popped up. He motioned for them to move away from the window.

Baranowski pulled a tank off his own back, leaving one remaining. He swam towards the back of the control room. He floated the tank onto the top of a stationary counter at the rear of the room and held it down with one hand. With the other hand, he yanked his knife off an ankle holster. He repeatedly smashed the base of the knife onto the regulator atop the tank. After a number of hard blows, a series of small bubbles began to ascend from the regulator. Baranowski took a final look, confirming that the tank was aligned correctly. Then he levered his arm up and down one more time, smashing the regulator completely off. The tank exploded forward like a torpedo through the water of the control room. Aimed directly at the cracked window, the projectile made violent contact, as intended. It was the straw that broke the camel's back. The splintered and damaged glass shattered immediately. David watched as thousands of shards of glass floated through the water like a slow-motion explosive shockwave.

The vault quickly gulped up a few more feet of water and reached parity with the rest of the floor. Vlad went to work on the rest of the window, using a hammer to smash a clear path through the remaining glass remnants along the window frame. After the coast was clear, David, Vlad, Baranowski, and Konstantin swam into the vault. They floated through the cracked glass and headed towards the huge pile of gold on the floor.

David arrived at the pile first and gripped his first gold bar in his hand. He observed it closely. Then he turned and began to help. The other three pulled along a daisy-chained trail of twenty weight-balanced, waterproof bags behind them. Konstantin guided the bags into place as Vlad and Baranowski began heaving the gold bars in. Each bag was filled until it could be comfortably zipped and then handed to David. David confirmed that the bag was balanced by either adding or releasing air from a small plastic lung they'd sewn into the outside pocket of each duffel. They continued to dutifully pack the floating train of bags with gold.

▪

Outside of Montgomery Noyes, chaos reigned in the shadow of the civic emergency that was unfolding. Throngs of ejected office workers gawked in groups on the sidewalk across from the building. A few police officers struggled to contain the scene. One street to the side of the major commotion, the soda supply rental truck finally drove away. Its tires splashed through the water backing up out of the drains outside the building.

Moments later the city finally arrived. Multiple utility trucks converged on the scene. DEP and Con Edison workers suited up near various manholes. One team pulled up a manhole near them. But all they found was water flush with the street level. *Shit.*

The amount of policemen grew exponentially. Numerous squad cars arrived simultaneously. As the police began to establish an official cordon around the premises of the building, Jake Rivett ripped up the street in his motorcycle. He was quickly followed by Villalon in a black SUV. Jake parked his bike and hopped off. He found a pair of police officers milling about.

"Make sure these ladies don't leave the car," he commanded the officer as he flashed his badge. The officer glanced into the back of Tony's SUV and noticed that Cat and Marina were stowed there, their expressions a mix of resentment regarding their own personal situations and amazement about the state of affairs outside.

▪

David, Vlad, Baranowski and Konstantin swam back through the first sub-basement and into the elevator shaft. David looked up. The water had continued to rise while they were in the vault. Obviously the city hadn't discovered their water-main stopper yet. David noticed that the elevator he'd seen above was becoming submerged. The screams from those stuck inside were growing in ferocity, but apparently no one was aware or able to help them from above. David looked down and watched Vlad, Konstantin, and Baranowski descend even deeper down the shaft, past the second sub-basement and towards the very foundation of the building. Already a certified bank robber, David wasn't going to be party to a mass murder as well. He made a decision.

David swam vertically, up to the elevator. He maneuvered himself against the side of the elevator until his BCD snagged on the cabling behind him and he couldn't move farther. David wriggled out of it, making sure to attach it to the elevator. He hung his mask with the BCD and emerged from the dark water, pulling himself onto the surface of the top of the cab. He climbed atop the machine and noticed that there would only be inches of air, if that, left inside the elevator itself. He could still hear urgent banging emerging from beneath the roof. David pulled a panel off to spot a handful of screaming, terrified office workers.

"Thank God!" they screamed, thinking that he represented an official rescue. David helped them all climb up onto the roof, one at a time, until all of them were standing atop the elevator like castaways on a small island.

"How do we get out of here?" one asked David, starting to realize that he was a one-man band.

"Where's the rest of your crew?" another asked.

"I don't know," David said as he shrugged, "anyone else in there?"

The panicked inhabitants of the elevator looked around.

"Where's that lady? Wasn't she in here too?" one replied.

David took a deep breath and descended into the submerged elevator. After a brief moment, he emerged pulling an elderly woman in a heavy wool suit. She wasn't moving. Another man on the elevator kneeled down and began to administer CPR. After a number of deep breaths, the woman slowly started to stir. She began to hack and cough up water, but she was alive.

"What do we do now?" one of them asked.

"That's an excellent question," David said. "Keep yelling. They'll get you out eventually."

"What!"

"You're alive. Count your graces," David said before he slipped down against the side of the elevator and disappeared back into the water.

▪

In the maze of pipes below Montgomery Noyes, two Con Edison workers held flashlights and walked down a massive, dry sewer line with confused looks on their faces.

"Why's it dry?" the Con Edison worker in a yellow safety helmet asked, noticing only a small stream of water below his feet when there should have been a few feet of fast-running water. Then the two workers turned a corner and saw the back end of Vlad's massively inflated tunnel plug, completely obstructing the drainage tunnel.

"Um. Holy . . . fuckin' . . . crow," the other emoted.

▪

In the back of Villalon's police SUV, Cat and Marina perched on opposite sides of the second row with upset looks on their faces. With similar temperaments but for different reasons, they weren't speaking to each other. Each sat in silence.

Marina watched the commotion outside, which had turned from a civil emergency into absolute pandemonium as the police, then local newscasters, and finally the crowd began to realize that something abnormal was occurring below the surface of the city. Marina's face suddenly scrunched up as if she'd heard something. She listened again. There it was. It wasn't a noise—it was a rhythm. A minute and faint but identifiable vibration ran through her body. Her eyes bounced down towards her purse, which was sitting on the floor of the car by her feet. She reached into the bag and pulled out her phone. The Froggie Finder app was going crazy. "User1: Location is . . ." She noticed that the glowing dot on the app's map was within twenty feet of her.

"No way . . ." she murmured to her herself, piquing Cat's interest as well.

"What is it?" Cat asked.

Marina didn't reply directly. She scanned the crowd frantically through the tinted window. She couldn't see David anywhere, even though the Froggie Finder was supposedly right nearby. She started to pound the glass of the car. "Hey! Get the detective! Get Jake!" she screamed.

Outside, the officer standing guard heard Marina's clanging against the window. He leaned towards the glass and screamed back, "Shut up, lady! I don't have time for your bullshit!"

▪

Vlad, Baranowski, and Konstantin swam through the completely submerged foundation level of the building. They followed a small pipe along the floor towards an intersection with a much larger drain main, where a human-sized hole had been torched. Baranowski swam through the hole. Konstantin followed. About to enter, Vlad turned and noticed with alarm that David wasn't there. He hesitated. The heist wouldn't be complete unless David was with him. But luckily David swam frantically around the corner towards Vlad a few seconds later, giving the thumbs-up sign as he did. Vlad grinned.

▪

In a regional water center on the outskirts of the city, a supervisor in a hard hat sprinted down a metal walkway. He finally reached a row of wheels and their connected pressure valves. After consulting a schematic on the tablet in his hands, the supervisor located the valve he was looking for. He began to spin the wheel clockwise, finally closing it. Then he stepped left and did the same with another. He continued to work on the valves, slowly decreasing and finally stopping the water supply into a ten-square-block area of Manhattan, of which Montgomery Noyes stood at the epicenter.

▪

In the stairwell above the sub-basement levels, Roger O'Neill watched the water begin to slowly subside.

"Call me off my nut, but I'm going back in," Roger yelled.

"Roger, are you crazy?" his assistant asked. "You could get stuck down there."

"The water's going down. I'm not insane—I'm an O'Neill."

Roger ripped off his jacket and tie. He pulled his shoes off. And without any hesitation, he dove into the water while the assembled security and staff around him gawked. No matter what you thought about Roger, he put his money where his mouth was. He was impressive—the true definition of a man.

▪

Perhaps unlike Howard Bergensen, who finally arrived in his limousine after slowly navigating the police cordon outside the building. He stomped up through the front stairs, pushing aside cops and security alike.

"Where the hell is Roger?" Howard asked as he flew down the steps into the basement level where the vault staff was standing. Long faces greeted him.

"Uh, he went swimming, Mr. Bergensen," one finally replied.

"What the hell is going on?"

"The flood, sir . . ."

Howard stepped past them to gaze down the stairwell below. The water had receded another foot, but when he finally saw it in person, a look of pure horror flashed across his face.

"The vault," he muttered.

"What was that?" the vault technician asked.

"The vault. They went for the vault."

"Huh? Who went for the vault?" the crowd around Howard asked, not sure if they should be more concerned about the nonsensical words coming out of his mouth than they already were.

▪

After swimming down one floor, Roger dipped underneath a low ceiling. Looking for air, his fingers clawed against a ceiling tile with its integrated vent. He ripped the metal panel off and ascended a few feet into the vent, where he found the air pocket he had been expecting. He breathed deep, gasping breaths. He pulled himself down again, and stroked back into the first sub-basement. It was pitch black, but he knew this corridor like the back of his hand. He swam toward the open door to the vault's control room at the end of the hallway.

▪

Two blocks from Montgomery's front doors, but still within the police cordon, David and Vlad stepped out from the back of the blue van. They were dripping wet, but so were a number of the groups standing outside the building. They fit right in.

After David and Vlad had departed, Baranowski and Konstantin also pulled themselves out of the manhole below the van and rose through the hole in the floor of the closed vehicle. They slowly rotated the steel floor panel down, covering up the hole. They worked their way into the front seat, started the ignition, and drove the van away from Montgomery's headquarters.

▪

By the time Roger finally made his way into the control room, the water had receded and a void of oxygen had appeared two inches from the ceiling. Roger rotated his feet up in front of him and floated to the top of the space in order to breathe. He inhaled the air carefully, afraid the water would swell into his open mouth. But it didn't.

Roger somersaulted down to gaze at the vault ahead. The last time he'd been in the control room, the window was simply cracked. Now the glass was completely broken. He swam back towards the ceiling for more air. The water's recession had reached a crescendo. It spilled from the room and slowly revealed the rest of the space. As Roger took another breath, his toes finally felt the surface of the floor below. It was only then that Roger noticed a scuba tank lying on the floor in the middle of the vault.

▪

Baranowski drove the blue van down the street, with Konstantin in the passenger seat. Unfortunately, they hadn't been parked enough streets away to avoid the police roadblock. In front of them were three angled and parked police cruisers and a few menacing cops holding automatic rifles and shotguns.

Jake stood with the officers, inspecting each car as it attempted to exit. Drying his hair off with a towel, Baranowski rolled down his window.

"Hey, officer. What's going on here?" Baranowski asked calmly, emitting a big ol' warm smile.

▪

The water inside the vault at hip level, Roger stood easily. He gazed at the vault and was finally able to take a good, long look at the situation. The window was smashed and the stack of gold that the Stacker had mistakenly placed in front of the window was gone. Roger fell to his knees just as Howard Bergensen waded into the control room behind him. Howard's eyes blew wide when he resolved the destruction.

"What happened?" Howard asked Roger.

"I don't think this was just a flood," Roger replied. "We were robbed. We were fucking robbed, Howard. So what's our procedure? What do we do?" Roger asked.

"I dunno," Howard replied. "What does a dead man do? As for me . . . I'm going to order myself a truffle pizza. Then I'm going to savor it while I write my goddamn resignation letter to the board."

▪

The police officer in front of the roadblock gazed suspiciously at Baranowski.

"Why are you's all wet?"

"We were doing work next door—painting that kitchenette right there in the basement. It filled up with water in about ten seconds. What the heck happened, officer?" Baranowski replied.

"I need you to open the back," the officer commanded him.

"It's a bunch of paint. We're just driving through, sir," Baranowski said.

Without pause, the officer pulled his gun and aimed it at Baranowski. "Open—the—back." This was serious business, staring into the oblivion of a gun barrel.

"You got it. No problem at all. I'll just get out and walk, okay?" Baranowski slowly exited the driver's seat. He walked around the side of the van. His normally confident fingers nervously gripped the handle to the back of the van, preparing for what was about to come. Baranowski swung open the back door of the van. There was nothing—no gold—only paint supplies as promised.

"They're good," Jake said as he nodded at the officer, who allowed Baranowski through.

▪

David and Vlad joined a large pack of the office building's workers, queuing through a security line set up by the cops. They approached and were quickly frisked by a couple of busy policemen who didn't give them much of a second look. One of them patted David's pockets. Feeling something bulky, he asked, "What's that?"

"My cell phone," David replied. The policeman nodded his head, and they walked through to freedom.

David and Vlad half-jogged down the street and into a nearby parking garage. They quickly located Vlad's Mercedes and burned rubber out of there.

▪

Still inside the cordon, Marina watched her Froggie Finder application miserably as the tracking dot quickly moved away from their location. The transponder blinked south through Manhattan and headed towards the Brooklyn-Battery Tunnel. She kept knocking incessantly on the window of the car, but the officer outside had stopped responding after her first few volleys. Desperation flashed across Marina's face. She grabbed the front seat's neck brace with one hand and her seat with the other. She faced the window.

"What are you doing, honey?" Cat asked.

In the current moment, Marina actually didn't feel the need to ever express a single word to her former best friend forever. She used her upper body to propel both feet into the window. She only cracked the glass. She went for it again, this time completely breaking through with her feet. She pulled herself back into the car, reached out and opened the door from the outside.

Marina dove out of the SUV and onto the street. The officers had already noticed. They pounced, but Marina didn't care. She wanted to get Jake's attention, and she knew the best way to do that was to let out a bloodcurdling scream of epic proportions. As the officers attempted to wrangle her down, Marina fought like a banshee and yelled like one, too, "Jake! Detective! I know where they are!"

Turning his head from about fifty yards out, Jake Rivett finally took notice of the ferocious Belov woman.

THIRTY-TWO

DAVID AND VLAD REACHED the other side of the Verrazano-Narrows Bridge and found themselves in Staten Island. Vlad navigated the Mercedes into a back alleyway of an industrial zone off Richmond Terrace. There was a garage ahead. Inside was another rental box truck. Vlad and David stowed the Mercedes and jumped into the truck.

∎

A mile southeast of Port Richmond, water pumped ferociously into the Silver Lake Reservoir. The rented white truck drove up, and Vlad and David emerged. The coast was clear. They approached the drain output pipe they'd visited the previous day. They removed the last of the already loosened bolts and rotated the cover aside. Water rushed over a large dark clump at the bottom of the drain. Vlad reached into the mass and pulled out an underwater bag. He unzipped the bag. It was filled with gold bars. And there were nineteen more bags to pull out.

Vlad laughed like the bastard he was. David was quiet. He'd pressed the Froggie's button earlier, but salvation had not shown its face. Maybe he just wasn't smart enough for this. He was beginning to wonder if there was anything at all he could do to pull himself out of the sinkhole. It didn't seem likely. That's the nature of the cascade. Once inertia's forces pick a direction, it only takes a push of the finger, or a smack of the enter key, to send one over the event horizon with no hope of traversing the other direction. David had learned this all too well. Now he was wondering if in his haste, he'd gone and ruined himself completely.

He stared at the gold. He didn't want any of it. His body quaked with fear when he thought about what he'd just done. He should have listened to Marina. He was positive that he'd learned his lesson. He just wished it had sunk in earlier. And while David was contemplating all of this, Vlad wasn't. Vlad was talking. Because Vlad hated silence and it made him antsy.

"We are complete legends now, David. Whole street's going to know our name," Vlad said.

"Which street?" David asked through his grimace. Victory was bitter, and the tragedy was becoming unbearable. The two of them continued to pull bags out of the drainage output and load them into the truck.

"They never knew what hit 'em, and they'll definitely never know who!" Vlad ranted.

As he listened to Vlad drone on, David couldn't help but think about the original truth teller in his family—his mother Veronika. She had warned him. She wasn't explicit. She wasn't a mind reader. But she was prescient. He replayed the lesson in his mind. David still remembered their conversation from years before as if it were happening in real time, because it had been the last night that Veronika would ever say a word about David's father.

THIRTY-THREE

Ten Years Prior

THE MORNING OF THE Cash & Loan job, David still hadn't decided to participate. It would be swift, easy, and it would pay Vlad back for protecting his hide. But that didn't make it the right thing to do. The paradoxes ran deep, and registering one's manhood in the game of life was extremely complicated.

It was a Friday morning. David was sitting in his mother's kitchen and worrying. Beyond the immediate decision ahead, he had college to consider. Stony Brook's colorful pamphlet was sitting on the counter in front of him, projecting a perfectly sanitized and successful version of the world. He could almost taste the university experience, like the sensation of sodium on one's tongue a few blocks from the beach. But Stony Brook was still quite far off, with walls of the necessary cash piled up as obstacles between.

Veronika prepared pancakes for him by the stove. She'd even located a cup of blueberries to mix in, which he liked, although he preferred chocolate. Veronika had requested David visit her that morning, and yet she wasn't saying much. Both of those facts were unusual. She was tense. David wondered if she'd heard something, somehow, about Vlad's plans. He didn't want her to be worried about him. All that was required was two snips of a wire. Then he'd be free from Vlad's clutches and even score a little cash to go along with it—not that he could tell her any of that.

Veronika loaded up his plate and brought it over to him with a glass of orange juice. She sat down at the table, which David found awkward. Generally she would spend the majority of her weekend sitting in the back den, watching stories on the television and smoking cigarettes.

"What are you doing?" she asked. Her eyes peered deeply.

"Huh?" David replied in between mouthfuls of pancake.

"Your girlfriend called. She's worried about you—says you're taking too much risk. Doing what all the other kids are doing. What does she mean? Tell me."

"Mum, I'm the good guy. I'm fine."

"Marina doesn't call me to exchange pleasantries, Davyd."

"Let me worry about myself," David replied.

"No. You deserve more. I'm sorry I couldn't get you out of the neighborhood. That's the truth. And I'm not saying that just because you're my blood. I tell you . . . because of who you are—who you can be. You're not Papa. You're different. I don't know where it came from, or how. But I love Marina because she sees it too. You're the one who'll get out of here. You'll excel. You can become something completely different from what's going to happen to all of your friends."

"If you're so smart, Mum, what's going to happen to them?"

"Same thing as your father. They're going to blow out bright—be kings for a night, or a year or two. Maybe a decade if they're lucky. And then, one by one, they're going to start to disappear. They'll die—in prison, on the streets. And if none of that happens, they'll be miserable and paranoid. They'll become freaks of nature. That's what you want?"

"I'll never let that happen."

"That's what Papa said to me every single night when he left. I'd sit back there on the porch and I'd wait. You don't know how many times I'd wake up in the morning and he still wasn't back. How horrible it feels to wake up and cry . . . And you know what? He was wrong. I was right. One night, when you were tiny . . . He just never came back." Veronika's eyes moistened in front of David. "But the police did—three days later. Know how they found him?"

"No . . ."

"Underwater—in cement up to his knees. He was murdered, and none of his friends would peep a word. The cops told me all about it . . ." Veronika began choking up. Both stunned and sorrowful, David moved across the table to comfort her.

"I kept calling the police, tryin' to figure out what was going on. I had you to take care of. Had to figure out how to tell you that your daddy was gone. But I called over and over again, even though they had nothing to say. They were 'still working on it, missus' for weeks. Eventually this detective comes over. He tells me there's an update. He sat right there at the table where you are. They tracked the barrel—the one full of cement. Came from a waste management operation on Cropsey. Guess what's right next door? Arseni's boxing gym. That was the only clue. And unless someone came in from the cold and told 'em the truth, that's as far as they were gonna get. He didn't say it, but I know why he was here. He just wanted me to know. He wanted to tell me that my husband was killed by his best friend."

"Are you saying that Arseni . . ."

"I don't know, Davyd," Veronika said. She shook her head. "Doesn't matter anymore. But the world's full of liars and stocked with masks."

David figured that telling him the story allowed Veronika to close the book on her past. But it opened a whole new page for David. And right then and there, he had made his decision.

THIRTY-FOUR

Monday

DAVID AND VLAD FINISHED loading up the box truck and exited the reservoir's empty parking lot. They ripped through New Jersey and headed west on I-280 towards the wilderness of upstate. In a brief and rare moment of silence between Vlad's rants of ecstasy, David found the time to ask the question that had been bothering him.

"Did you know Tyler Stanton was murdered?"

"No," Vlad announced after a long pause. "When did you hear that?"

"Saw it on the news."

"I know he was your friend. Sorry. Who knows what trouble he got himself into? Always more going on than anyone realizes, ya?" Vlad said as he put his arm over David's shoulder. "We did it. We really shittin' did it. Didn't we, partner? Didn't we!" Vlad screamed with delight as he held the steering wheel.

■

An hour later, the box truck careened along the Delaware Water Gap, a river running between dueling mountain ranges and delimiting the border between New Jersey and Pennsylvania. Since he was a good ninety miles from New York, time finally slowed down for David. Whereas the entire heist had seemed to pass in a split second inside the vault, his body was beginning to regain balance, and his adrenal glands normalized. It was the first time in two weeks that he had a chance to take a breath and look around.

What he saw was downright beautiful. The box truck rolled down the country road, next to the clean rushing water of the Delaware River, framed by a luxurious patchwork of amber, red, and yellow fall leaves in the forests above. The sun glided over the surface of the immense mountain range behind them, illuminating the scene of what must have been a massive battle millions of years before as these geological formations took shape. Vlad craned his neck and searched for a particular driveway. He found it eventually and guided the truck onto an unmarked gravel road. They headed towards an old abandoned quarry situated next to the river.

Vlad slowed the truck down to a crawl in order to navigate the bumpy and uneven dirt road ahead of them. David eyed the iron ruins of a long industrial steel catwalk strung across the high cliffs leading down to a rocky bank below. After a few more minutes, David and Vlad finally arrived at a small gravel lot at the base of the quarry.

■

There was an eighteen-wheeler packed with bananas and parked there already. Working to create a space between all of the fruit, Konstantin waved from inside.

"You sure this is going to work?" David asked Vlad.

"Absolutely. The hard part's over. What we're doing next, I'm really good at. I got a long life to live. I wouldn't do anything to jeopardize that."

"I do too," David responded.

"I know. You have to trust me, David."

"I have."

"And look where it got you." Vlad smiled brightly.

"Don't really know where that is yet . . ."

"Give it a rest. Relax."

"All right."

"It'll all be over soon," Vlad said.

Vlad parked the box truck. He and David disembarked and walked towards Konstantin. As they paced towards the banana truck, in which the gold would be smuggled across the country, David heard a sound behind him. He looked back. Baranowski was controlling an excavator with two huge chains wrapped around the scooper. But that wasn't all. The chains were lifting up a light-green Honda Civic in the air and rotating the vehicle towards them.

David stared at the car. Something about it was familiar, but he couldn't quite put his finger on it. Then he saw the license plate on the back and a logo printed on the plate's frame: "Stony Brook Alumni." It was David's car.

"What's going on?" David asked with alarm. He turned abruptly towards Vlad to find a pistol aimed directly at his face.

"This is where we end, my peach," Vlad said solemnly.

"Vlad . . ."

"I'm not delighted about it."

"What are you doing?" David asked plaintively.

"Right now?" Vlad shrugged. "Actually, nothin'. I'm sitting on my couch with Cat—eating pirozhkis. But you? I made sure the truck was rented under your name. You're the only one on any of the building's surveillance cameras. And your partner, Tyler . . . You murdered him to cover your own tracks, with a gun that only has your prints on it. Remember, when I tossed it to you in the safe house?"

The truth began to spread across David's consciousness like an out-of-control wild fire. It all began to connect, and his gut tightened as if he'd had been slammed with a bat.

"You bastard," David said. "What the hell did I ever do to you?"

"Shame of it all is you got away with it—free and clear. But it was dark out. You crashed," Vlad gestured to David's car. "Your body will be found in the river, with a car full of gold. But not all the gold. I mean, shit. The rest must have went down the river. In the muck . . . Ya? Did you really think that we could do all this without puttin' the crime on someone? That person is gonna be you. Come on, you knew there was no way you were getting out of this. I can—it's in my blood—but not you. This ain't who you are. That's the way life really works, David. It's just like your flash crash. What are those stocks floatin' on? Nothin'—thin air—everything can be destroyed in an instant. It can happen to anyone, at any time."

"I don't deserve this," David said. "We're friends." David eyed Konstantin and Baranowski, who were watching the interaction intently. "You're going to let him do this? He could turn around and do you, too!"

"Don't worry about them. They're loyal. It's you that's the problem. You always thought you were better than me. But you're not. We're the same, David. We're two poor kids from the neighborhood. The difference is I never forgot it," Vlad responded.

"I never looked down on you," David said.

"Right. You hated me instead. And you betrayed me—left me high and dry."

"Don't you get it? I didn't hate you. I hated me. I didn't want to be the smartest hood in Bensonhurst. You're not doing all this because I stopped running with you, are you? That's insane. I had to do that for me. It had nothing to do with you." David grew angrier. "Just 'cause I got an education, got a job . . . What does that matter to you? What does it mean? We're friends, Vlad. No—you were my best friend."

"Three years in the pen because of what you did." Vlad spit onto the ground in disdain.

"The Cash & Loan? I was a kid, Vlad. That was *your* plan, *your* bag—

not mine. You had to hold the risk on that one. Told me so yourself. You know that. You never would have gone to prison if you hadn't decided to up the ante and go after that business. I had nothing to do with it. Don't lay that on me."

"Wrong again, pal. I went to jail because you chickened out. And you didn't even have the respect to tell me that you pissed your pants and weren't going to cut the alarm. But the truth is . . . it's not just prison, David. That's not the worst part. This wouldn't have happened if I was just angry 'bout the pen. It's what came next," Vlad gazed hatefully at David. "The worst part is that you didn't come. You didn't visit. That's when I knew for sure how you felt about me. You hated me for a long fuckin' time. Shit. That's why we didn't talk for years—because you didn't want nothin' to do with me. Until Mikey came along and you and Marina decided he needed friends from the neighborhood. Right? I'm supposed to just take that? You want to turn me into your little errand boy? Life ain't like the bank. You don't get to just keep taking a little bit off the top—not for free. But the truth is that's what I always was to you. And now you're gonna be that for me."

David didn't respond.

"I'm not your goddamn convenience. You're right, by the way. You were my best friend—until you weren't. Until I realized you'd do anything in the world to not be like me. I had to mourn losing you. I cried." Vlad paused for a moment. "So now you know it all. Story time's up. Get in the car," Vlad said as he gestured with his gun.

David watched as Baranowski lowered the car back down to the ground. Vlad opened the door. With no choice, David did as he was told and sat in the driver's seat. Vlad pointed his gun at David, who scrambled to delay his fate.

"Well, if you're going to do this, at least don't keep me wondering," David said. "It was you all along, wasn't it? That was your mask in the incinerator? So there were no women at all—no Asians, right? The whole thing was you guys, from the very beginning—all of it. Marina told me the cops were looking for masks. I didn't understand that. But I should have known. I just couldn't bring myself to believe it—couldn't turn my brain that direction. I didn't believe that you'd betray me like this. You . . . you kidnapped my family," David finally said it out loud.

"You really were genetically blessed with a large lump of grey matter," Vlad said, confirming David's suspicions.

"You're a piece of shit."

"I enjoyed it," Vlad said with a shrug. "Got to see Marina naked. Always wondered what she'd look like. Can't fault me. I'm a man. You got a babe, bro. Don't worry. I'll take care of her."

"You're going to pay," David steamed.

"You're right again. And I'll have a hundred million dollars to do it."

"But why the armored car? That's way out of your comfort zone. How did you even know about . . . Why did . . . You don't know what a flash crash is. You couldn't have . . ." David trailed off as the endless possibilities piled up inside his mind.

"I should actually thank you," Vlad opened up. "Gig came around. A middleman set me and Howard up. Because I knew you, that made it really easy. I terrorized your family and robbed that armored car. It was beautiful. But that's not why I wanted to say thank you."

Vlad opened a small black medical case that Konstantin had handed to him. Inside was a hypodermic needle and a vial of knockout agent. Vlad prepared the device in front of David as he continued to explain himself. "That penishead Howard Bergensen only paid me five hundred grand for the FDR job. So when you told me that the score was worth a hundred million, I became deeply, deeply offended. I hate being lied to. Only I get to do that, ya? So I had to steal it back. The perfect crime—take from someone who can't report it. Now, of course, I needed you to pull it off. And to make everything just that much more refined, I'm going to use you to seal the deal."

"Wait . . . Vlad . . ." David stalled.

"Nah. I've been waiting a long time for this. I'm done with all that," Vlad said, about to deliver David his final fate via a needle prick.

"Hold on. One more thing. When we were teenagers . . . The Cash & Loan . . ." David said.

Vlad hesitated with the needle. "What?" he asked.

"The newspaper back then said all the bills were gone. You hid the stash, didn't you?" David asked.

Vlad shook his head, "No. Fuckin' pigs were always wrong about that. It was fine with me for the street to think it—"

"I thought that's how you paid your debt down. What happened? Where'd you store it all?" David asked.

"I got in there, my peach. And the cash room . . . It was clean. Nothing was there. I guess my source was wrong the whole time. And I didn't have any time to look around. 'Cause the alarms had gone off, thanks to you, and the police were already outside."

"There's a reason you never found that cash," David said nervously as the needle vibrated an inch from his neck.

"What?" Vlad asked. The needle stopped shaking.

"How do you think I paid my way through college?"

Vlad's eyebrows twitched nervously. Surely that couldn't be. David was messing with him. All of a sudden, Vlad wasn't sure if perhaps David was the type of man who looks like a sheep but acts like a lion.

"You were my first counter trade," David said.

David's hand rose abruptly. He was still holding the yellow taser gun that Vlad himself had insisted upon. David didn't need to think. His instinct was to shoot, which he did. He aimed at Vlad's face, and the two tasers impacted Vlad's neck, diving half an inch into the flesh. Vlad's body stiffened in a split second as thousands volts of electricity coursed through each vein simultaneously. He fell to the ground like a lump.

David kicked out the Civic's door and reached down for Vlad's gun, which was lying on the gravel next to him. Konstantin wasn't armed, so he turned and sprinted back towards the eighteen-wheeler before David could swing the gun his way. Baranowski was scrambling to jump out of the excavator. David shot at the glass cab of the excavator, shattering a window but completely missing Baranowski.

David sprinted away from the flat parking area and towards the top of the old quarry. He smashed his way through a wooden gate and hustled up a set of rusted stairs. Hearing a squeak at the gate, he turned and discovered that Vlad had recovered and was chasing after him.

After David reached the top of the stairs, he leaned over the metal gangplank. He saw Vlad coming up the stairs. He took another shot. Missed. David scampered along the metal walkway, hearing Vlad in rabid pursuit behind him. David turned again, pressing the gun trigger just as Vlad swung a piece of two-by-four wood at David's hand. Vlad knocked the gun away and launched himself into the air, impacting David directly in the chest and holding on. David lost his balance on the metal walkway, his body flipping over the low railing separating them from the quarry. Vlad fell along with him.

The two men tumbled down the rough rock face, rolling about a hundred feet along a slope towards the sheer edge of the quarry proper. Neither of them had any weapons. David scraped his hands along the side of the rock quarry, his fingers ripping against the stone, before finally holding on to a piece of rock that held his weight. Vlad wasn't so lucky. He couldn't stop the fall. He rolled over the edge of the cliff, unable to gain equilibrium.

But at the last moment, just as Vlad was about to fall another hundred feet through the air onto granite below, David instinctively stuck his hand out. He wasn't sure why. It must have been something deep inside his subconscious. He wasn't saving Vlad; he was saving the little boy he used to know and love. Having caught Vlad and prevented his imminent death, David held him suspended in the air. The two men stared at one another, their eyes locked in a death embrace.

"Please. My peach. Don't . . ." Vlad pleaded.

"Who was the middleman?" David asked angrily.

"Huh?"

"Who set you and Howard up?" David insisted. Vlad's sweaty hand began to slip.

"Who?" David demanded angrily.

"Joe—the Pie Man," Vlad finally revealed. "Please. I'm begging you."

"The pizza guy? How did he know Howard?"

"You've seen his walls. Joe rolls at the highest levels. There ain't a CEO, movie star, or athlete who hasn't shaken Joe's hand at some point in life."

David didn't know what to do. If you murder a monster, does that make you a saint? Or do you become what you hate? Vlad had wanted to kill him, but that didn't mean David had to do the same. David could right the boat. It was his turn, and he had a chance to save a life. He wasn't a killer.

David pulled Vlad up. No good deed goes unpunished. The second Vlad was safe, he immediately lunged after David and straddled him. He burrowed his two thick hands deep into David's windpipe, strangling the lights out of the quant.

All of a sudden, a bullet whistled through the air and impacted Vlad's head. Vlad ricocheted backwards as a stream of blood erupted from his cranium. His entire body arched behind him, shoulders and head leading the rest of his body like a high jumper. Vlad flopped backwards and plummeted over the edge of the quarry to his death.

David panted in exhaustion. He struggled to crane his neck upwards towards the sound of the gun above.

"This is the police! Get your hands up, David!" Jake Rivett screamed, holding a carbine at the top of the rock embankment. Smoke articulated from the end of the gun. Jake slid down the embankment towards David, finally reaching him after a bit of struggle. David put his arms up in the air in surrender.

"Are you going to arrest me?" David asked.

Jake took a long, stern look at David as he loomed above the quant. "No, I am not. Because I'm the law, and you . . . You're an innocent man."

"Not so much . . ." David said.

"What do you want?" Jake asked cryptically.

"From what?"

"Life."

"My family."

Jake evaluated David's response. "I believe you, David. And that's between you and them. But hell if I'm gonna be the guy who destroys your little boy's world—especially after what I think you've been through." Jake paused for a moment. "But don't get too ahead of yourself. We'll be spending a whole bunch of time together on the debrief."

▪

A police car stopped in front of the Belov house in Bensonhurst later that evening. David stepped out and looked up expectantly at the front door. He was awestruck by how badly he'd craved this moment. He'd perpetually held up hope, and the return to ordinary had finally arrived. If one didn't get killed by the crash, the only place to go was back up. And average was wonderful. It was his life, and it was just inside the door.

Marina stepped out first. Mikey followed behind, holding her hand. David ran up to them and wrapped them both into a hug. He was trying to talk, but the words didn't come out. He pulled the Froggie Finder from his pocket. The nose still glowed.

"I told you Froggie would come in handy," David said as tears filled his eyes and Mikey jumped up to hug him deep and long. "I love you, Mikey."

"Never go away again, Daddy."

"I won't."

"And don't do anything crazy," Mikey added.

David glanced up at Marina. She smiled and shrugged. He was right. "I love you both so much. Nothing like this will ever happen again. I promise," David said. This time he really meant it. Tears filled David's eyes as he hugged his wife and son tight. He would never let go.

THIRTY-FIVE

One Month Later

A DIGITAL VIDEO PLAYED on a small screen in front of David.

"Please say your name for the camera," Jake Rivett's voice said over the image.

The Pie Man, Joe Raffaeli, stared directly at the camera with a disappointed and downtrodden expression cast over his face. He was sitting in a stark interrogation cell. This was a confession.

"Joseph Angel Raffaeli," Joe finally said.

From behind the camera, Jake pushed him further. "Yeah. And what's your nickname? What do they call you on the streets?"

"The Pie Man. I make pizza."

"Do you know Howard Bergensen?"

Joe hesitated for a long moment and then said, "Yes."

"Do you know Vlad Zhadanov?"

"Yes," replied the Pie Man.

"Did you facilitate payments from Howard to Vlad?"

"Yes."

"Explain—in detail," Jake urged.

"Howard needed a job done. He came to me. We've had an off-the-books relationship for twenty years. He knew I was the king of the streets. Vlad ran the best crew in town. All I did was bring two interested parties together so they could make a deal."

▪

The digital feed flickered. In Jake's office inside One Police Plaza, David watched the remainder of the video with a revelatory expression on his face. The Pie Man laid out exactly what had occurred, including Howard's copying and subsequent forgery of his own driver's signature for Tsunami's incorporation documents. When the admission was finished, Jake turned the television off and addressed David.

"Even the masters of the universe have to come down to Earth," said Jake.

"I have one question. Why would the Pie Man talk? I met him. He's about as original gangster as man can be. They don't speak. They take what they know to the grave. Don't they?"

"You watch too many movies," Jake replied, "but you're not wrong. He didn't say a thing until we found his freezer tapes. Thanks for that. The Pie Man's like everyone else. Once he knew we had his insurance, he was willing to make the best deal he could. He's only looking out for himself."

"So when are you going to arrest Howard?" David asked.

"Case needs to be rock solid," replied Jake.

"You have it there." David nodded at the screen.

"Between us? The DA's a prick and we got a new boss, this chick, who's on my ass about dotting i's and crossing t's. Our team is working through all the videos from Joe's freezer camera. It's a huge cache. Gonna bring down a couple big criminal networks in the city—not just Vlad. It'll be a couple more days."

"When?" David had to know.

"You know I can't tell you that," Jake said.

David stood up defiantly. "I need to go home to my wife and my child and tell them that I'm there for them now—that I'm going to protect them for the rest of their lives. That they are never going to have to worry about masked men barging into our house and terrorizing us, because the person who started all this is behind bars. Tell me when I can tell them that and be telling the truth. Tell me when my son can stop being afraid."

Jake thought about it for a moment. "Next Monday morning," he said. "You didn't hear it from me. And I didn't tell you that because of you. I'm telling you for Mikey."

"I know," David replied. And he did. "Thank you."

"It's chill," Jake said. David turned to leave, but Jake stopped him. "So what about your family? You'll be okay for a job and stuff?" Jake asked.

"We'll be fine," David said.

"How come?"

"Because whenever I make a trade, I make a counter trade," David said and allowed a sly-wolf grin to escape his lips.

▪

Montgomery Noyes loomed like a dark obelisk supporting the sky. Having left the police station and walked just a few avenues to the west, David stood across the street. He observed the nexus wherein his American dream had fallen into the abyss. He took a deep breath and ran across the street towards the entrance.

▪

David entered the third elevator on the right. After he'd pressed a floor number, the door began to close. A businesswoman raised her hand for him to stop the elevator. But David jammed the door-close button before she could get her hand in.

"Sorry. Something's expecting me," David said as she approached and crossly gave him the middle finger.

The doors closed and the elevator rose. If one were particularly diligent, one would recognize it as exactly the same elevator in which David had saved multiple Montgomery employees from drowning to death. David treated it like a normal elevator ride. He turned his back to the surveillance camera and played on his cell phone.

But in actuality, he was opening up the emergency call box in the elevator. He found a red telephone and a fire extinguisher inside. David moved the items to the side. Hidden behind them was a black bag hanging from the nose of the extinguisher. David loosened the chord that kept the bag closed and reached within to pull out what was inside. His hand emerged with two gold bars, each weighing about eight pounds.

David slipped the gold bars inside the pockets of his jacket. That was it. Time to go. No need to remain at Montgomery a second longer. He started to repeatedly jam the button for the lobby, whistling quietly as he rode the elevator for what he knew for sure would be the last time.

▪

At a downtown CashForGold retail store, David sat at a desk inside a private office. A licensed gold dealer sat across from him and weighed both gold bars on a scale and then stared coolly across the table at David.

"Why me?" the dealer asked.

"What do you mean?"

"This is troy gold—COMEX marked. Each bar's a hundred ounces. You probably already know that. But this isn't what I see on a daily basis. Normally I'm talking to old ladies selling off their ex-husband's guilty anniversary earrings."

"Does it matter?"

The gold dealer thought about it for a moment and then smiled. "Not one bit, sir. That's the magic of this commodity. Gold is gold, and that's all she wrote." The dealer glanced at a computer quickly. "Current troy-ounce spot price is eleven sixty-five. Bar's worth about a hundred and sixteen thousand dollars. I can offer you two hundred for the both of them."

"Two hundred? That's, like, fifteen percent less . . ."

The dealer shrugged, knowing that he was about to personally net thirty thousand dollars in one afternoon. "This is a retail business. You're probably here because you want to walk out of that door with a check that will clear, right now. So whaddya say?"

"I'll take the check," David said.

The dealer consulted his computer. He finally printed and handed over a cashiers check for two hundred thousand dollars to David. David accepted the paper with a handshake. The dealer slipped the gold into a red velvet pouch. David watched it disappear with a whimper, not a boom. He'd finally closed the position and wiped his hands clear of that risk. But he wasn't done.

▪

The afternoon was wrapping up, but David had one more destination in mind. He hustled down Liberty Street in the central bowels of Wall Street, looking for a particular address. He entered another nameless, faceless Wall Street building, built in the seventies and consisting uniformly of steel, glass, and cash.

David ran his finger along the businesses listed in the lobby, until he found the one labeled "Hurlbut Kentmere." Seventh floor.

▪

David emerged onto another brokerage firm's trading floor. It had many of the same elements as Montgomery Noyes. Traders in Brooks Brothers yelled into phones in front of their triple-monitor setups. Harried assistants and trade specialists paced around the floor. Tape prices scrolled around the walls, and CNBC was muted in the background.

David was standing in the lobby looking for a receptionist who didn't seem to be there, when, of course, Rick Stanfield popped into view.

"David! Heard you might be comin' by today. You like Kentmere? Just super, ain't it?" Trader Rick pummeled down the hallway, pulling David in for a huge bear hug. Rick smiled at a pretty assistant passing by. He leaned in. "Did you know at these second-tier places they don't even make you sign a sexual harassment pledge?" Rick asked.

"I did not."

"Yeah. It's like the eighties, but with worse coke," Rick said as he guided David into his office. "It's hilarious. They think I'm some sort of god because I worked at Montgomery. So I got my own corner office. I guess that's what they call success, eh?"

"They always said you traded like a cat," said David as he sat down.

"Did they?" Rick asked.

"Yeah, Rick. Everyone knew about you before they met you. First man in, first man out, every time. And they heard you yelling before all of that. But that's another story altogether."

"Well, not much has changed, Davey-boy." Rick laughed and then bellowed, "So how can I help you?"

"I want to open a trading account," David said. He reached into his pocket and pulled out the check for two hundred thousand dollars. He placed it on Rick's desk.

"Two hundred? A little smaller than I'm used to working with, but no problem. I'll add you to my book—give you the friend-and-family discount."

"How much leverage can you give me?" David asked.

"Really? You don't strike me as a guy who craves the nitro. Don't you think a nice dividend-paying buy-and-hold or index would be good for this?"

"If you don't give me leverage, I'm walking out of here."

Rick checked David's face to confirm he was serious. "Atta boy," Rick said. He checked a monitor in front of him. "Twenty to one?" he replied.

"Make it fifty on the equity side, and I also want to throw in some options."

"Fifty? What's your play? Is it mortgage-backed security calls? A rate-twist butterfly spread? Some sort of hedged covered call? You got an edge somewhere? Something you wanna tell me at the gyro stand outside?

What?" Rick asked.

"Short the lion—Montgomery Noyes," David said.

"Really?"

"Yes."

"How big?"

"Every single dollar," said David.

"I don't know, brother. Financials are on a tear this year. They spent a whole long time in the shitter after the recession, and now they're coming back hard with rates. And, yeah, Montgomery had their bad news with the gold crash and the robbery, but that's already baked into the price. You don't wanna be chasing."

"I'm not chasing anything," said David.

"You're serious? A full naked short on the bank? You know that if it moves the wrong direction, that'll wipe you out completely. Right?"

"I'm not an idiot, Rick."

"Just asking. I'm not your fairy godmother either, but I gotta suck your balls a little here, 'cause those short bussers at the SEC might get pissed if I helped you lose absolutely everything," Rick said.

"The trade needs to be in by the end of the day. Will you do it for me or not?"

Rick thought about it for a moment, but there was an obvious response bubbling up. He was Rick Stanfield, after all. "Fuck it. Of course I'll place the trade," he finally said as he extended his hand to David. "You came to me because you know I'm cray cray and I'll fuckin' try anything once, didn't you?"

David shook Rick's hand with a wry smile. "Ya," he said.

THIRTY-SIX

Monday

IT WAS EARLY MORNING in the Hamptons—six a.m. An arrow balanced menacingly on a recurve bow's rest. Tension coiled along Howard Bergensen's arm. Archery required many of the same skills as trading. One had to control emotion—mollify the nerves. It was critical to wait until the right moment and then strike without hesitation. And after all the calibration and expectation, there was nothing more satisfying than watching an arrow arc through the air and blast out the center of the bullseye right through the X.

Howard released the arrow. It smashed into a target fifty yards down a long field in the backyard of his Hamptons house. It hit blue—way off the bull. Not even close. Howard rested the bow on the grass. Something had distracted him. What had he heard? He stared over the huge berm separating his property from the ocean. But there was nothing—only waves of reed grass blowing in the light wind.

Then a head appeared over the stalks—and a few more. Jake Rivett and Police Chief Marks emerged from the green blur. Howard thought about notching another arrow and lifting the bow. He could do some damage—keep them at bay. But he didn't. He was paralyzed. He'd always wondered what this moment would look like and how it would feel. He knew it would happen. The market had no soul and in the end, that was his problem, too. Howard was quickly surrounded in the middle of the field by a circle of officers and federal agents.

"What's going on?" Howard asked angrily.

"Howard, you're under arrest," Marks said solemnly.

"Do I need to read you your rights?" Jake asked.

"Don't worry. I'm not going to talk," Howard replied.

"Well, you're getting them. The legal system can be tricky. I guess you know that. Wouldn't want to let a snake escape back into the grass over a technicality," Jake said. "You have the right to remain silent . . ."

▪

A few hours later on the same Monday morning, life had returned somewhat back to normal for the Belov household. David stood at the stove and made pancakes for Marina and Mikey. The television was playing in the living room. Even though Mikey wanted his cartoons, David had insisted on CNN.

"New York's finest were out in force in the Hamptons this morning," the announcer on CNN began. David stopped everything. He turned abruptly to the television. The shot onscreen was from the perspective of a news helicopter, circling around Howard's immaculate Hamptons home. The place was crawling with police on the ground.

"The vice chairman of capital markets at Montgomery Noyes and street veteran, Howard Bergensen, was arrested today for multiple civil and criminal charges. Including armed robbery and murder," said another anchor as Howard was escorted into a government car by Marks. David could make out Jake Rivett in the background, a lone man in a leather jacket climbing onto his motorcycle and disappearing offscreen.

"Meanwhile, Montgomery Noyes' stock has crashed over thirty-five percent on the news. Makes sense. Bergensen's name had become practically synonymous with the old-line institution."

David was glued to the screen. He didn't realize that, back in the kitchen, the pancakes were burning. A thick field of smoke rose from the bottom of the pan while David gawked at the television. Marina jumped off the couch in alarm.

"David! The pancakes!" Marina tossed the charred mess into the sink. She placed another pan on the burner.

"Isn't Mommy forgetting something?" David asked. He held up a bag of chocolate chips. Mikey's eyes blew wide with anticipation.

"You want to do the honors, Mikey?" he asked.

Mikey grabbed the bag and succeeded in pouring half of them into the pancake mix before Marina could stop him.

"That's enough, honey!" Marina exclaimed.

David stared at Marina with a devilish grin. He lunged at the pancake mix, tossing the rest of the chocolates into it. Marina pretended to be disappointed but couldn't help smile as David and Mikey high-fived one another.

Then David's cell on his hip rang. He picked up to hear Rick's booming voice.

"You are a glorious and astounding ivory pearl burrowed deep under the most rancid ocean muck imaginable," Rick screamed.

"Tell me the good news," David inquired.

"It worked," Rick said.

"What's my size?"

"Last tick? You're worth . . . over twenty-three million dollars. What do you want to do, David?"

David gazed over his family and smiled. "I want to cash out," he said.

</END>.

ENJOY *FLASH CRASH?*

Dear Reader:

More Rivett is coming fast. The sequel to *Flash Crash* is *Never Go Alone*. It's available in paperback or Kindle from Amazon. As usual, each book in the *Rivett* series is a thrilling standalone, but reading them all pays the most dividends.

Reviews are the **lifeblood** of an independent author. If you enjoyed *Flash Crash*, I would be extremely grateful if you would post your review on **Amazon**, **Goodreads**, or any other preferred site.

Pulling your hair out in anticipation of the next Jake Rivett thriller? Have no fear. Just sign up for the latest announcements!

Stay up-to-date with Denison's latest musings and news:
DenisonHatch.com/signup/

BUY *THE JAKE RIVETT SERIES* ON AMAZON!

ABOUT THE AUTHOR

Denison Hatch is a screenwriter and novelist based in Los Angeles. Although he lives in the proverbial desert now, he is originally from Delaware—land of forested valleys, corporate shells, and DuPont gunpowder.

Denison has a number of feature and television projects in development, including his original screenplay, *Vanish Man*, which is set up at Lionsgate. A graduate of Cornell University, Denison lives with his wife and big dog in a little house in Hollywood.

Flash Crash is Denison's debut novel, and the first in the Jake Rivett series.

**Stay up-to-date with Denison's latest musings and news:
DenisonHatch.com/signup/**

BUY *THE JAKE RIVETT SERIES* ON AMAZON!